SKY QUEEN

SKY QUEEN

A NOVEL

JUDY KUNDERT

SHE WRITES PRESS

Published June 2019
Printed in the United States of America
Print ISBN: 978-1-63152-523-0
E-ISBN: 978-1-63152-524-7
Library of Congress Control Number: 2018964897

For information, address:
She Writes Press
1569 Solano Ave #546
Berkeley, CA 94707

Interior design by Tabitha Lahr

She Writes Press is a division of SparkPoint Studio, LLC.

To my husband Pat,
thanks for all your support along the way.

1

KATHERINE RELEASED A SIGH and leaned into her standing yoga position and a forward yoga position. This was her usual routine to start her day after a red eye flight. Now, her body zoomed with ideas. Snapping her fingers and moving to the psychedelic rhythm of the record playing on the record player, she drifted into a surrealist chant of the things she had to do. "Finish prepping for my midterm exam. Pack for my trip to Greece. Take—"

The click, click, click of her roommate's four-inch heels tapping on their bedroom's hardwood floor quashed the music. The scent of Jungle Gardenia perfume floated down the hallway and into Katherine's nostrils and made her sneeze. Charlotte bounced into their bedroom and tossed her treasured Pucci purse on her twin bed.

Katherine's roommate looked gorgeous in an emerald-green satin costume. Like a gust of wind, she dashed to her dresser on her side of their bedroom. "It's rush time. I have the early

7 p.m. shift at the Playboy Mansion. Hefner has a special party tonight." She paused to catch her breath. "I have to dress for work here tonight since I and five other Bunnies are doing a publicity gig in Lincoln Park. It's for a Chicago Tribune article about Hefner's Playboy Mansion." She paused and nodded to her friend. "Hey! You'll get stoned just listening to that stuff. But it looks like you've already succumbed."

Without waiting for Katherine to respond, she gazed in the mirror and plopped a rabbit-ear headband atop her upswept auburn hair.

Katherine lifted her shoulders and stretched her arms to the ceiling. Leaning back on her pillow, she yawned and sighed, "Oh, hi, Char. I was just finishing my final review of my class notes for my exam before my afternoon San Fran turnaround. I'm wiped out, but I think I finally know about Oedipus, Prometheus, and all those other spectacular Greek gods."

Charlotte wrinkled her nose. "Yuk. Why do you spend your time on that stuff? Greek gods? Hey, remember what you told me, that we'd have a blast in Chicago?"

Katherine rubbed her temples and released a deep breath. "Yeah, and we're having fun. Who got us tickets to the Monkees' concert next month?" Katherine glanced down at her class notes and gave her friend a half smile. *Jacob Burckhardt's History of Greek Culture will bore Charlotte, but I'll share it anyway.* "The Greek gods got me thinking about life and times today. For some reason, studying this stuff made my dad pop into my head. He was always telling me about working and living in the Windy City, where he fought for the rights of people, like the ones who lived in the Cabrini-Green public housing projects. And now my dear father is still helping others. You know, he spends a couple of weekends a month offering his legal services to the Chippewa in the Chippewa Valley. Look at me, what have I done with my life? Who am I helping?"

Katherine organized her notes and textbooks. Seeking silent approval, she nodded toward her parents' picture centered on her dresser. A sterling silver frame set off the handsome couple, a tall, handsome blond Germanic man with a determined look standing next to an exotic, raven-haired woman with bronze skin and high cheek bones.

Charlotte wrinkled her brow, shrugged, and continued dressing for work. With ease, she inserted two foam rubber cups into her bodice to boost her cleavage.

She stood up and released a quick breath. With an abrupt turn, she grabbed her handbag from atop the pile of mod dresses, bell-bottom pants, and hot pants.

"Oops! Sweetie, I almost forgot. Here's the invitation that I promised you." She handed it to Katherine.

Katherine leaped up to reach for the glossy card. She examined the raised gold lettering: "*Si Non Oscillas, Noli Tintinnare.*" In parentheses was the translation: "If you don't swing, don't ring." The gold doorknocker and rabbit head proved it was an official invitation to the Playboy Mansion on Chicago's luxurious North State Parkway.

Katherine smiled and laughed about the promise of a new adventure. "Wow, Char, this is cool! I can't wait to see inside that place."

Charlotte rummaged through the heap of clothes, retrieved her fluffy Bunny tail, and threw it into her handbag. She jabbered on to her roommate as she grabbed her bow-tie collar and slapped it around her neck. "Aren't you thrilled about this invitation? It's a pretty unique one too. It's a press preview party for the Playboy Penthouse event. Lady, there'll be tons of celebrities hustling for some face time. To get your ticket, I told our publicity coordinator that you're a journalism student who'd like to write a feature article about the Playboy Mansion for a journalism class assignment. Chill out, girl. I know you're not studying journalism, but you can fake it."

Journalism student. Charlotte's words shattered Katherine's dreams of an exotic escapade at the Playboy Mansion. Gulp. In her excitement about the party she missed the date on the invitation. It glared at her like a Do Not Enter sign. "Yikes, I have a History of Greek Culture exam that night. What should I do?"

Katherine closed her eyes and released a breath. If her parents found out that she'd taken an incomplete for a course exam to go to a Playboy party, they'd call in her school loan and demand that she pay them back with triple interest. Katherine recalled her father's words when she left Beloit College to become a stewardess two-years ago. *'Don't forget your education.' And me, I promised myself that I would finish my degree. Is this not a promise to break? Hey, this Northwestern class is a one-time thing, I'll find a way to complete my program at Beloit. I'll still keep my promise? Charlotte went out of her way for me. We've been friends for so long. I don't want to harm our friendship.*

Katherine sighed. "It's also the night before the trip to Greece E. J. and I have planned." Katherine hurled the invitation on her bed, threw her hands on her hips, and turned to Charlotte to look for consolation.

"Katherine! You asked and asked for this invitation. It's a pretty incredible one too. Sarah Vaughn, Pete Seeger, Harry Belafonte, and lots more celebs are going to be there. I stuck my neck out to get this invitation for you. And now you're fussing about silly things. You should be jumping up and down with joy. Charlotte pursed her lips. With a shaking hand, she snapped the white wrist collars on each wrist She thrust her hands in the air and sighed.

Katherine wrinkled her brow and slipped her fingers through her hair. *I can't believe my personal sabbatical will be over soon. I've had experiences that I couldn't have in college. But with all my travels, new people and places, I let time slip by me. Two years to make up this incomplete course feels like forever. It's time to revisit my promise to myself. Do I still want my education?* Katherine tilted her head and gazed out the bedroom window at Lincoln Park. Her mind drifted back to that spring day in April 1965 when she'd bounced into her Beloit College undergraduate anthropology advisor's office to tell her about the job offer to become a stewardess. Her advisor tempered her congratulations on the job offer, while reinforcing Katherine's desire to finish her degree. She could still hear her words. "Katherine, you have too much to offer. You must continue your education." Katherine closed her eyes and recalled her advisor's support and belief in Katherine's dream. The advisor had given her a waiver to finish the one course at Northwestern. Now her two-year time limit was fast approaching. If she didn't complete the course now, she might not be able to continue working on her degree. What if her Northwestern University professor did not give her another incomplete for the course? Katherine raised her eyebrows and slipped her fingers over her lips. *Hm, maybe I can work something out with my Beloit College advisor. Impossible, perhaps, but I can make it a possibility. Char has been my best friend forever. And she did move to Chicago to be my roommate. If she'd stayed in Chippewa Falls, Wisconsin, she'd still be working at her mother's art gallery.*

"I'm sorry. I do appreciate all your trouble. I wonder if E. J. and I could come for an hour or so. We'll need some sleep since our flight to Greece leaves at 5:30 a.m. the next morning." Katherine placed a hand on Charlotte's white wrist collars.

"Don't put yourself out!" Charlotte pulled her wrists away, turned to the mirror, and gave herself one last check.

"Hey, I'm a real rat fink. I hope you'll forgive me someday. Remember all the fun times we've had? What about the time Dad got us tickets to the Packer/Bears playoff game and you left me high and dry and went off to that frat keg party in Madison?"

"Okay, okay, you're right. But hey, what's the problem? You're leaving for a vacation. You could sleep on the plane. And why do you even bother with school? I thought you left Beloit to become a stew and forget about school? All that studying is your hang-up." Charlotte sighed. "Maybe you and E. J. can make a quick pit stop at the party. There'll be so many people wandering around; no one will notice when you sneak out early. You'll have a fake press badge and remember to carry a small notebook. Chat up a few people and act like you know everyone there. Must go now. Don't forget, I'm moving to the Playboy Mansion. Ciao." Charlotte chuckled and slipped into her London Fog trench coat and waved to her friend.

Katherine exhaled a gust of air and stared at the invitation on her bed next to her class notes. Katherine tilted her head and chuckled when she surveyed her roommate's unmade bed buried under a mountain of leotards, hot pants, and bodysuits. Katherine thought that their beds were a metaphor for the young women's extreme opposite lifestyles—Katherine, a bookworm, and Charlotte, a glamor girl. *She'll never understand my desires. I only took a leave of absence from Beloit to be a stewardess for a grand adventure. She thought becoming a stewardess was the coolest thing I'd ever done. I still remember her words when I got accepted to stewardess training: 'That's the smartest thing you've ever done.'*

Glancing at the picture of her and Charlotte in their Girl Scout uniforms, Katherine remembered that her Chippewa great-grandmother, Hanging Cloud, and the tribe's noble medicine man, Soaring Eagle, had told her to act like a bird and fly high to the stars. They had also told Charlotte that the tribe's great white rabbit Manabush would lead her. Katherine sighed and wiped a single tear from her check as she reflected on her great-grandmother's and Soaring Eagle's prophetic instructions.

Charlotte's hectic clamor gave way to an enveloping calmness. The silence gave Katherine time to collect her thoughts and prepare for her workday. She bounced on her toes as she slid the closet door open to a line of blue uniforms—two summer ones and two winter ones. Each garment was draped in precise alignment on hangars and waited for its call to action. Today, she summoned the summer suit, the light blue boxy jacket, and a refined high-neck white blouse tucked into a free-form flared skirt. In less than two minutes, Katherine glowed and felt like a happy winsome young woman. She became an airline hostess ready to smile, entertain, and serve each lucky passenger who boarded her plane. Standing on tiptoes, she reached for her sugar swoop hat. It topped off her outfit in a way that suited her conservative taste. She appreciated that her airline maintained a traditional brand image and didn't put their stewardesses in sexy garb.

Katherine sighed when she thought about the first time Bunny Charlotte posed next to her in her official stewardess uniform. Her mind's eye flashed with a vision of her Cheshire grin. She leaned into a glamor pose with her white-gloved hand holding her standard headpiece, secured with a hatpin. "Don't I look sexy in this tailored blue suit, little blue hat, and my white gloves. Thousands of admirers storm me every trip. Cameras flash, wolf whistles howl, and hordes of autograph hounds surround me. I can't escape them. I get exhausted from all the attention. And you think you Bunnies are hot stuff. You'll never know what it feels like to have men tear themselves apart just to be near a sex symbol like me, the girl in the tailored blue suit with the white gloves. White gloves are much sexier that any white bunny tail." Katherine remembered how she thought her last line would ace her in a Second City comedy skit.

The ringing phone jarred her reverie. "Oh, hi, Emma Jean. I have some exciting news. Charlotte gave me an invitation to the Playboy Mansion press party. It's for the both of us. One thing, please don't panic; it's tomorrow night."

"Oh, bless her heart, that's wonderful. Please do thank her for me. I do declare. I'm not panicked. What should I wear?" Emma Jean's southern charm never failed to give Katherine a warm and cozy feeling.

With her practical Midwestern roots, Katherine responded, "Well, I haven't had time to think about that. We can go for an hour or so."

"Going to a party for an hour and then abruptly leaving is so impolite, Darlin, it's only proper to stay until the party ends." Emma Jean sighed.

Katherine squirmed. Her friend's warm southern drawl cooled. Katherine agreed with her. "Yep, but that's all, cuz we have an early flight the next day. Have to run now. I've got a 5 p.m. check-in."

"Sure, Darlin'. Happy landings."

Just as Katherine dropped the pink princess receiver onto the cradle, she heard a light tap on her bedroom window. A bright nebulous cloud enveloped three black crow feathers hanging fifteen stories up. Katherine's eyes widened as she surveyed the black plumes that fluttered and stalled outside the window right at her eye level, and she gasped. The swirling quills entranced her as she gazed at the feathers' soft float up to the heavens. She blinked and wrapped her arms around her shoulders and trembled.

Katherine's mind scurried for answers. She recognized the feathers as crow feathers, but there were no crows in

Chicago. *What does this mean?* She wished she could remember what she knew about crow feathers. Katherine didn't spend time pondering her Chippewa roots and their legend. Why should she? She was only one-eighth Chippewa and looked more like a blonde from German stock. She'd always wanted her mother's exotic elegance and beauty. People believed her mother came straight from Paris.

She could never become a full-fledged member of the Chippewa tribe, but her Native American genes were part of her existence. She wondered what made these roots intrude on her life now.

2

KATHERINE HELD HER BLUE uniform hat as she dashed through O'Hare Airport's maze of gray-flannel-suited businessmen. Her pounding heart drummed in sync with the clock at the flight crew desk. A stewardess could not be late for her flight check-in, not even by a minute. Katherine had a perfect record with no late check-ins in her file. The seconds ticked as she bobbed and weaved around travelers in front of retail shops.

Just then, she slammed into a man with shiny dark hair. He flashed Katherine a lecherous smile. She flinched when she surveyed him in his slim-fitted jersey blazer over a black turtleneck shirt. Ick! *Not* the typical traveler. When she turned to rush away, she bumped his shoulder. *The Daily Racing Form, Chicago Sun-Times,* and *Life* magazines fell from his hands to the floor. His face turned stoplight red.

Katherine sighed and stooped to recover the man's magazines. She kept her head down as she grabbed the periodicals. Like her cabin crew hostess role she hoisted publications over her head and gave them to the man. Katherine rubbed her neck. *Reminder: An on-duty stewardess is ready to serve at all times.*

Katherine jumped up and flung her airline handbag over her shoulder. The bag opened with a jar and its contents—her bid sheet, her makeup-up case, a stewardess in-flight manual, a dog-eared *Ancient Greek Mythology* paperback, and the Playboy party invitation—floated like leaves on the wind from her purse. She shivered as the contents glided to a landing around his shiny black Chelsea boots.

Like the first snow of winter, her face blended with the crisp whiteness of her blouse. She swept her hands across her face and gulped.

The man touched his hand on her wrist and smiled. "Please, I owe you."

He leaned toward her. "Here ya go." Then he stopped and scanned the invitation before he loosened his grasp. "Do you know people at the Playboy Mansion? I got one of these yesterday. It's one big press party." His eyes skimmed Katherine from head to toe. She squirmed when she sensed his x-ray vision targeted at the top button of her uniform jacket. She wanted to slap his hands and say, "I'm as untouchable as those Playboy Bunnies." He grinned and returned the envelope.

Katherine blinked at his diamond pinky ring when she grabbed the envelope. A red flag warning: do not trust men with pinky rings. Charlotte's voice echoed in her ear, "Stay clear of them. They're total sleazebags."

But, she thought, *he does read* Life *magazine, and I don't get super bad vibes from him.* "Yes, I'll be there. Sorry, but I gotta get to my check-in.

"Bye, Miss Roebling," he said with a sly smile. "Hope to see you again."

Katherine's nostrils flared. Touching her name engraved on the gold wings pinned to the ultra-prim neck-high white blouse, she winced and thought. *Why don't they add my phone number too?*

Katherine rushed through the terminal while the omnipresent smells of stale popcorn and roasted hot dogs floated in and out of her nostrils. When she arrived at her crew lounge, she grumbled under her breath. *Because of that guy I'm two minutes late. This is the first stain on her otherwise golden record.*

Katherine gripped the handle of the crew lounge door. She paused and rubbed the Thunderbird amulet hidden under her blouse, behind her stewardess wings. Touching this precious turquoise stone gave her strength, reminding her of a legend her great-grandmother told her. "Over ten winters ago, our tribe members danced and rejoiced when the rains came. Our tears of joy mixed with the rain and fell into Mother Earth to become the SkyStone." Katherine swallowed a deep breath and released a web of worries into the invisible protection of the Thunderbird's powers. Airline regulations stated no jewelry. To Katherine, this was not jewelry. The necklace was a talisman, part of her existence.

Glancing back, she surveyed the caravan of harried faces sprinting to their flights. Katherine had the urge to follow the frenzied crowd, hop on an airplane, sit back, and enjoy the trip. She sighed and lifted her shoulders. The stark crew lounge door opened to Katherine's fate—an angry desk supervisor and a late check-in.

The pilot from last month's flight glided right after her. "Hey, Katherine. I saw you talking to that young Chicago mafia guy. Are you scheduled on my Las Vegas junket today?"

Katherine moved along. "No. I have a San Fran turn around, and I'm so late for my check-in." Her mouth quivered. "What makes you think that guy is a gangster?"

"He has that 'I'm from Vegas and speak bookies, gambling, and babes' aura. I fly these junkets often since I'm junior. And, these types of guys . . . I'm not saying they're *bad*. He's different. Not like Iowa farm boy pilots, which I am." He tipped his pilot's hat.

Katherine smiled at the aviator. *He must think I'm a sweet innocent girl who needs help with evil characters.* "Wish me luck."

He laughed and shouted after her. "Have a blast. See you on the Vegas trip."

Las Vegas, he must be joking. Katherine cringed at his parting comment and dashed up to the sign-in desk.

The new crewman glanced up from his paperwork and smiled.

"Katherine Roebling, checking in for San Fran flight 219. I got detained in the terminal, so I'm a few minutes late."

"Late? You're not late. That flight canceled two hours ago. Now you're on the Las Vegas flight that departs in two hours at 17:00 p.m." The crewman laughed. "You deserve a gold star for an early check-in."

Katherine pursed her lips to suppress a scream. A gambling junket assignment was like a tempest. "This is a layover flight. My San Fran was a turnaround. I don't have an overnight bag."

The crewman winked and slipped the sign-in sheet to Katherine. With an extra nudge from his chubby hand, the clipboard bumped her breast. "You know how it is: 'the number one rule for a good stewardess is to expect the unexpected. Sign in and prepare to board your flight with a smile that ignites the cabin with a happy glow.'"

Katherine's brow furrowed as she signed the sheet and remembered the next rule: Don't complain and don't explain. "You're right. I can shop for the things I need when I get to Vegas. Drop lucky coins in the slots. I'll have a fab time."

The crewman leaned forward and patted Katherine's hand. "That a girl. You don't know how lucky you are. You have a twenty-four-hour layover at the Sands Hotel in Las Vegas. I'd give my mother's gold teeth for a chance for a night at the Copa Club with those gorgeous showgirls."

Katherine giggled. "Well, if I see any of those ladies, I'll get them to autograph their picture for you. What's the equipment for this trip?"

The jolly man jumped up, grabbing Katherine's hand. "Gimme some skin. Oh, you're beautiful." He dropped back into his seat and perused the crew manifest sheet. "Oh, I got so excited about your trip. I wish it were I on that junket. Hey, your equipment—a DC-6." He paused to stare at Katherine. "This is your first gambling excursion. Keep your guard up with these high rollers."

Katherine stepped away from the crew scheduler and gave a hand salute. "Thanks for the tip. But those fellows might need help if they bother me. I *am* a star member of the Chippewa bow hunters, after all."

Katherine squinted and raised her left arm to aim at an imaginary red dot with an imagined bow. Katherine felt her muscles flex, and she held a clear vision of the feathered shaft. She envisioned a gentle breeze ruffling the meadow grass at the Beaver Creek Reserve, a special place where she practiced instinctual aiming and had learned to hit the bull's eye. She mentally released the arrow, and it hit her target. She used this technique to focus on goals in her life.

Hands clapped. A cheer erupted behind Katherine. "Wow. What strength and form."

Katherine turned around to see two stewardesses she'd flown with before. She couldn't remember their names. "Hey, you know you're safe with me on your flight," she said.

One of the women walked over and nudged Katherine's

shoulder. "Wonder Woman, sorry to run, but it's time to dash for our flight. Can you join us at Butch McGuire's next week? We're meeting the Cubs' rookies there. You athletes have lots in common." The stewardess pointed to the address book. "This is your number, right?"

Katherine loved the Cubs. And McGuire's wasn't a singles bar. It was the neighborhood living room for friends to gather. "Thanks. Call me, and I'll check my calendar." Next week. Katherine remembered the Playboy party invitation that she planned to put in E. J.'s mailbox before her flight. "I have to run now. Happy landings."

On her jaunt to the stewardess mailboxes, Katherine passed the dreaded weight check scale where the supervisor gave random weigh-ins. A chill overcame her every time she got a notice to come to the supervisor's office for her weigh-in. Today, given her long sprint in the airport, she wanted a weigh-in. Her uniform skirt's waistline felt loose, an extra inch of room. She must be five pounds less than her required weight.

Katherine shook her head and closed her eyes. Memories of last winter's preflight weigh-in still made her stomach churn. The vision was like one of Scrooge's visits to the past. She relived the weigh-in with the tall, well-groomed supervisor—her chignon, the smirk on her face, the lilt of pleasure in her voice: "Oh, dear, you weigh 146 lbs. I have to ground you until you lose that pound. We can't have chubby girls; you know the importance of appearances. Come back next week for another weigh-in." Never again did she nibble an unwanted extra ounce of fat.

A few doors past the scale, she arrived at the stewardess mailboxes, crowded in a cubbyhole a few feet wider than an airplane galley. Katherine peeked inside Emma Jean's message-jammed mailbox. She crammed the gold-embossed Playboy party invitation in the last sliver of space. Emma Jean Hasting, the ultimate Southern belle, seemed misplaced as a jet goddess. A Playboy party would be a very different party for her. To Katherine, their friendship was yin and yang, which enriched them both.

Turning from her friend's mailbox, Katherine confronted the company bulletin board. The notice-laden corkboard was the company's way of delivering the marketing message to their frontline image-makers—their stewardesses.

Katherine tilted her head as she scanned her company's recent advertisements. The airline's marketing message for their stewardesses, which was to smile and please their passengers, 75 percent of whom were male, gave her the shivers. She wrinkled her nose and read the ads, each with smiling stewardesses.

"We've improved everything on our nonstop to Chicago, except the stewardesses. We know when to leave well enough alone," one said.

Katherine rolled her eyes.

The second displayed a smiling stewardess holding a gourmet banquet on a tray. Under it, the caption read, "The perfect wife to be." Katherine shrugged and rushed away from her employer's marketing tactics. *Hey, these tactics would make a good cultural anthropology paper.* She grinned and shrugged. *Maybe I should be a cultural anthropologist.* Katherine pursed her lips and clenched her fists. I have to decide soon. *Though, if I don't complete my degree, what will it matter? Who needs another person to dig up old history; especially, a woman?* Katherine sighed and lifted her shoulders, ready for her stewardess duties.

Strolling to her gate, she pondered her fate and the standard stewardess life path: spend two years as a stewardess, meet a guy, get married, have kids, quit flying. She thought of Thoreau:

"Most men lead lives of quiet desperation and go to the grave with the song still in them." That's the same dismal life for most women these days, she thought.

No. That life was not for her. A bigger dream waited for her just beyond the horizon. Visions of mystic goddesses spinning the threads of her fortune danced in her musings. Was it a cord of luck or fate that had jerked her from her studies at Beloit College? And was it luck or destiny that had landed her in Chicago as a stewardess? Katherine chuckled. *Maybe it's training for me to become a cultural anthropologist.*

Katherine thanked the magical karma ties that had brought her childhood friend Charlotte from Chippewa Falls, Wisconsin, to Chicago. Katherine appreciated Charlotte's gift of the coveted invitation to the Playboy press party to her and her friend, Emma Jean. Emma Jean and she weren't party girls, but an event at the Playboy Mansion on Chicago's Gold Coast? A one-time event that neither young woman could pass up.

Charlotte had told her about the celebrities invited to the party. She remembered holding the bright apple red card to the light to read the ornate lettering. Emma Jean had screamed when Katherine translated *Si Non Oscilla's, Noli Tintinnare*: "If you don't swing, don't ring." But Charlotte told her that was just Hefner's message to fit his image and not to take it literally. Katherine breathed a sigh of relief. She hoped to see different places, people, and cultures. To understand the world and find herself at the journey's end. She nodded in agreement with Euripides' saying, "Experience, travel—these are an education themselves."

Katherine mused, *I'm not a Playboy swinger or a Vegas kind of girl, but doesn't every experience enrich me? They're adventures, yes. I won't be judgmental. Accept people as they are and respect them.*

At the Las Vegas gate, the agent jolted Katherine back to the job at hand. "You're working on this flight, right?"

Katherine summoned her best stewardess smile, the one that made her cheeks ache. "Yep. And I'm looking forward to it."

Katherine sauntered across the tarmac to the boarding stairs. At the top of the stairs, a stewardess greeted her. "Are you Katherine? We have a full load, so I hope you're ready for a real blast." She motioned to Katherine and waved from the galley. "Here's our flight manifest. I try to get these high-roller flights wherever they come. I've gotten to know many of these guys. I'm the A stew, so I'll take their tickets. Since you're the most junior, you'll run the meal trays. And there is one more stew. She'll do the drink orders. Are you ready to check the back galley?"

Katherine mustered a half grin. "That's fine with me. I haven't worked a junket, except for a Jobs Corp flight to Atlanta."

The A stew swept her blonde locks off her cheek and laughed. "Aren't those Job Corp charters a bunch of fifteen- or sixteen-year-old boys?" She waved her finger across Katherine's wrist. "These junkets are packed with *real* men. You know the kind. They wear gold all over themselves and have rolls of that green stuff in every pocket." She winked and whispered. "And they're generous with us sky queens."

Katherine offered a half smile at her bigheaded senior stewardess. With a quick brush of her hand, she stopped her chuckle. "I better check the galley. Who's doing the emergency demo?"

"I give all the announcements. The gentlemen all tell me my voice is sexier than Marilyn Monroe. Either one of you can do the demo. Just let me know."

Katherine shrugged and walked out of the forward galley. "Sure thing. I'll check in with you later."

Proceeding to the back of the plane, Katherine did a mental check of emergency exits and evacuation procedures. She checked the in-flight first aid bag and did the regulation galley check. First, in-service meal drawers crosschecked with her in-flight manual.

Katherine peeked out from the galley and waved to the A stew, who motioned that she was ready to give the safety announcement. Katherine smiled and grabbed her props: the oxygen mask and the seat belt. With a quick hand brush, she made herself ready for show time.

Keep smiling; she told herself when she stood in front of the passengers. As the A stew whispered her throaty announcement, Katherine released a breath and smiled at the only two passengers who looked remotely interested in learning the safety details.

When she finished her demo and dropped the mask, she gulped. Another passenger glanced up. She took in a deep breath. It's my lucky day to run into that guy from the airport. He gave her a nodding approval and smiled. She gathered her poise and told herself to act professionally. He was a passenger, and she had to talk with him.

Katherine rubbed her moist palms against her uniform jacket as she greeted him, "Welcome aboard. What a surprise to see you again."

He dropped the *Racing Form* on his tray and offered his hand to Katherine. "Hello, Miss Roebling. Seeing you twice, this must be my lucky day. You ran off, and I didn't get to introduce myself." He paused and coughed. "I'm Dominick Rizzo. And what should I call you instead of Miss Roebling?"

Katherine's mind rushed for a smart answer, but her professional side took command. "I'm Katherine." She glanced up and smiled. "Please excuse me, but we're about ready for departure. Have a great trip."

He raised two fingers to his forehead and gave her a salute. "Happy landings. Maybe we can get together in Vegas for a show or something. Let's check before we land."

Katherine gave him a nod and rushed back to sit down on her jump seat for takeoff. Her heart pounded louder than her thoughts dashing around her head. *This jerk is creepy. When the plane lands, maybe I can hide out in the galley. Stay calm. He's nothing; he's just another guy to blow off, and that's easy.*

While the plane climbed to cruising altitude, Katherine leaned backed and closed her eyes. Soaring over the clouds still thrilled her. It gave her a sense of freedom.

The co-pilot's greeting that the plane had reached cruising altitude was the okay for her to attend to her passengers,

In the galley, she wrapped herself in her serving smock and checked out the meal service. Her fingers glided over the list of delicacies: lobster cocktail, Melba Rounds, Mignon of veal, rice pilaf, butter broccoli, Parker House roll, chocolate layer cake, coffee, tea, or milk.

A deep male voice bellowed behind her. "Hey, does that look delicious."

Katherine turned to face a ruddy, balding man wearing a snug white silk shirt unbuttoned to his navel. "It looks sumptuous." He aimed his eyes below her neckline. "The meal, I mean. I'm a beef guy, but the chicken I'll do for a snack. So you're Miss Roebling. Pleased to meet you." He gave Katherine a slight elbow jab. "I'm the Big Buck; everyone gave me the name on these junkets. I'm in seat 10A. Stop by."

He's a charmer. He's like the guys our stewardess school instructor mentioned during the passengers-to-avoid session. Katherine smiled. "Please excuse, I have to start the meal service. Hope you have a pleasant flight."

Katherine rolled her shoulders, straightened her back, and smiled; she was ready to make every passenger feel at home. As she strolled down the aisle, she grinned at passengers reading and sleeping. It was a regular flight, just another workday. Then, like an unexpected cyclone, three nasty creatures greeted her. Katherine narrowed her eyes and squinted when she spied them in row 20. She soon found out that Big Buck was a choirboy compared to these craggy, greasy, vermin calling her. "Hey, come on over here."

Katherine rubbed her Thunderbird. "Yes, gentlemen?"

The creepiest one, his shirt unbuttoned down to his navel, grease plastering his hair, grabbed her hand. "Yeah, we need fire water."

"This is a Vegas trip," the other said. "Where are all the cigar-store Indians guarding the slots? Don't you have them on board to get us in the mood for our gaming spree?"

The man next to him shoved his elbow into his side. "Hey, Sam, tell her one of your jokes."

Katherine's face turned red.

He cleared his throat. "The fastest thing on a reservation's the beer truck; the second fastest thing's the Indian chasing it."

Three filthy mouths opened to release roars of laughter, spit flying from their mouths. Passengers on all sides turned and gave Katherine a look that said, "You have one lousy job."

"Excuse me, gentlemen," she said, "I have to check on the other passengers. I'll check back later."

Creep number one reached into his pocket and pulled out a shot glass. "Hey, take this with you and bring it back with the full four ounces, babe."

Katherine moved to avoid his pinch on her backside. "Yes, sir."

Katherine scurried by passengers and averted her eyes from their pitying stares. When she got to the galley, she glanced at the shot glass and held back her first instinct: to fill it with hot water, walk back, and pour the water on his head.

Instead, she rested her hand over the Thunderbird. Her heart jerked as she surveyed Native American images on the shot glass with despicable inscriptions. 0 oz. Low man on the totem pole, 1 oz. Squaw, 2 oz. Brave, 3 oz. Medicine Man. The most intimidating was the 4 oz., a reclining Indian with the caption, "Happy Hunting Ground." Katherine peeked over her shoulder and threw the shot glass in the trash.

Katherine sighed and looked outside the galley. She delivered all the lunch trays, served all the airline quota of drinks, and survived her unpleasant Vegas passengers. She took a tour of the cabin, As she passed by the passengers were either snoring, reading, or playing poker. It was a safe time for her to take a brief escape. A vacant airplane bathroom was a haven, a place to get calm. As soon as Katherine closed the bathroom door, she took in a deep breath of smoke free air. Her nose twitched with pleasure since the air wasn't full of the cigarette and cigar smoke that permeated the cabin. Katherine scowled at the mirror and wrinkled her brow. She touched her Thunderbird and closed her eyes. *I have to figure out a story for the lost shot glass.* Childhood memories of Chippewa Falls and the Native American citizens boosted her defiance.

Katherine unlocked the bathroom door and heard a soft crunch. A black crow feather touched the toe of her blue three-inch pumps. No one was near her. She swallowed and pressed the glossy black feather against her chest then bowed her head and slipped the mysterious plume inside her purse. Katherine looked up and smiled and whispered. *Thank you, Great Spirit, for watching out for me. I will need this for good luck and protection.*

After finding the feather, nothing could get her down for the rest of the trip, and the captain's pre-landing announcement came on sooner than she expected.

As she walked through the cabin to make a final passenger seat belt check before landing in Las Vegas, she flashed a bright smile to the passengers. The Cheshire cat grin reflected the rapid flow of thoughts scampering through her mind. A desire to hop through the cabin pushed her down the aisle.

Katherine finished her cabin check, settled into the jump seat, leaned back, and wondered how this trip might have been her best trip. *At 30,000 feet, I received the message about the reason the feather floated past my apartment window. Now I remembered what my Great-grandmother told me that a crow feather means strength, wisdom, power, and freedom. I must discover the reason for this omen and sign. What does this mean?*

3

CHICAGO'S WARM SPRING BREEZE beckoned to the hibernating dwellers, calling them from their dwellings. They emerged from their lakefront high-rises, townhouses, and three-floor walk-ups to gather at their favorite pubs after a day spent enjoying Lake Michigan.

Danny O'Brien was a newcomer to the Lincoln Park neighborhood. Six months ago, he moved from his Southside home and discovered an acceptable parish home and favorite pub: St. Michael's in Old Town and John Barleycorn. Everything fit. A good Irish boy needed his church and his bar.

Danny glided from his three-story walk-up apartment to John Barleycorn. He waved at his neighbors walking their dogs down Dickens Street. When he entered John Barleycorn, he ogled the charming young women mingling at the bar. Danny's whole body reacted to the sight of these attractive young women, prompting his face to flush and his groin to tingle. He wanted to dance a jig. He looked up, winked, and touched Lucky McCool, his lucky charm leprechaun in his pocket. Since Danny was five years old, he'd kept McCool with him since he helped him feel Irish.

Pale ale and stout odors wafted through the room. Raucous laughter from the Tuesday-night softball crowd drowned out the classical background music. Huddled in the back room of the historic tavern, they clinked their mugs of suds. Locals told tales of hearing the former bootleggers' bottles rattling in the corners of the bar. The locals relished telling their jokes about John Barleycorn's past, as diverse as a Chinese laundry and a speakeasy.

Danny's brother, one of the softball players, waved. "Hey, Danny, grab a brew."

Danny raised his hand and ordered his favorite drink. Guinness Extra Stout flowed down his throat. With each sip, it kindled louder laughter. In his amateur boxing days, a cold Guinness after one of his many KOs affirmed his victory.

Danny sauntered to his brother's table to join him and his teammates. With shouts of laughter, they reran their winning plays. "You made a great double play in the fifth," one guy yelled to Patrick, Danny's brother.

"What the hell gave you the idea to steal home on that bunt play?" Patrick asked his fellow teammate.

"And whattaya think of Billy," another said, "the strike-out king?"

Danny sat and smiled at the winning team. "You guys did it tonight?"

His brother grinned and turned to Danny. "That we did. And I've got even better news. You've got an interview at the Playboy Club tomorrow at 11:00 a.m. I gave them the full rundown on your amateur boxing career and bouncing at Murphy's. You have one foot in the door. Getting the next foot inside the club is up to you."

Danny gave his brother a shoulder punch and beamed. "I'm ready. What should I do?"

Patrick, a private practice attorney, understood the workings of Chicago. In his practice, he confronted the Chicago machine politics and the "Chicago Outfit." His motto was "stay clean." Five years Danny's senior, Patrick had stepped in to raise Danny when their policeman father got killed in the line of duty.

Patrick looked like Danny's twin brother. They both had a muscular build, a ready smile, and balding-yet-handsome good looks. Patrick winked at Danny. "Well, you can handle yourself with the Outfit, so you're okay there. Just keep your cool if you see FBI in the club or the mansion. They read every issue of *Playboy*. They say it's for research on the *Playboy* philosophy and that counterculture malarkey. As for those Bunnies, you can look at them and protect them, but don't touch them. Use your muscles on the drunks and perverts, and you'll be a champ."

"I'll try my best."

"And remember Dad's warning: 'If you see a lady in distress, move with caution.'"

Danny furrowed his brow and considered his brother's last comment.

4

THE BRIGHT KITCHEN LIGHT jolted Katherine awake. She needed lots of coffee this morning. While the coffee pot percolated, and her English muffin toasted, she yawned and stretched. The flight home from Vegas was uneventful, but the flight there still rattled her thoughts.

She had to admit the Copa Room was fantastic. Showgirls dressed in red sequined evening gowns and long white gloves sang and danced. The ladies oozed talent and charm. After the antics on the flight, Katherine had appreciated the musical extravaganza. Life was a blend of good and bad. The Copa Room show was good. The obnoxious antics of the few grown men were the bad. Overshadowing everything was the feather and the message it gave Katherine to find its purpose in her life.

Katherine smiled as she paged through her journal of experiences. She found a quote that she liked from Ernest Hemingway's *A Movable Feast:* "By then I knew that everything good and bad left an emptiness when it stopped. But if it was bad, the emptiness filled up by itself. If it was good, you could only fill it by finding something better." Now she'd tasted the tainted life and didn't enjoy the queasy feeling it gave her. Katherine curled her lips and pressed her hands to her stomach. *Those men with the "injun" shot glass and their comments about a drunken "injun."* She grabbed her Thunderbird necklace and wrote a note. *Next time, I will defend my people.*

Her brow wrinkled with the distant memory of her first experience with attacks and ridicule of Native Americans. She closed her eyes and heard the three teenage boys on Chippewa Falls' Main Street joking. *"What is an empty Budweiser on the side of the road? An Indian artifact. And what is a half-empty can of Budweiser on the side of the road? A rare Indian artifact."* The jokes darted from her ears straight to her heart. She clasped her chest to stop herself from bursting into tears.

Katherine closed her notepad. She glanced at the photo of the Las Vegas showgirl who'd autographed it for the best crew deskman in the whole world. Katherine stared at a glob of strawberry crimson. She'd accidentally plastered the performer's head with blobs of jam. *Oh, no, that friendly crew desk supervisor promised he'd do anything for me if I got him an autograph from a Copa girl, but not one with a splash of jam on her forehead. Now, he'll give me Las Vegas junkets until I get another autographed photo without a jam blot on it for him.*

The apartment buzzer startled her. She pressed the speaker button. "Hi, Fred."

"Yes, Miss Katherine. I have a flower delivery for you. Should I bring them up now?"

"Sure, Fred. Thanks."

Katherine put her finger to her lips and reached for the doorknob. *Who would send me flowers?*

"Dazzling flowers," Fred said. "Do you know how much yellow roses and one orchid cost? I know, cuz my mom works in a flower shop."

Preoccupied with her delivery, Katherine waved. "Oh, yes. Thanks, Fred, see ya later."

Katherine left the front door ajar and walked to her living room. A few minutes later, Emma Jean waltzed through the unlocked door.

"Hey there, Darlin'."

Katherine turned with a jerk. She dropped the delivery card on the table and greeted her friend. "Hey, lady. How did you get in here?"

"Well, for starters, Fred knows me. He said that he'd delivered flowers to you. Who sent them?" Like a gazelle, she glided over the beanbag chair to pick up the unread card.

Katherine admired her friend's ease and poise. She'd learned how to sit tall in a saddle with aplomb. Those southern women popped out of their mother's wombs with grace and refinement.

Katherine retrieved the card and laughed. "I bet they're from my parents." She smiled.

"There's no mystery."

Katherine flashed a playful grin. She held the card in her hand and started to read it. Her confident smile changed to jaw-dropping shock. "Oh, my God! Oh, no. It can't be. I spoke with him for five minutes."

Katherine threw the card on the table.

Emma Jean chuckled and shrugged her shoulders. "Well, I reckon you've eliminated your mom and dad as suspects."

Katherine sighed. "They're from a passenger on the gambling junket." She skipped telling the details of her run-in with Dominick at the airport, and her dismay when he appeared on her flight. *I'm going to ignore him, and he'll go away.* "He thanked me for being so pleasant and looks forward to seeing me tonight."

"Tonight! Did you forget the Playboy party? Darlin', it's not proper to cancel prior commitments. I'm dressed and ready to go. I spent lots of time and money on this outfit. Don't you just love it?" She waved her hands in the air, sighed, and collapsed on the sofa.

Katherine thought Emma Jean was a fashion goddess. She did look great in her red mini skirt with a white lace blouse and paisley fishnet tights. "You look fabulous."

Katherine took in a deep breath to wait while Emma Jean relaxed.

"Girlfriends are forever, Emma, you tell me that story all the time. I still remember what you taught me about how to deal with men. Men are like buses. If you miss one, you can always catch another. He meant that he'd look for me tonight at the Playboy party. You know it's kinda like when a guy says I'll give you a call. Have you ever waited around for calls?"

"Okay," Emma replied with exaggerated exasperation. "So, tell me. Is he a musician, an actor, a member of the press, what?"

"Well, he's not any of those types." Katherine nibbled her nails. "He may have family connections from Italy. He mumbled something about his dad's name." Katherine coughed. "If I heard right, he said his last name was Rizzo. He coughed and said his name in one breath. It sent chills through me and landed like a boulder in my stomach. My instincts shouted loud and clear on this one."

Katherine turned away from her friend to gaze out the window as the L train moved along its 100-year-old tracks. It prompted her to review her list of things to do in Chicago, including riding all the Chicago L lines with all its rainbow of colors. Checked off her list were the brown and purple lines. She liked the humming sound of the train wheels as it clanked over the old tracks.

I'll avoid any involvement with Dominick, she thought to herself. *He may be a decent guy and* might *not be a gangster. But I'm not wasting time to find out.* Her face turned red. *But what would Mom and Dad say if he is? Chippewa Falls would shun me from town forever.*

Emma Jean's faced turned white. "Wait. Do you mean Vinni 'the Butcher' Rizzo? He's up there with Al Capone and Frank Nitti, Katherine! You don't want to mess with them!" Emma Jean giggled. "Of course, I'm a proper southern girl, but I do adore dark, handsome men." She wrinkled her brows. "My neighbor, Dave, works for Mayor Daley. He spent an hour telling me tales about the Chicago Outfit while we sipped wine. They do terrible things, like Chop Shop stuff. Do you know, they have the nerve to steal peoples' cars, tear them apart, and then sell the vehicle parts?" Emma Jean flinched and wrinkled her nose. "And they do something like off-track betting. He won't tell the worst things that they do. He said it wasn't fit for lady's ears. But he did say they were involved with the Central Intelligence Agency. He said those thugs are the biggest of Chicago mobster legends. Oh, my heavens, what about your parents? My mama and papa would ban me from the family if I dated someone like that. They're carpetbaggers. Scalawags!"

Katherine rolled her eyes and scanned from left to right. *Hm, Dominick had* The Daily Racing Form. *And he was in a huddle with two guys on my flight to Las Vegas. They wore pinky rings, and gold chains flopped down to their navel.* Her chest sunk like a deflated bagpipe. *I can see Dad's finger waving at me.* Katherine pressed her clenched fist against her pursed lip. She sighed. "Hey, remember, my father was a civil rights lawyer in Chicago a few years ago. That's why I'm upset. And this is what I get for doing my job since our supervisors require us to talk to the passengers?"

Emma Jean raised her hand, "Darlin', remember, I'm a southern lady. Southern women are polite and speak when someone speaks to them first."

Katherine recalled her father's mafia stories. Some of his clients never got untangled from their web. "Okay, okay," she said. "Back to my party predicament. I'll just get busy with other people and ignore him. He may not even notice me." Despite her words, hoping for the best didn't wipe away her fear of the worst.

"Kate, Darlin', don't worry. It'll be okay. We'll have a ball tonight."

Katherine tilted her head and clasped her hands behind her neck. Something about Emma's voice wasn't coming off right. She glanced at her watch. Emma Jean had arrived pretty early to go to the party. *Something's wrong, and here I am fussy over nothing.* Then she noticed that her friend's makeup looked like a mess of smudges and smears, something this Southern belle *never* allowed to happen. "Emma Jean, are you okay?"

"It's Mama. I'm not telling her where we're going tonight. I tell Mama everything. She's my best friend. She believes I'm a perfect Southern belle. Even my being up north and working as a stewardess causes Mama to get the vapors and faint."

Katherine raised her brows and chuckled. "You're over twenty-one. I don't tell my mom and dad everything. And they expect that I won't. They trust me."

"But this is different. Northern families let their daughters go wild. Mama still thinks that I just go to cotillions and church socials at the Methodist church and then rest under a parasol under a magnolia tree and practice my Southern belleness. You know I'm born and bred to wait on the veranda for the proper boy to take me home to the South. There's no veranda in Chicago, and I still want to go tonight. Bless your heart for letting me blubber on."

Katherine scratched her head. She couldn't relate to Emma Jean's preordained Southern belle pattern for living. Compared to Emma Jean, she felt wild and free. She enjoyed being considered untamed. Her parents didn't give her a road map. They made her feel that she could become her own person and follow her uncharted path. I still see dad smiling at me when I graduated from Chippewa Valley High School and he handed me a note with a quote from our favorite author Henry David Thoreau: *Go confidently in the direction of your dreams, Live the life you've always imagined.* And my imagination tells me the sky is the limit. Wow, I'm like our school mascot, the mighty Hawk. I'm getting ready to fly higher than I've ever flown before. I have my own power and my own wings. "Hey, we all have different ways," she said. "If you're not comfortable with the party, you'll regret going tonight. I'm cool with that. We can go to McGuire's or somewhere else."

Emma Jean smiled. "Oh, Darlin', I'll just have to regret not telling Mama and Papa. You know, I never miss a party, even if it's at the Playboy Mansion."

Katherine recalled the first time she and Charlotte walked past the great brick and limestone Playboy Mansion on North State Parkway. They both wanted to live in the elegant mansion.

Katherine clapped her hands. "Hey, I have a good story. Remember my story about Charlotte and the Playboy Mansion?"

Emma Jean nodded. "Yes."

"Well, before Charlotte got the Bunny job, I researched the history of the mansion before the Hefner Playboy era." Katherine noticed Emma Jean's eyes glazing over. She leaned in toward her. "This is the point. I found out that a law partner of Abraham Lincoln built Hef's mansion. At that time, some of the guests were Theodore Roosevelt and Abraham Lincoln. You could tell your mother about the history of the mansion. It's impressive."

Emma Jean shrieked. "Darlin', if I mention Abraham Lincoln, she'd scream more than if I tell her I went to the Playboy Mansion."

Katherine laughed. "Don't tell Mama and let's go have an adventure."

5

A SPRING BREEZE ENVELOPED the women. Fresh green leaves dressed the trees that lined North State Parkway. Springs floral scents filled the air. The two friends chattered as they strolled by the elegant brownstones.

Katherine waved her hand to point at the homes and giggled. "These are Hugh Hefner's next-door neighbors."

Emma Jean glanced at her friend. "Would you like to live in a home like this someday?"

Katherine shrugged. "Not really. I don't know where I want to live. Living on Chicago's Gold Coast is fine for now." Katherine laughed to herself when she recalled her first impression of the Gold Coast. On her quest to find an apartment, the Playboy Mansion was the first home that appealed to her. Of course, she didn't know it was the Playboy Mansion. It had a regal appeal like an understated beauty without fake adornment. Katherine smiled. *Wow, was I a poor judge of places. I hope I'm better at judging people.* She liked the friends she'd made at Butch McGuires, the neighborhood parties, and the Lincoln Park Zoo's volunteer events. Katherine sighed. Chicago was a great place. Wherever she went, Chicago would be in her heart.

The women continued their stroll as they passed the Ambassador Hotel. Katherine cheered. "Hey, the Pump Room is where we have to get our next big dates to take us."

"Yes, even Mama tells me that I must go to the Pump Room. She loves Frank Sinatra's song 'My Kind of Town'. He has a line in the song about the Pump Room. Mama insisted that when I go there, I must get lots of celebrities' autographs."

They arrived at the Playboy Mansion, a grand limestone and brick facade designed by David Adler, a Chicago architect, wreathed in an ornate eight-foot wrought iron fence. Katherine's eyes twinkled. "This belongs in an English country village. Where are the sheep grazing in the nearby green pastures?" she asked as she opened the iron gate to the mansion. "Yikes. I almost forgot!" Katherine reached inside her purse to pull out the fake press badge. She pinned it to the strap on her purse. "There, I hope it's not too visible."

"Darlin', are you really going to interview people?"

"Only if I need to as a cover. Charlotte said the publicity woman might look for me." Katherine released a breath and jerked a spiral notebook from her handbag. "Since Charlotte told me to look the part, I have this pad in case I have to act like I'm really a student journalist." Katherine gulped. "Remember, my fake story is our ticket to this party." She smiled at her friend. "Cross your fingers that I'll never have to write a real article for this event. I want to write about serious stuff like ancient Greece, not a lowbrow story about a Playboy party!"

Emma Jean chuckled. "As Papa would say about your situation, it's like getting caught with your pants down. But if you're faking it as a student reporter, you can still interview people that you'd like to meet. You can play it like the old Southern belle ploy of the dropped hanky in front a man she wants to meet."

Katherine wrinkled her brow and tapped her finger on her lips. "Hey, I could also use it to avoid someone."

Emma Jean winked. "Like that gangster guy?"

"Yep."

Emma Jean turned to her friend. "Darlin', how do I look?"

Katherine wanted to tell her to forget the Aqua Net hair spray. *Maybe she could tell her that it's not good for the environment or that it made her look stiff and not as feminine and alluring as she could be.* She scolded herself for criticizing her friend. She really did appreciate her. Her gooey black bouffant hairstyle was part of her mystique. And everyone loved how her deep blue eyes twinkled when she laughed. "Geez, you look fantastic. When you make your grand entrance, every guy will turn to you and forget those curvy Bunnies."

Katherine turned around and squealed. "Look! There's Ernie Banks. He's going to the party! Wait till I tell Dad."

Emma Jean gave her friend a wink. "Will your papa be impressed that you saw him at a Playboy gala?"

Katherine's heart pounded. "Well . . . he might be impressed with the Playboy party more than Ernie Banks."

A statuesque Bunny with gleaming white teeth opened the massive double doors and welcomed the young women. She looked dramatic in her black satin corseted Bunny costume. Katherine remembered Charlotte's comment that the black outfit was a mark of achievement for a Bunny. Katherine offered a half smile and a sweaty handshake.

The young women entered the elegant, turn-of-the-century mansion. Its classical stateliness was unexpected backdrop with the cacophony of The Who and festive laughter. They noticed every detail of the wood-paneled room and ogled the variety of partygoers, from celebrities to politicians to famous athletes.

The lady guests' fashions ranged from bathing suits to snug mod dresses, and the men were in tailored suits with narrow lapels and skinny ties. Emma Jean threw her hands to cover her open mouth. "I can see my dear parents' reactions if they knew about the goings-on in this place. Mama would faint on the couch, and Papa would aim his shotgun at these rascals." She paused and sighed. "Do I have to put on a bathing suit?"

"Maybe later if we decide that we want to slide down the firemen's pole to the underground swimming pool. According to Charlotte, we don't have to change. I think I'll pass on the swim suit and stay out of trouble."

Katherine wanted to find a safe place to hide, to mix into the safety of the crowd. She spied the circular stairs leading to the giant ballroom. "Let's follow the crowd to the ballroom. That's where the action starts."

Emma Jean gawked over her shoulder. "Oh, no! Katherine, look down there." She pointed to a dark-haired man in a tuxedo jacket with a busty bikini-clad young woman on each arm.

Katherine shrugged. "Oh, that's Hugh Hefner. That's his style."

"That's style?"

Katherine chucked. "Yes, if you run a mega sex empire."

"Sex empire? What decadence!"

"Yeah, I agree. Hey, forget Hefner." Katherine glimpsed the mobster and ducked her head behind a group of guests climbing the stairs. "Oh no, that's him on the sofa. Hurry. I can't let him see me."

After each step, Katherine kept her eyes on the next step. With her foot on the last step, her mind focused on finding a safe place away from Dominick. Katherine forged ahead up the stairs and peered over the bobbing heads.

Katherine took one quick glance over her shoulder at the leopard-suited Bunny with sunglasses leading people up the circular stairs. The euphoric crowd bounced and twisted to the Watusi as the throng drifted into the grand ballroom like a giant helium balloon. Then, she spied him. Her shoulders tightened. Her heart bounced against her chest. *I might be safe. He looks comfy lounging on that huge black leather sofa with four women encircling him. Yuck, Emma Jean will vomit if she sees him. In fact, I want to vomit too.* His thick dark wavy hair swept over the collar of his pink shirt. *A gaudy orange, green, and black paisley tie aren't our style.*

Katherine tapped Emma Jean's shoulder and whispered. "Dominick is here. That's him on the black leather sofa."

Emma Jean sighed. "Katherine! That guy attracts sleazy women with his black velvet bell-bottoms. He's despicable."

Emma Jean shivered when she saw him leer with a plastic grin as he turned from one woman to the next. He reminded her of a sheik with his harem, each woman competing for his attention.

Emma Jean tugged at her friend's arm and pointed at the womanizer on the sofa. "Well, Darlin', is that your Dominick fella?"

Right after Emma Jean's words left her mouth, the notorious ladies' man noticed Katherine. He waved and ascended the stairs to meet them.

Katherine crouched and dropped to the floor, moving her hand over the carpet is if she were searching for something. *I have to think of a way to avoid this jerk. I don't want him to ruin our fun. Maybe he'll find someone else in the ballroom.* She tugged on her friend's skirt to get her to join the search. "We've got to crawl over there and mingle with the people around that hors d'oeuvre table. Just keep feeling on the carpet and pretend to look for my contacts."

After crawling halfway across the floor, Katherine felt a tap on her shoulder. She froze and took in a breath. With a nonchalant air, she looked up and smiled as Dominick's paisley tie tickled her nose.

"Katherine? What ya doing? You okay?" Dominick said as he proffered his hand.

"Oh, hi, I'm looking for my contacts. Thanks." Katherine refused to extend her hand.

Dominick nodded and continued through the crowd with an, "Okay . . ."

Emma Jean raised herself halfway. "Katherine, don't you think we can get up now? I'm ready to move on, this is silly."

Katherine tugged her skirt and whispered, "I know, but we'd better act like we're still looking for something. Just a couple more feet, and then you pretend you found something on the floor."

Emma Jean shouted, "I found it!" Emma Jean jumped up and feigned handing a contact to Katherine.

Katherine raised and sighed. "This looks fake."

"Oh, no, Darlin', I could have found it sooner. We're here for fun, not stress. Forget about him. Isn't that what you said you'd do?"

Katherine skimmed the massive spread of food, an array of gourmet cheeses, fruits, smoked salmon, and prime rib. A Playboy Bunny ice carving stood at the center of the sumptuous morsels.

Looking over her shoulder, Katherine released a sigh. "Hey, we need a table surrounded by a big crowd nibbling food to blend in with them. Okay?"

Emma Jean glided through the massive ballroom like a queen hoping to command the attention of admirers.

"Darlin', isn't this beautiful?" she said. "Why this room—it's as big as a polo field full of men."

Katherine bit her lips. For now, her mind wasn't on working the room to find a celebrity or possible date. She wanted to escape the scuzzy guy and vanish into the crowd. The size of the room made Katherine feel safe. She felt she could disappear in here. She grabbed a handful of grapes.

Out of the corner of her eye Katherine noticed Danny O'Brien as he wrinkled his brow and touched his lucky leprechaun charm in his pocket. She wondered how unusual he seemed compared to other men wandering around the ballroom.

If she could peer into his mind, she'd find her answers. Since it was his first day on the job, he wanted to make the best impression possible. It was his business to perform as a gentleman toward the Bunnies and protect them, but if there was no danger, his job was to keep his cool. His instincts were strong, but he felt superstitious reinforcement when he touched his lucky leprechaun. Hey, what's up? Danny sensed the leprechaun's message to turn his face toward the lovely lady, who looked helpless. He always trusted his secret companion.

With a determined glide, he walked to her. "Excuse me, miss. I'm Danny O'Brien. I work here, and I just wanted to see if you're okay."

Katherine gasped for air. She swallowed a grape. Hm, he must have seen me acting like a drunken fool floundering on the floor. Wiping her mouth, she responded, "I was looking for my lost contact, and my friend found it. Thanks for your concern, but I'm fine now."

Danny bit his tongue to avoid asking more questions. He remembered his brother's words: "If you see a damsel in distress, move with caution." Instead, he just smiled and nodded. "Very good. Do let me know if you need anything."

Katherine released a breath and walked to a serving dish of Swedish meatballs. She saw Dominick huddled with two sleazy fellows wearing the standard uniform of white silk shirts opened to their navels. Gold chains hung to their belt buckles. And yes, they each wore large diamond pinky rings. Dominick slipped a five-inch wad of cash in one of the guy's hands. Her heart raced like a thoroughbred racing to the finish line. Her shoulders tightened. She scouted around for shelter, but it was too late.

Danny had his eye on Dominick because his brother had educated him on the mafia and their signs. From a distance, Danny observed Dominick slipping a wad of cash into the suspicious man's suit pocket and motioning him toward the circular stairs. Dominick's shady companion dashed down the stairs. Dominick ran his fingers through his hair, threw his shoulders back, noticed Katherine at the appetizer table, and sauntered up to her. "Hey, Katherine. Would you like a drink?"

Katherine cocked her head and glimpsed at Danny O'Brien as he cast squinted eyes at Dominick. His glance said it all. She could almost hear him say, "Get away from that viper." She wanted to run away.

6

KATHERINE CRINGED AS DOMINICK yanked her against his paisley tie, grabbed her arm, and twisted her wrist into a captive lock. Like a glutton, he swallowed her lips in a kiss that nearly made Katherine gag. "Hey, sweetie," he whispered, "have you been trying to hide from me? You got my flowers, didn't you?"

Katherine gulped. "Oh, thank you so much. I forgot myself. I was busy looking for my contacts. I wanted to come over and tell you how much I appreciated them. But I didn't want to interrupt Mister Popular." Katherine forced a half smile as she slipped her hand over the neckline of her red velvet mini dress, feeling reassurance from the turquoise necklace snuggled under the fabric. She gulped and searched for something, a safety net, or an escape route. Her father's smiling face burst forth in her mind's camera. He whispered his favorite John Wayne saying, "Courage is being scared to death and saddling up anyway." She raised her back, offered a cold stare to Dominik, and tilted her head toward Emma

Jean. "Would you like to join us?" *Now, why did I say that? I should have said it was nice seeing him, but we have some friends to meet.*

Right on cue, Emma Jean motioned to Katherine. "Golly, look over there!" She fanned herself and squealed. "Mr. Handsome, Dean Martin, is in the game room with a pool cue in his hand. And, oh dear, a chubby, gray-haired woman cornered him. Let's cut through that large fireplace and rescue him. Quick, he's going somewhere else. Come on, Katherine."

Dominick grabbed Katherine's arm and glared at Emma Jean. "Hey, babe, get lost. Go find your own playmate."

Katherine's heart pounded; her blood roared through her body like a runaway train. *I have to be calm and smooth with this guy. His steamy breath reminds me of a dragon with flames flying out his nostrils.* She paused with a firm glance at her friend and looked toward the celebrity. "Go ahead and get Mr. Martin's autograph and I'll be there in a sec. Remember, I'll need it for my article." *Okay, I'm ready to be a super reporter. I have a great escape plan.*

Emma Jean giggled and patted her friend's arm. "Oh, Darlin', that's a fantastic idea. Mr. Martin is so handsome. I'll offer to bring him a mint julep and show him real Southern charm."

Dominick grumbled under his breath and pulled Katherine to him. "Tell your sidekick to stay away from us. I want one special woman at a time. Capisci?"

Katherine's knees wobbled. Dominick's dark eyes shot bolts of fire. They reminded her of the rattlesnakes she ran from as a young girl playing in the Wisconsin meadows. "Please excuse me, but I need to talk to that person, so I can write an inside scoop on this first Playboy Penthouse event." Katherine pulled the press badge from her purse strap and pasted it right over her heart. She flashed a wide-toothed smile. Finally, she dug inside her purse and waved the spiral notebook in front of Dominick's face. "I'll be quick."

Dominick's scowl made Katherine flinch. "I promised my roommate, the Playboy Bunny who gave me the invitation for tonight, that I'd write an article about the event. It's for my friend since she went to the trouble to get me this party invitation. You understand friendship and keeping your promises to them, don't you?" Katherine thought about the mafia's rules on friendship.

Dominick released her. "Sure, I do. I can visit with a couple of old friends over there. Get your story. I'll take you somewhere after."

Dominick winked at Katherine and slapped her ass. Katherine wanted to slap his face and run away, but that Danny guy would come and make a scene, so she made a hasty retreat.

Katherine rubbed her shoulders as she made her way away from Dominick. Sweat oozed from every pore in her body, and her breath stuck in her throat. Katherine's muscles tightened, and her eyes darted from left to right; like a deer glaring at a hunter's spotlight. She couldn't move. She had negative panic; the kind scared passengers experience after a plane crash. Her instructor in stewardess school emergency training class had told her to use her hatpin to poke frozen passengers out of their seats after a plane crash. Now she needed someone to give her a pin poke.

I'm trained to get people out of burning airplanes. I can do this. I'll find a person to interview and make my escape.

She surveyed the crowd. Two women in bathing suits strolled past her toward the underground pool. A line of half-naked people in swimming suits lined up to slide down the brass fireman's pole.

On her way to the crowd, Katherine made the mistake

of turning around and sighting Dominick's dark eyes focused on her. Her clammy hands dropped her notebook.

She turned from his stalking eyes and stumbled over the feet of a waiter wearing a red jacket. She tumbled to the floor, and her black sling pumps flew off her feet. Her face warmed to a red the shade of the waiter's crimson jacket.

Not her prince charming, but he held her black slippers in his hand for assistance. With a profound foreign accent, he smiled. "Do you want to sit?"

Katherine focused her dazed eyes. *Right now, his offer is my best option. As Dad says, take the ball and go with it.* "Yes. Can I go somewhere away from here?"

"Yes." He nodded toward a swinging door. "The kitchen. Okay?"

After the embarrassing nosedive, Katherine wanted to take refuge. Speechless, she nodded.

———

Chefs were shouting orders and waiters zooming in and out of the swinging door provided sanctuary.

She felt safe here but wondered what she'd tell Charlotte. That she'd spent the evening in the Playboy Mansion's kitchen? She turned to her host. "Thank you for helping me. My name's Katherine."

He motioned for her to sit on a stool in the pantry with the linens. "My name is Angelos." He smiled. "Please sit here. I'll get you something to drink."

Katherine's heart pounded in rhythm with her eyes as she searched to find an exit out of the kitchen. Her manners took over, and she postponed her escape. She wasn't sure she was ready to return to the wolf's advances. "A glass of water would be fantastic."

While she watched him drop ice into a glass of water, it occurred to her that he might be the perfect person to interview. *Hm, and his name is Angelos. That's almost like an angel. Is that an omen?* She whipped out her notebook and pen.

Angelos handed her a tall tumbler of water with ice that clinked against the crystal glass. "I have to get back to work. But you can stay here a bit longer."

Katherine's hand shook as water slipped over the rim of the chilled glass. "Thank you, but I should get back to the party. I don't want to get you into trouble, you've been so pleasant. But could I ask you for one more favor?"

The soft scent of garlic butter floated in the air. Turning her nose in the direction of the scent, which was a sizzling plate of escargot resting on a nearby table.

Angelos reached for the plate and offered it to Katherine.

She ran her tongue over her lips. Her stomach said yes, but her head said no.

"Oh, no, thank you. Hey, will I get you in trouble? Is that your boss staring at us?"

Angelos glanced at the annoyed maître d'. "I told him you're Mr. Hefner's friend. He said it's okay for you to stay here for a while, but I'd better get moving." He paused. "Will you be okay? Let me know if I can do anything for you."

"I'm a journalism student, and I'm writing an article about the Playboy Mansion and this event. When you have time, could I interview you? I'll be quick. Can you spare two minutes?"

Angelos smiled. "I'm a student too. I'm not sure why you'd interview me, but I'd love to."

Katherine grabbed a pen from her purse. She twisted on the stool, hoping to summon a question. "Great. You understand then. I have many questions, but I'll just ask one. Okay?"

Angelos glared at the scowling maître' d' then back at Katherine. He rubbed his chin. "One question is fine. Then, why not give me your phone number? You can ask me more questions later."

I already got myself in trouble with Dominick . . . but what choice do I have? She scribbled her name and number and handed a tattered page to Angelos. He tucked it in his pocket and smiled.

Why didn't I write a fake name and number? Katherine cursed herself. *I'm not interested in him.*

"Okay," she said. Since Angelos had a charming accent, Katherine wanted to ask about his home country. Instead, she stayed with her fake story about the Playboy Mansion and the press party. "I bet lots of guys are jealous of you with this job at the Playboy Mansion. How did you find this plum job?"

Angelos faced turned red, and he gave her a half smile as he answered with a thick accent. "Well, I'm from Athens, but I have lots of Greek relatives who live in Chicago. One of my uncles knows lots of Playboy Club members." He chuckled. "I think it's what you say, 'It's who you know, not what you know'."

Katherine jumped off the chair and squealed. "Athens!" She put her hands to her mouth. "My best friend and I are taking a trip to Athens. We're leaving tomorrow. I'm so excited about seeing everything there, especially the Oracle of Delphi."

Angelos winked. "Is there room in your suitcase for me to hop in and go with you?" He lifted his chin. "I spent my summers as a tour guide on Mount Parnassus. I know secrets about the Sanctuary of Apollo." He sighed. "I miss my family." He paused and smiled. "Please call on my parents. They love having visitors from America for dinner."

Katherine hesitated. What a neat idea to have dinner in a local's home, but Angelos was a stranger. A kind stranger so far, but he could be anyone. Her brow moistened again. She imagined Emma Jean's chiding and finger pointing as she screamed, "Darlin, he's a stranger. You don't know his family. Just think of the mess with another dark-haired stranger."

Katherine searched for a polite answer. "That will be super, but we're on a prearranged tour."

Angelos grinned. "You can meet them when they come to visit me. My parents are part owner of my uncle's Greek restaurant in Greek Town." He winked and continued. "They're coming over to check in on their investment."

Katherine envisioned sizzling saganaki and licked her lips. "Thank you. I love Greek food."

"I'll call you. And you can tell me all about your trip, too."

He nodded toward the door. "Since you're Hefner's friend, you can stay as long as you want."

Katherine raised her hand to her mouth and whispered. "Sorry to bother you. Does this kitchen have more exits?"

"No, just a fire escape, and we're on the third floor."

Katherine sighed as Angelos left the kitchen. Before she could muster the courage to get up from the stool, she spotted two waiters rushing from the kitchen's revolving door into the dining room. Like Buckingham palace's changing of the guard, the Bunny who she'd seen talking with Dominick dashed through the revolving door into the kitchen.

For a hands-offs Bunny policy, she was acting pretty close with Dominick, like more than just friends. Katherine gulped and snatched up a nearby copy of the *Chicago Tribune*. She lifted it high enough to watch the Bunny move around the kitchen. With typical Playboy Bunny finesse, the young woman sashayed through a drooling crowd of servers and chefs. With Bunny pizzazz and a standard Bunny dip, she waved her manicured hand over an array of desserts on the silver-serving tray. She selected two brownies and nibbled on one as she walked toward Katherine.

"Howdy, Katherine. What are you doing in here? Dom's hunting for you and Charlotte just asked me if I'd seen you."

Katherine lifted the cool tumbler against her cheeks and put a finger to her lips. "Shh, I had a minor accident in the ballroom, so this friendly waiter brought me in here to put myself together." Katherine cocked her head. "How did you know about me, Dominick, and Charlotte?"

The statuesque blonde put one hand on her hip and the other well-manicured one on her well-endowed breast. "Well, Dominick is a good friend. Charlotte happened to walk by when Dominick asked me if I knew you. They are both looking for you." She offered a hand to Katherine. "I'm Debbie. It's nice to meet you."

Debbie put her hand on Katherine's shoulder and stared into her face. "Okay, sweetie. You'd better get back to Dom soon. And I should tell Charlotte where you are."

"Oh, no. I'll be okay. I need a break from all the action. Do you need a break?"

Debbie pulled up another stool and smiled. "You have no idea how much I wanted to escape tonight. If anyone asks me, I'll say I had to help you. Shouldn't I go tell Dom that you're in here?"

Katherine scanned her face. She appeared genuine. "I'm not with Dominick. I met him on my flight the other night, but he's not my friend. Are you a friend of his?"

Debbie smiled. "Wow. I sorta liked you before because you're Charlotte's roommate, but now . . . well, I've always had a crush on that guy. And I was jealous that you might have a thing with Dominick when I saw him getting close to you in the ballroom. I know who he is and who his father is, but he's different."

Katherine's heart pounded, and she put her hands on her chest. She had a solution. "We can work together."

Debbie wrinkled her brow. "Do you want to be a Bunny? I wanted to be a stewardess, but I failed the first interview."

Katherine took another glimpse at Debbie. She looked like a corn-fed girl from Nebraska with that natural, platinum blonde hair, and those sapphire blue eyes that didn't need those false eyelashes.

"No. I meant we might work something out with you and Dom." Katherine smiled and laughed. "Now that you mention it, I always thought it might be fun to be a Bunny." Katherine paused and envisioned a full load of passengers. They didn't compare with the glamorous and famous people mingling in the ballroom. She chuckled. "I'm ready to be a Bunny for a night. Why not?"

Debbie squealed. "How cool. I'm a stewardess for a night. I love your dress. But I'd like to wear your classic blue uniform."

Katherine shook her head. Her blue suit couldn't even compare with a Playboy Bunny suit. The idea occurred to her. "Hey," Katherine said to Debbie, "since you want to be with Dom, and I want to be polite and not just avoid him, let's switch places."

Debbie moaned . "Well. I need to keep my Bunny job. I love living in the mansion. I only pay fifty dollars a month for rent. There's always a party. I meet celebrities and people from all over. I don't want to go back to be a receptionist."

Katherine took another look at her. *She's shapelier than me, but we are the same size.* "Let me explain. Charlotte got an okay from the club's publicity coordinator for me to come to this party to write a story. Do you know the promotion coordinator? Is she here tonight?"

"Yeah. Everyone knows that woman. She's the one who can make you famous or nothing. I talked with her before I came in here. Do you want to be a centerfold?"

Katherine rolled her eyes and looked up at the ceiling,

wondering if her father would burn the centerfold picture or swear to never speak to her for months or maybe years. "No, I don't think I'd make much of a centerfold, but I thought she might help us. Since I'm a journalism student who's trying to write an article about the Playboy Mansion." Katherine felt like either a real actress or a good liar. "If I explain to her how trading places with you would make a great story, she might go for it. And you might receive good points with her for helping me. You might even be a star."

Debbie beamed. "Let's do it! I'll find her now. If she says yes, you have to work my whole shift."

Katherine waved at Debbie who dashed out the revolving kitchen door. She released a silent giggle. *Boy, I am an intelligent girl. I wonder if I'll be a Bunny for a night?*

Within minutes, Debbie flew through the revolving door and rushed over to Katherine. "She said yes and loved the idea and thought it would make an interesting story since there are all kinds of reporters writing and interviewing the guests. She only said yes because you're Charlotte's roommate and probably know how to act like a Bunny. Of course, you'll have to be cautious and not get caught doing anything out of order. Act like a smart Bunny and stay calm. She said to tell you if you do anything wrong, Charlotte may suffer the consequences."

Katherine flung her hands over her face, wondering what she'd done. She didn't want to write any article about the Playboy party and especially not one with a Bunny-for-a-night angle. And what about Charlotte if she messed up? Would she get fired? *Hey, a Bunny isn't any sexier than a stewardess. Most airlines want stewardess dressed like Bunnies, so I can do the job. But that article will remain an untold, unwritten story.*

"I'm supposed to stay until 2:30," Debbie informed her. "After that, we change into our swimming suits and mingle with party guests. Many of them stay around to hang out at the pool with us."

"Okay, but I won't be swimming. First thing tomorrow morning, I'm hopping a plane for a trip to Europe. My girlfriend . . . " Katherine paused. *Golly, I have to get a message to Emma Jean. I'll surprise her when I find her mingling in the party.* "Hey, I've got your shift covered. Go have fun with Dominick."

Debbie's eyes grew into large round circles. "Wow. European vacations. I'd like to be a real stewardess. Not just for a night."

Katherine and Debbie hugged. Debbie had found a way to experience a life out of her Bunny suit, and Katherine had procured a date for Dominick. She sighed. *I'll never see him again.*

Following Debbie's directions to a place where she could change into the Bunny costume, Katherine slipped out the kitchen's side door to a small supply closet. With one small overhead light, Katherine examined herself in a dusty mirror. She cocked her head to the left and right and watched the Bunny ears wave with her motion. Her wavy blonde hair and emerald green eyes were a beautiful match for Debbie's forest-green satin Bunny suit. Patting her Bunny tail, she released a deep breath and opened the closet door to the ballroom. She was ready to be Bunny Katherine for a night until she heard a familiar voice shout her name.

"Katherine! What are doing?" Charlotte grabbed her arm. The two friends stared eye to eye in frozen silence.

Katherine's heart missed a beat, but her mind rushed to the rescue. "I'm working on the 'story' about the Playboy press party. I came up with this smart undercover idea. Oh, and don't worry, your publicity coordinator gave me and your friend Debbie a green light to switch roles." She gulped and winked. "Don't I look fantastic?"

Charlotte shook her head and laughed. "Yep." She

paused. "But you know that you may be stuck with actually writing an article. Well, have fun on your secret gig. And you and Emma Jean have a blast in Greece. We'll have to catch up later."

Right then, Katherine's mind was bursting with excitement for her European vacation, so any worries about writing a real article slipped into Katherine's dark pit of never-mind-right-now. "Thanks. I'll send a few postcards. Wish you were coming along with us."

As the two young women gave each other a hug, Katherine noticed Danny O'Brien's Irish eyes smiling toward Charlotte.

7

STREAMS OF SWEAT FLOWED over the young black boy's face while Danny O'Brien cheered over the ropes. His heart pounded in rhythm with the howling crowd. He wanted to shout instructions but bit his tongue. His boy was on his own. He taught all he could. Now this was Luther's moment to shine.

Luther, the swarmer, overpowered his opponents with his boxing skill. Danny mimicked Luther as he bobbed and weaved. An instinctive rhythm moved Luther's feet from left to right while he coordinated his jabs at his opponent's weak spots. Swish, swish, his hands whistled with each blow, slamming his opponents as they bent and bowed to the master. Then, Luther stood his ground to move with his power-heavy cross hit. Like a maestro orchestra conductor, Luther finished his victory with a sneak hook straight from the hip to land the final defeating punch. Like Danny instructed him, Luther bent down to shake his vanquished opponent's hand while he breathlessly rested on the rope. Danny's eyes glistened as he howled while the crowd cheered on his protégée.

Danny raised his fist to the ceiling and danced a jig. He checked the Silver Gloves schedule. He switched between laughing and smiling; he was so thrilled Luther had advanced to the final prizefight. He loved this more than any paying job. If he could keep one kid out of trouble and show him there were better places for him, he could sleep in peace and rise with a smile each day.

Boxing provided Luther with a sneak peek into a new world, with a couple of hours a week at St. Andrews away from Cabrini-Green's public housing. He wanted to see Luther become the next Mohammed Ali after he finished high school and graduated from college. And he hoped maybe his Irish luck would get him a scholarship.

He and his brother still laughed when they remembered the first set of boxing gloves their dad had given them. At ten, Danny was short and skinny. Kids made fun of him. The bigger guys pushed him into lockers. At lunch, even the girls took his food and threw it in the trash. But when he and his brother sparred with each other, Danny grew desperately hungry, and the more food he ate, the bigger and stronger he got and, soon, he became a skilled fighter. Danny's victories grew like spring blossoms. He won fighting matches against his brother, kids in school, and competitors in the ring.

Luther ran over to Danny for a towel and a swig of water. "Did you see me? I'm a contender!" He paused and asked, "Could I be the next Mohammed Ali?"

"You bet, kid," Danny said, nudging his protégé on the shoulder. "Now take a shower. We'll talk later."

As Danny walked toward the parking lot, he lifted his chest to catch a breath. He smiled and whispered, "Mom, even if I didn't become a priest, I'm helping my fellow man."

Danny pulled out of St. Andrews' parking lot. He maneuvered his red Mustang GT 350 Fastback around the turns on Lakeshore Drive to Wrigleyville. He opened every window to welcome the evening spring air drifting off Lake Michigan. He smiled at the thought of tonight's game between the Cubs and the Reds. He wanted to give himself a pat on the back for doing a good deed. Tonight, watching his favorite team counted as the best reward for his act of kindness.

Parking off Addison Street, Danny gave himself a reassuring smile in the rearview mirror and grinned an approval.

At the entrance of the Cubby Bear Lounge, the odors of stout and ale drifted out to the street. Meeting his brother at the Cubby Bear before a Cubs game was a tradition, starting when Patrick took them for a "first" beer at twenty-one.

Danny spotted Patrick at the bar with two of his attorney friends. His brother waved and pointed to the empty chair next to him. "Hey, coach, your chilled Bud is now the temperature of warm piss."

Danny nudged his brother's shoulder and grabbed the mug. "I'm cool. I don't want anything to put a jinx on Fergie Jenkins, not even that Billy Goat. His hard slider might turn into a slow ball."

Patrick, his buddies, and Danny clinked mugs and cheered. "Cubs! Cubs!"

Danny looked up to the bar's top shelf lined with Guinness Bottles. He slipped his hand into his pocket rubbed his Leprechaun Lucky McCool. Danny raised his chilled mug and gave McCool another squeeze for the Cubs.

Patrick smiled. "Hey, how was your first day at the club?" He paused and turned to his friends. "Guess what? My little brother works at the Playboy Club and Mansion as a bouncer. Anytime you gents want to visit Hef's place, just ask me, and I can arrange it."

"That's right. Paddy got me the job, and it's the best. A few nights ago, I got to work the Playboy Club Press Party. It overflowed with press, celebrities, gorgeous Bunnies, and—"

Patrick interrupted with a shout. "Stop. Didn't I tell you not mix with or touch the Bunnies? You're a working stiff; don't mess with the merchandise."

"Yeah. I remembered."

"Sure," Patrick said. "And the other ladies, any problems with them?"

"No, I did as you said. I didn't rush in and save any women in danger. But I did my professional duty for one lovely lady. An Outfit guy attempted to devour her with outrageous advances. Being a proper gentleman, I asked her if she needed any help."

"Hey, now, I told you to keep your nose clean with those goons and their molls."

"I performed like a champ bouncer. I left her alone and just used my hawk eye on her for the club's reputation. I noticed that the mafia fellow had her marked, but she looked around the room like a frightened animal. Then, zip, she fell to the floor. Then she disappeared, and, no joke, she came back an hour later the mystery woman as a Playboy Bunny! I don't know how it happened, but she lost her party clothes and appeared as a dynamite Bunny. I scratched my head. I didn't report her. I heard your voice telling me to stay clear. A regular Bunny couldn't have served drinks any better. She was fab but squirrelly."

"Well, I doubt you'll ever see her again," Patrick said.

"Yep. That's the end of her story." He glanced at his watch. "Hey, we better get over to the park. Let's beat the crowd."

Danny walked over to Wrigley Field with his brother and his friends. He still got chills when he came near the

"Friendly Confines" of the diamond-shaped park. A wide grin wiped across Danny's face as he lifted his nose to the sky to sniff the blend of popcorn and hot dogs coming from the concession stands. His heart danced with all the summer odors floating around the ivy-covered wall. Something twitched in his mind and diverted him from his ballpark reverie to that sweet blonde lady turned Playboy Bunny. She'd vanished from his mind until tonight. A thump popped in his throat; he wished he hadn't told his brother she'd acted goofy. She was different. His intuition said she was more than just a beautiful face. And she was beautiful Charlotte's roommate. He realized that he'd misjudged Katherine when he'd thought she hung out with the mafia. *If I run into her again, I'll apologize,* he thought as the game got underway.

8

ANCIENT LIMESTONE ROCKS crushed under their feet on the sacred path to Apollo's Sanctuary. A charming Greek gentleman escorted Katherine down the road. Her skin tingled when she stood at the foot of the temple. Her heart's tempo zoomed like The Who's song, "I Can See for Miles and Miles."

Was it Angelos? *He filled my mind with images and inspiration about ancient Greece. We only talked at the Playboy Mansion for twenty minutes. Thank goodness, he didn't get fired. I don't know how his boss thought I was a real Playboy Bunny. Hm, we should have talked more in the kitchen when I was just a frightened lady needing protection.* His enthusiasm for his country had impressed Katherine. He knew all the Greek myths. She remembered his entertaining story where the nymph raised Zeus on milk and honey had come alive. As he told the story, Katherine could taste the milk and honey.

After she'd read the Greek myths, something had stirred in her. She'd had to visit Greece to find something. She didn't know what she'd discover, but the Oracle of Delphi had given answers for centuries. She wondered if the wise one could give her an answer even if she didn't know the question. *Maybe I just wanted to visit the Plaka.*

The Greek sun glistened over the tumbled pillars and monuments that had stood for many centuries.

Her sexy escort turned and smiled. "Over there is the Oracle. I'll wait for you with our friends."

"Thank you."

Katherine stopped to get a view of the Gulf of Corinth. She needed time alone on the sacred Parnassus Mountain, here at the Oracle of Delphi where ancient leaders came to receive the Oracle's prophecies for their future. Her knees buckled, and her heart raced. Was it a dream or did she sense something? She overheard Emma Jean's Greek escort telling her that she was gorgeous last night. Emma Jean giggled. *My date said I was like a Grecian goddess. That tops beautiful. But I'd rather be a Chippewa princess.*

The winds swirled around Katherine. Black crow feathers floated above the Oracle's column.

I must be imagining it. But there's Soaring Eagle. What's the reason for his presence? A vision of herself as a child appeared. The younger Katherine followed Soaring Eagle, the shaman from her Native American ancestors' tribe. Hanging Cloud, her great-grandmother, walked next to the great leader. They led her to a crystal waterfall. Its clear water glistened, flowing over beige and pink rocks. Sunlight magnified sparkling water drops, and a soft mist floated from the boulders and fell to the fresh grass, covering it like diamonds on velvet.

Katherine walked toward the vision of Hanging Cloud. Her delicate child's hand touched her great-grandmother's smooth, intricately braided raven hair. Soft scents of cedar surrounded Hanging Cloud.

Hanging Cloud removed a turquoise, orange, and ivory blanket from her shoulders and placed it around Katherine's shoulders. Her great-grandmother raised her old hand and directed Katherine's attention to Soaring Eagle. A soothing breeze drifted with the rhythm of a stream as it moved toward its reunion with the Chippewa River. Soaring Eagle's chant—a request to the Great Spirit for protection for Katherine—harmonized with nature's symphony.

"*Eagle. Fly high, touch Great Spirit. Share your medicine, feel me, and know me, so that I may know you too.*"

Raising his hands to the sky, he paused and bowed his head. He removed feathers from his headdress and waved them over his heart. With gentle strokes, he moved the plumes around the crown of her head.

"*This is my sign. I am here to cleanse and protect you. When you feel these touches, you should know that I am near to warn you. And know that I will always stay with you to guide you on your journey.*"

Shrill squawking and cawing penetrated Katherine's mind and shook her whole body. A mystical vision circled her. Her mind's eye saw a spectacular view. Soaring Eagle's magic prepared a sacred fire as he twirled and chanted. He raised the smoke as a message to the ancient spirits. Each spirit handed Soaring Eagle the revered turquoise, green, and yellow feathers. Wind puffs rustled each feather, helping their magical splendor glisten brighter in the sunlight. Soaring Eagle's message hit her inner being. He warned her to leave the Oracle's entrance. She had to obey.

Katherine pondered her vision. What had caused Soaring Eagle to appear? She had to find Emma Jean. After she had taken a couple of steps, a soft nudge on her shoulder made her jump. She looked around—nothing in sight. Then a beam of light directed her eyes toward an eagle flying down to touch a saying carved on a nearby rock, "Know thyself." Seven ancient philosophers and lawgivers had inscribed that saying on the entrance to the sacred Oracle, so it had to be important. Katherine scanned the sky like a telescope to discover eagles on the horizon.

Katherine's Greek champion tapped her on the shoulder. "Are you okay?"

"Sure," Katherine replied.

"You look pale, like you might faint. Why don't I find some real nourishment for you? We Greeks eat baklava for energy and zest. Crunchy walnuts and pistachios over the fluffy pastry and buttery sweet sauce are gifts from the gods."

New ideas buzzed around Katherine's mind. Her heartbeat thumped in her ears, but her stomach remained silent.

Katherine tried to hide her feelings and fight the rush of tears. "I'm fine, just tired from sight-seeing yesterday and the fun time with you guys." She paused and looked at the sky. "I wonder if any eagles have flown over Mt. Parnassus since the legend of Zeus."

Emma Jean rushed over and touched Katherine's forehead. "Yes, Darlin', I wondered if you were okay too. You look lily white. What's this silly talk about Zeus and eagles?"

Katherine rolled her eyes and cast off Emma Jean's hand from her forehead. "Thanks for your concern, but I'm full of energy." She took in a deep breath and smiled. She couldn't share the experience she'd had with Hanging Cloud and Soaring Eagle. What had happened to her was sacred. *I wait for my guidance.* Katherine felt a calm knowing that everything would fall into place. "Zeus is the major player in Greek mythology. When we have time, I'll share the most interesting Zeus stories with you."

Katherine gave her Greek gentleman an elbow nudge. "Last night was a blast."

Emma Jean put on her southern charm as she gazed her sexy escort with her fluttery thick eyelashes and alluring smile. "Oh, my Lord, yes. Thanks for showing us the best of Athens at night. I loved the way you Greek gentleman dance. I had a ball."

The highlight of the evening had been Plaka's nightclubs. The cobblestone streets had echoed with sounds, scents, and tastes from centuries of life-loving people. The Greek food was magical. They drank ouzo, ate lamb, devoured flaming cheese, and nibbled stuffed grape leaves. The vibrant Greek atmosphere buzzed with the music, the belly dancers, and Greek men lining up to dance the Kalamatianos with Emma Jean. She'd wanted to join in, but her date had kept her on a tight rein. She was glad that Emma Jean had received overwhelming attention from the Greek "gods" waiting for time with her. She thought Emma Jean even relished the day-long tour of the Parthenon since they'd met charming Greek gentlemen on the tour. Katherine would never forget Emma Jean's comment, "Darlin', you never told me how excellent museums are for meeting men. Let's go to them more often."

Katherine glimpsed one of the Grecian studs reclining on a tumbled pillar. She nodded to Emma Jean to join him. "You wore him out last night. Go join him."

Emma Jean sauntered over to the bronze-skinned, wavy-haired young man. Patting his shoulder, she sat next to him. "Bless your heart. You were such a gentleman. You make those southern boys look like rude Yankees."

He raised his arm and wrapped it around Emma Jean's waist. "Let's rest here for a while."

Katherine turned to her escort and smiled. "Okay, it's time for a short pause. Please excuse me."

Katherine relaxed under the cloudless sky, the gentle breeze bringing peace with it.

Like three chirping birds on a power line, Emma Jean and the two Greek gentlemen bantered over their fun night of dancing and partying at Plaka.

Katherine opened her eyes and smiled. The gentle breeze touched her chin to lift her eyes upward. An eagle glided overhead and flew lower to rub Katherine's head. In a rush, the majestic bird slipped away with a gust of wind and vanished through an illuminated cloud.

No one will believe what happened to me. Everything builds on something. I knew something had inspired me to study Delphi my last semester at Beloit. It's been almost two years since that course, but I'm here now. A personal muse directed my journey to Greece.

9

CHARLOTTE'S JUNGLE GARDENIA–soaked note paper made Katherine's eyes water. Her vision blurred as she read her roommate's letter.

Kate Dear,

You must tell me every detail of your trip. Boy, it'll be strange not to have you nagging me that my side of the room is so messy. I'll be here for a few more days since I can't move until the other Bunny moves out. My closet at the PB Mansion is so small that I need to get rid of some clothes. If you want them, I'll give you three or four of my designer dresses. You need style, girl. (Joking!) Anita, my replacement roommate, plans to move in next month. You'll enjoy her. She's neat and quiet.

By the way, an exotic-sounding guy with a sexy foreign voice keeps calling for you. He sounds interesting. Is he Greek? Greek men are such a blast. I think he's the

*waiter at the Playboy Mansion. If he is, you're a lucky
lady. The Bunnies fall at his feet.*

Love Ya . . . See You Soon,
Char

Katherine laughed to herself. *I did fall at his feet.*

Katherine released a deep breath and wiped a trickle of
tears from her cheek. Her friendship with Charlotte spanned
over twenty years, almost as long as they'd both been on earth.

She wiped her tears and whispered, "What's my
problem? My best friend is moving two blocks from this
apartment. I'm the free spirit. I've got wings and light feet.
Nothing or anyone can keep me fettered, but Charlotte gave
me roots and a place to land."

Katherine folded the paper and called her parents to tell
them that she was home.

"Hi, Mom," she said, "I'm home."

"Thanks for thinking of us with your daily postcards.
We got to enjoy your trip. We loved the letters with the
Parthenon, the Plaka, and the Oracle of Delphi. It looked
like you had a fantastic time."

Katherine wrapped the telephone cord around her
finger. Her stomached quivered. "Oh, Mom, it was thrilling, and I can't wait to tell you and Dad my exciting tourist
stories. Can I talk to Dad?"

"No, honey, he's at work. He can't wait to speak with
you. Oh, and your midterm exam, aren't you glad you to have
that behind you? We bet you aced it. We miss you. When
are coming for a visit?"

Katherine's face tingled. It had been two weeks since her
midterms. Grabbing her hair, she wanted to scream. She'd forgotten to contact her professor to take the makeup exam. *I better*

make a decision. Katherine chuckled. *I'll keep taking classes or find a better plan. Do I need to solve this now?* No. Right then, home beckoned her. She could smell Mom's baking. Katherine licked her lips. Oh, for a cream-filled, chocolate, best-of-heaven pie.

"Mom, when you have time, could you send me a box of your delectable éclairs?"

"Can your nose smell them baking in the oven right now?"

Katherine raised her eyebrows, "Hum, maybe. It's sniffing fresh lavender too!"

Her mother laughed. "I sewed some new lavender sachet for you. I found fabulous Aqua French Toile de Jouy at Alison's Fabric Shop, and I had to buy it for you. I have your special French goodies box ready to go."

"Oh, Mom, I can't wait to get it." Katherine cherished her parents. She needed Wisconsin's fresh air and time with her parents to recharge. But a trip home had to wait. "I'd love to come back to see you and Dad. I'll bid a schedule with a block of days off soon. Do you guys have any particular plans in the next month?"

"No." Katherine's mother cleared her throat. "I saw Charlotte's mom at the library event last week. She mentioned that Charlotte gave you an invitation to a Playboy party, so we're happy that your life is full. Parties, work, and school? How do you manage?" She paused. "Oh, one thing, you father worried while you were in Greece. The turmoil that erupted in the Middle East concerned him. Your dad gets overprotective if there is danger within ten feet of you. He fights the urge to call out the militia."

Katherine's father kept up with world events and expected her to discuss current events with him. Now that she was on her own, the television remained dark, collecting dust. Real life was more intense and exciting. Once in a while, she might glance at a newspaper when a passenger left one on their seat.

Katherine shrugged. "Yeah, Mom, I'm still his little girl." Katherine thumped her fingers on her desk. "Hey, Mom, I have to get ready for flight to New York I just wanted to check in with you and Dad."

"Bye, sweetie. Have a safe trip, and we'll call this weekend. Love you."

"Bye." Katherine dropped the receiver in the phone cradle and screamed.

Now, what do I do? How can I tell Dad I didn't take my midterm? That I went to a Playboy party instead and hid from a mafia boss's son and met a Greek man? Boy, if Mom and Dad knew what a bimbo they'd raised. Why am I always stumbling into one daffy mishap after another? I am an intelligent woman and destined for bigger and better things.

Katherine sighed and padded into the bathroom. After a long trip, a luxurious bath was a welcome reward. The gardenia-scented bubble bath always cleared her mind. It reminded her of Lake Wissota, where she and friends spent long summer afternoons drifting on its soft waves beckoned her. Throwing off her pink jumpsuit, bra, and panty girdle, Katherine smiled at herself in the mirror. Patting her bare bottom, she sighed and shouted, "Freedom," pondering who hated corsets more—the women who wore them or the men who had to fight the modern-day chastity belt.

Holding the nylons with the garter belt dangling over water brought the memory of her first check ride. Her rear still felt the sting from when her supervisor swatted her for the girdle check. *Someday I'll be free of this body trap.* She flung the corset into the bedroom and made a wish for it to disappear.

The bubbles tickled her feet as she tiptoed into the inviting foam. Slipping under a blanket of warmth and fluff, she closed her eyes to focus on her calming, measured breaths. Calming waves lulled her into a peaceful reverie. She sailed to the Chippewa Falls waterfalls with its pine scents and soft breezes wafting through the trees. Her memories of the bright Wisconsin sun illuminated her vision.

Like a dolphin leaping from the ocean deep, Katherine lifted herself from the refreshing water. With a fluffy white towel wrapped around her midsection, she did her usual shimmy to dry herself.

WLS-FM played the top hits that urged her to dance. *I've got it*, she said to herself. *Get a plan for my life. Not like now. It's fun to hop on planes, explore new places, and meet interesting people, but there must be a bigger plan waiting for me.*

Gliding from the bathroom to the bedroom, Katherine sang one of her favorite songs from The 5th Dimension, "Up Up and Away."

She tossed her multi-colored serving smock and stewardess manual into the airline regulation suitcase. The value of her stewardess training taught her important life lessons. For example, always check for the location of the nearest exits. You never know when you might have to get out in a hurry, whether it be from a burning plane, a lousy relationship, or a flaky lifestyle. Or the fact that it's always best to toss excess baggage. If you can't carry or stow it, then leave it. And the most important lesson: keep emotions at bay. Don't respond in anger. Count to ten and make every effort to refrain from rude, unkind remarks. Smile and reply. Keep calm. Just because it says first class doesn't mean the people are.

Katherine took in a slow breath and released it with a sense of freedom. Life and its adventure called out to her.

Ready for another day in the blue skies, Katherine glanced in the mirror and reviewed her mental checklist: blue sugar scoop hat secured with the hatpin, lipstick perfect, and no runs in her nylons. She smiled. *I can't wait for a new journey.*

10

"WELCOME ABOARD OUR FLIGHT 19 headed to New York." Captain Jack Armstrong's voice drifted over the PA system. "The skies are clear; winds are calm. Get ready for a smooth flight tonight and enjoy the hospitality of your charming stewardesses."

Carol, Katherine's first-class flying partner, chuckled as the DC-8 climbed to flying altitude. "Hey, let's get everyone drunk, and then you and I will seem like every man's dream women."

"Okay, but if the kids barf, you can clean it up."

"Geez, I remember you from last month. Didn't you puke when you handed that mother the air sick bag for her little boy?" Carol asked.

Katherine gulped. "Yeah, don't remind me. I can't take blood or vomit."

"I have my issues too. Flying scares the pants off me," Carol said.

"Oh? Why'd you become a stewardess, then?"

Carol leaned closer and continued. "I'm on my way to Hollywood. My head waitress job at Chuck's Truck Stop in Spotted Horse, Wyoming, was a dot in the road on the way to Deadwood, South Dakota. Customers told me how beautiful I was and that I should go to Hollywood. I thought I should become a stewardess and let someone discover me."

Katherine gave Carol a half smile. *How could that woman even pass the airline stewardess appearance standards? Did they notice her pointed nose, bug eyes, and frizzy hair? I'm not catty, just honest.* Katherine felt like biting her tongue. She reminded herself not to be judgmental. "Yeah, that makes sense."

Carol nodded toward the cockpit. "Hey, how about a night of clubbing in New York tonight? The guys up front wanted me to ask you. It'll be a blast with Steve, the second officer. He's a regular at the best clubs in Greenwich Village."

"Darn it," Katherine said, feigning disappointment. "I have a date tonight."

"Emma Jean mentioned you met a New York guy the last time I flew with her."

The hair on the back of Katherine's neck bristled. She wondered why her best friend had told this chatterbox that Adam was her "New York guy." *He's my friend and nothing more.* "She did? What did she say?"

"Oh, not much. Emma Jean and I bumped into him at LaGuardia. He likes you. We could see it in his eyes when Emma Jean mentioned you. And you met him on a flight. I never meet guys on my flights. How did you get him to keep asking you out?" Katherine recalled her stewardess life lesson. Find an exit for when you need to remove yourself from unpleasant or dangerous emergencies. "Oh. I'll tell you later. I have to do a galley check for the meal service."

Adam Goldstein's bronze tan glowed from his Key West beach vacation. Katherine limited her "layover city friendships"; she wasn't a sailor with a guy in every port. Adam called her when he came to Chicago, and Katherine bid New York layovers often. Katherine appreciated their casual friendship. A long-term relationship wasn't even on her radar. Solo flying was the life for Katherine with many places to see and things to finish before she clipped her wings.

Adam drove away from the St. Moritz, passing by a clear view of Central Park's meandering tree-lined sidewalks. He smiled at Katherine. "Stewardesses must rate with this prime hotel location. That's why the flying public says fly girls enjoy a glamorous life."

Katherine chuckled. "Yeah. It's a thrill around every corner. Everyone expects us to greet them with a warm smile, escort them to their seat. Then we serve them hors d'oeuvres, steak, and lobster with their favorite drinks. After a gourmet meal, we give them a choice of music and a down-filled pillow." Katherine paused and chuckled. "I'm sure that's what the young soldier thought when I dumped his hot goulash in his lap on a flight today. It was an accident. I went back to the aircraft galley and cried. He was a soldier and a gentleman. If he'd been a jerk, I might have let the food dish slip on purpose."

Adam grinned. "He was lucky. Did you give him extra attention?"

Katherine shrugged. "Well, I don't know. I treated him the same as all my passengers. But he asked for my address as he deplaned. Maybe he plans to write me up and send a nasty letter to my supervisor."

Adam shook his head. "I bet you'll find a bouquet of roses when you get home."

Katherine had had enough of all the talk. It was time to change the subject. A copy of the *New York Times* flashed an alert. She grabbed the paper and read the headline: "Cease-fire in Syria Accepted; Israelis Hold Golan Heights; Soviets Break Tie to Israel." She thought this must be the trouble in the Middle East her mom had mentioned. Adam was Jewish and was more aware of events in Israel than most of her other friends. *Why didn't I pay more attention when Mom cited this Middle East conflict on our phone call?* When she had plans to see Adam, she should have something to discuss with him. She added to her to-do list: *Pay more attention to the world around me and the people in it.*

Adam noticed her reading the newspaper article. "Marc and Sarah Cohen, the couple we're meeting for dinner, are classmates of the reporter for that story. Most of Sarah's family come from or live in Israel, so Marc and Sarah keep up with what happens to their people. It's a great day for Israel."

Katherine's stomach flipped; her inadequacy wobbled. She had no comment and wished she'd talked to her father. He filled his mind with current events, plus the historical background. She took a deep breath and remarked. "My dad followed this war and the well-deserved victory for Israel."

She stared out the car window as Adam sped past the Electric Circus on their journey to the Lower East Side. She wondered if black crow feathers would appear to flutter around her. Adam stopped at a red light and turned to Katherine. "On your next trip, let's make it an Electric Circus night."

Katherine smiled and winked. "Sounds cool. I'll have to find the right clothes and listen to Frank Zappa before we go."

Adam beamed. "Tonight, you'll love it; the restaurant is full of New York history. The name is appropriate. The Bridge Cafe is on the waterfront at the foot of the Brooklyn Bridge. It's the oldest surviving tavern in New York haunted by the ghosts of its pirates and brothel history ."

New York was in its own league. Everything moved faster, and the scents of the city made it come alive. Summer odors distinguished each neighborhood, and the heat squeezed the scents and smells together, from the aromas of the outdoor cafes to the urine smells from the subways. Whiffs of concrete and dust from the buses and cabs that clogged the street made Katherine cough. Park Avenue was better with its air-conditioned buildings and perfumed shoppers.

Adam smiled at Katherine. "You'll get used to it."

Katherine giggled and winked. "Hey, I'm still sampling all the tastes, sounds, and smells of Chicago. I can't savor two cities at once." *Now, why did I say that? I can take in as many sights, sounds, and sensations as I want. My senses are ready for an overload.*

Adam swung his hands up and pointed at the Bridge Cafe. "If I have you figured right, you'll be ready for a scenery change in a New York minute. Here's the grand old lady on the waterfront."

Seagulls soared like a banner waving above the 200-year-old landmark. Katherine peered through the evening mist to check for black crow feathers floating around. She smiled. "I can't wait to meet Sarah and Marc." Katherine blinked to adjust her eyes from the bright sunlight to the dark wood-paneled interior of the restaurant. Adam took her arm and walked her to a stylish looking couple. The woman's simple long-sleeved purple shift dress made a statement that she dressed with ease and purpose. Katherine gave Marc a silent shout-out. Yeah, no gray flannel suit, just well pressed chinos, white shirt, and penny loafers.

Sarah and Marc rushed over and hugged Adam. "Hi, Adam." The couple turned to Katherine and squeezed her hands. "And you must be Katherine," they said in unison.

Katherine shook their hands, but she wished she could give them a hug. "I'm thrilled to meet you. Adam told me you are the most charming and fun couple that he knows."

Sarah motioned to Katherine for her to sit on the velvet bench. Sarah's scent reminded her of Charlotte's fragrance: Jungle Gardenia the aroma known on every corner of the globe.

They covered all the small-talk topics while they ordered their drinks. Katherine braced herself and charged into a more substantive conversation. She wanted to seem like an intelligent woman, even if she'd be treading into deep water where she might drown. "I saw the article in the New York Times today. What good news for Israel to have a cease-fire with Syria."

Katherine released a deep breath and smiled at Adam when he rescued her from the conversation's deep waters when he added his comment. "It's a strategic win for Israel. More secure borders with the occupation of the Golan Heights, the West Bank, and the Sinai Peninsula. But Israel still needs recognition as a country."

For more than thirty minutes, the threesomes debated the pros and cons of the Six-Day War between the Arabs and the Israelis. Adam took a breather and turned to Katherine. "How are doing?"

Katherine nodded. "Great. I have a better understanding of the conflict, but it's still complicated for me to grasp everything."

Sarah turned to Katherine. "I hope we didn't bore you."

"Oh, no. I learned so much from your conversation. Thanks for letting me listen and learn. I'm not Jewish, but I'm discovering how amazing the Jewish people and their history are from Adam. He's good to suggest books for me to read."

Adam smiled. "And you'll help me understand your Chippewa ancestry."

Sarah and Marc glowed with broad smiles. "A blonde Native American?" Marc asked.

Katherine's memories bubbled to the surface. Her tall, blonde German looks had always concealed her Chippewa ancestry, Her chest tightened and reminded her that she'd neglected that part of herself until she'd gone to a Native American civil rights lecture at Beliot College. Perhaps Soaring Eagle's appearance was to warn her not to forget her ancestry.

"Yeah. People always think I'm making it up. I'm German on my father's side and my mother's French Canadian and Chippewa. My great-grandfather, a wealthy fur trader, fell in love with my great-grandmother from the Chippewa tribe. They had two weddings: a tribal wedding and a grand wedding in France."

Adam pointed to Katherine and smiled. "When we first met, she said we were cousins because the Chippewa were one of the Lost Tribes of Israel."

"Hey now. I still wonder if the Native Americans are the Lost Tribe of Israel," Marc commented.

"Me too," Sarah chimed in.

Katherine's people instincts were strong, and she wanted to spend time with Sarah and Marc. Sarah felt like a kindred spirit, and Katherine felt as if they had been friends all their lives.

"Well, my interest got charged when I did a high school research paper that explored Thomas Jefferson's request for Lewis and Clark to research the religious beliefs of the Native Americans. He even wrote a special letter to Clark asking him to search out the Lost Tribe of Israel. Who knows? Life is full of mysteries."

Katherine savored her quiet time and enjoyed a special breakfast at Rumplemeyer's restaurant in the St. Moritz. The morning sun glowed around the dining room and cloaked Katherine in its warmth. She munched on breakfast, and her taste buds danced with each crunch of the Belgian Waffle covered with whipped cream like a snow-capped mountain. Katherine wanted to smile at everyone. Then, she spotted an unwanted sight—Carol, her flying partner.

Carol rushed to her booth and joined Katherine without invitation. "Howdy." Carol glowed. "We had a blast last night. You shoulda joined us. Hey, why don't you come to Bloomingdales with me? Then we can have lunch at Bergdorf. I can't afford to shop there, but a girl can dream."

Katherine took in a deep breath and reminded herself that her time off was her own time. "Gee, thanks, but I have other plans."

Carol winked. "Oh, you and that guy." She waved her hand to fan herself. "I understand. When you're hot, you're hot."

Katherine thought her visit to the United Nations was her business. Carol would never understand. "Well, yes." Katherine crossed her fingers under the table for her little white lie. "So I'll meet you at the crew car this afternoon. Thanks for the invite, though."

Katherine grabbed a cab to head to the United Nations building. The taxi driver stared in the mirror and interrupted her thoughts. "Miss, you should be on Fifth Avenue shopping. The UN won't be any fun for you."

Katherine shrugged and smiled. In her mind's eye, she saw her father smiling down on her. But he fought for the rights of others. Her knowledge of the United Nations came from Alfred Hitchcock's movie *North by Northwest*.

Katherine paid the taxi, turned, and encountered a

crowd chanting, "Hey, hey LBJ, how many kids have you killed today?" Groups of worried parents carried placards that read, "Stop the War in Vietnam." The out-of-place parents attempted to slink through the throng of longhaired hippies and shorthaired draft dodgers. She reached for a placard, but before she could get a hold of the white cardboard square, a black crow feather drifted past her face. She crawled on her knees through the crowd to get inside the United Nations' main entrance. Her heart pounded in her ears and drowned out the competing chants of "Hell no, we won't go" and "Love our country, America, love it or leave it." A United Nations guard lifted her up and helped her inside the United Nations building.

Katherine quivered as she surveyed the lobby of the United Nations. Racing past her were men in dark suits. They dressed the same, but their faces were different. Worldwide cultures created a collage of skin colors, facial features, and hairstyles. Each person's real life blended like a map of the world.

A crowd gaped at a stained-glass window in the public lobby. The window mesmerized Katherine. She joined the group of tourists as one of the United Nation's tour guides explained the image in the glass: a striking young woman with black hair spun in a chignon with olive skin and deep brown eyes, smiling at the crowd of tourists. She looked like a stewardess in her tailored navy suit and white-collared blouse.

"This is a gift from a United Nations staff member and Marc Chagall," the guide said, "the French artist and designer of the window. He called it *Kiss of Peace* and presented it in 1964 as a memorial to Dag Hammarskjöld, the second Secretary-General of the UN. Mr. Hammarskjöld and fifteen other people died in a plane crash in 1961 on their way to a peace mission in Zambia." She paused and cleared her throat. "The memorial is fifteen feet wide and twelve feet high with several symbols of peace and love. If you look close enough, you'll see the young child in the center kissed by an angelic face, which emerges from a mass of flowers. On the left, please notice, below and above motherhood, there are people struggling for a peaceful way of life. The musical symbols in the panel evoke Beethoven's Ninth Symphony—Mr. Hammarskjöld's favorite."

While the tour guide answered the crowd's questions, Katherine's eyes moistened. She remembered the morning her father had come to awaken her with tears in his eyes because of Dag Hammarskjöld's fatal accident. The hair rose on the back of her neck as she stared at the stained-glass window. She heard her ancestors calling her.

Katherine narrowed her focus on her life plans. She could get a job as UN guide. Could she become part of finding peace in the world? And what was the meaning of her friendship with Adam? When he'd driven her back to the hotel, he'd asked her when she planned to transfer to New York. If she got a job at the UN, she could learn to understand people from different cultures and find ways to help them. *One of those one hundred and three countries need my help.* She wanted to find her way through her hopes and dreams.

A wave of hot and cold chills swept over Katherine. Drums pounded in her head. Her stomach bounced. She stumbled her way to the ladies' room and released a sigh when she opened the door, and a single chrome chair greeted her. Like a desert wanderer in search of water, she landed in the chair and dropped her head to her lap and drew in a deep breath. *So many roads, so many paths. Which one is mine to follow?*

11

THE BREAKFAST CROWD at Third Coast Coffee Shop bustled and hummed as spring burst with birds singing. The exciting Chicago lakefront events enticed crowds to stop at one of the Rush Street watering holes after basking in the sun and sand on Oak Street's beach. Chicago's sandy beach welcomed the bikers, walkers, and sunbathers. It was happy times on the beach again for all those hibernating Chicagoans who had hidden under their blankets during the extended subzero winter chill that froze the city.

Emma Jean and Katherine didn't notice the line of people waiting for their table. They had too much to talk about, and they hadn't finished eating the fresh strawberries and Danish pastry with heaps of cream cheese.

Emma Jean wiped fluffy white cheese from the corner of her lip and smiled at Katherine. "Oh my, you have nothing to fret about, Darlin'. Fainting is a typical southern lady's way of calming oneself. But you're the only woman to faint at the United Nations. What a silly place, since there weren't any gentlemen to rescue you. Oh, Lord. Why didn't you go shopping on the Avenue? That's what I do on New York layovers. I especially love my Bloomingdales. Of course, I can't afford it, but my dream is to shop all the time at Bergdorf when I meet my true love. He'll have to take me to New York for shopping."

Katherine twisted her love beads as she nibbled on the last fresh strawberry swimming in sugar and cream. "Eureka! That's why I fainted. I've been around you so much that I became a southern girl for a split second. I got overstressed and overheated. I'm conflicted. I want new adventures to learn about other people's cultures. That's one of the reasons I majored in anthropology. Don't you want to learn about people from different cultures?"

Emma Jean sat upright and patted her friend's hand. "Aren't you sweet? You remind me of Mama. She wants to help every stray puppy, even if they pee all over her yellow jessamine. Why meet people that are so different from you? Maybe you should spend more time looking beautiful and learn how to paint or play the piano. Or, like me, read poetry and dream of Mr. Right appearing in your life to sweep you off to his castle."

Katherine thumped her fingers on the table and rolled her eyes at her friend. After releasing her deep sigh, Katherine glanced at her watch. "Okay. Thanks for your advice, but I have to meet Angelos for lunch at his relative's restaurant in Greek Town." Katherine paused and thought about her and Emma Jean's trip to Athens. Katherine's heart leaped like when she and Emma Jean danced in the Plaka. She could hear the bouzouki playing. A smile slipped across her face.

"Darlin, you've got the smile of a girl in love."

Katherine shrugged. "Love? Not for a guy but our trip. Didn't you love Athens? And all those ravishing Greek men that swarmed around you?"

Emma Jean rolled her eyes, "I don't have to go to Greece for that. You know it happens to me wherever I go." Emma Jean sat back, jutted out her chin, and winked. "Besides, Greek men aren't on my marriage market list. You know they only marry Greek women."

Katherine tossed her hands in the air. "Marriage market! I'm in the banquet-of-life market." She paused and smiled at her friend. "For now, I agree with Epictetus saying, 'One must not tie a ship to a single anchor, nor life to a single hope.'"

"I know the life, the friends, and the country I want. Give me a southern gentleman and an antebellum house on the Ashley River." Emma Jean took in a deep breath and exhaled. "If you keep flying your kites willy-nilly, you'll get caught with your pants down."

Katherine shook and laughed. "I'm not worried about getting caught with my pants down. I'm a warrior woman, ready for adventure. Just like Aristotle said, 'Travel is worthwhile.'"

"Travel to the beach is just right for me." Emma Jean nodded her head. "What else is there?"

"Learning about other people. We don't have all the answers. I got up this morning, and the idea came to me that I should give Angelos this book. Since he shared the myths of his culture, I thought he might like to learn something about our cultural history."

Emma Jean's lips twisted, and her brow wrinkled when she scowled at Katherine's book. "*To Kill a Mockingbird*. Will he want to read that? Never mind. I have to get to Bonwit Teller. That's where you should be going too, Darlin'."

The two women waved at each other and headed down Dearborn Street in different directions. Katherine clutched Harper Lee's bestseller under her arm. She turned and rushed back to catch up with her friend. Katherine halted and sighed.

Why do I need her approval? She wants to do something frivolous like shopping, and I want to share books and knowledge. I'm not acting like a strong, determined woman. Holy cow, she almost made me into an elegant southern lady. My decision: follow my secret message that tells me to be strong and think on my own. Emma Jean and I have different roads to walk. This is my journey.

12

KATHERINE HOPPED OFF the Blue Line at the University of Illinois' Halsted stop. She looked on both sides of the track for Angelos. Many young Greek men with bronze skin and wavy black hair walked by her and smiled. It was like visiting Athens.

Katherine walked toward the stairs. Then a gentle tug on her sleeve pulled her in another direction.

"Hey, lady," a man with a Greek accent said. "Where are you going?"

Katherine turned and raised her hand to slap the stranger. "Oh, hi, Angelos. I was looking for you."

"You looked ready to slug me." He laughed.

"Oh. Well, what can I say? Unconscious self-defensive action in strange territory."

"Hey, this is Chicago's Greek Town. Certainly, no stranger than Athens."

"I agree. This area is like being in Athens." Katherine rubbed the back of her neck. "Well, I thought you were a stranger trying to pick me up or molest me."

"I'm sorry. I didn't meet your train because my class ran late."

Katherine, the great adventurer, didn't want to appear frightened of this new neighborhood. "Don't worry. I thought that's what happened. How was your class?"

"My uncle George was the instructor today. He's a humorous instructor who gets his message across."

"Is your uncle a professor at the University?"

"No, he's an engineer but comes to lecture our math class once a month. He wants to meet you. We Greeks are family oriented—loving and welcoming to each other's friends."

Katherine wrinkled her nose, cocked her head, and pondered his comment. What did he tell his uncle about her? Or did he want to fix her up with his cousin? "Do you have many relatives living in Chicago?"

"Just a few, maybe twenty or so. And you?"

Katherine reached for her Thunderbird necklace and rubbed it. "No." She sighed. "But my roommate is my best friend from my hometown. I'm an only child, but Charlotte is better than a real sister."

"Do you get lonesome?"

Katherine pondered the question. *I enjoy my time alone. I can read and study what I want.* She agreed with Albert Einstein's quote: "The woman who follows the crowd willingly usually goes no further than the crowd. The woman who walks alone is likely to find herself in places no one has been before." Katherine touched her Thunderbird necklace again and recalled the treasured Native American proverb: "Listen to the wind; it talks. Listen to the silence; it speaks. Listen to your heart; it knows."

Katherine turned to Angelos, "No, not really."

Angelos shrugged and grabbed Katherine's hand. "Well, let's eat lots of good Greek food."

Katherine's eyes widened remembering the sumptuous meals she and Emma Jean had enjoyed in the Athens Plaka: grape leaves stuffed with beans and vegetables and lots of lamb, along with the pleasure of sipping ouzo. Her nose wrinkled. Lunchtime, will they serve ouzo? She warned herself, *If we have that delicious drink, remember to sip it slowly and don't gulp it.*

Angelos rubbed his ear and leaned in to whisper. "I hope you like ouzo. Since you were in Athens, you probably realize that ouzo drinking is one of our cultural rituals. Even though it's lunchtime and ouzo drinking usually starts later in the afternoon, I asked my uncle to waive that rule for you. So, would you like some ouzo?"

Katherine winked. "Of course, who would turn down a glass or two of ouzo? I think drinking must be why Greeks are so smart, handsome, and wealthy."

Katherine chuckled and breathed in the savory scents of the Halsted's Greek restaurants. The welcoming, sizzling scents of saganaki and gyros danced in the air. Like a supernatural gift from the Greek gods, the ambrosial aromas transported Katherine to the Parthenon, the Plaka, and the glimmering, white buildings of Athens.

"Does Greek Town make you homesick for Athens?" Katherine asked.

Angelos opened the door of the Greek Islands Restaurant for Katherine. "Oh, no, you'll see. I have many loving relatives here; they make me think I'm—"

As they entered, a red-faced, cheery man in a white apron ran up to Angelos shouting, "Opa!" He took Katherine's hand and gave it a light kiss. "Beautiful lady. Welcome! Angelos' friends are my friends."

Angelos eased close to Katherine and retrieved her hand from his uncle's grasp. "Uncle Tasso, this is my friend, Katherine Roebling. Can we sit at the table by the window?"

His uncle smiled like a half moon on a warm spring night. "Oh yes." He led Katherine and Angelos past the laughing, chattering lunchtime regulars to a reserved table. "You're honored guests. Please enjoy yourselves."

Angelos nodded at his uncle. "Thank you. Please bring us your lunch meal and two ouzos."

His uncle smiled and lifted his hand to salute his nephew. "I will bring the ouzo now." He turned to a waiter and shouted, "Opa!"

Roasting gyros aroused Katherine's senses and awakened her sleeping hunger pains. The bouzouki music made her want to grab Angelos, his uncle, and anyone who wanted to move with and dance the Kalamatianos. Something else had happened to Katherine in Greece—her love of Greek myths had come alive. She had learned that they weren't just ancient stories with dusty covers. They were more like new best sellers with real life stories. How had they known so much way before Christ? She leaned back and smiled at Angelos.

Angelos touched Katherine's hand. "Did my uncle come on too strong?" Katherine blinked. "Oh, no. He just makes me want to return to Greece!"

Angelos smiled. "Even today, Greece is the center of the earth. Don't you agree?"

Katherine stared at the restaurants' murals with scenes of the Parthenon and the statue of Athena and smiled. Then, her Thunderbird amulet tickled her chest. Katherine flipped it over her neckline and rubbed it. *Hm, is there another center of the earth? My Native Americans believe that the center of the earth is Turtle Island or North America. There can't be two centers of the earth, can there?*

Angelos pointed at her amulet. "Is that necklace original art? Did your boyfriend give it to you?"

Katherine chuckled and released her grasped on her

talisman. "No. My great-grandmother gave it to me. The Thunderbird is significant to our tribe."

Angelos began to unbutton his shirt. Katherine wrinkled her brow. He lifted his hand and said. "I'm a gentleman. I also have something special from my grandmother." He lifted a sterling silver chain away from his chest and showed a blue bead with an eye painted on it. "Greeks believe it wards off the evil eye." He slid it back on his chest and buttoned his shirt.

Katherine smiled. "The evil eye?"

"Yes. In Greek, they call it *matiasma*. It comes from someone's jealous compliment or envy. If you catch the evil eye, it makes you feel afflicted of body or mind." He shrugged. "People say it's superstition. But the Greek Church recognizes the *matiasma* and offers prayers for those who suffer from the curse."

What he said about the evil eye made her think about the meaning of her amulet. Her Thunderbird wasn't just an insurance policy; it was part of her inner core—her Chippewa core. Right now, she kept this to herself. He was a lunch date. Nothing more. She was here for a good Greek meal and a Greek experience, not to share her deeper personal self.

She lifted the Thunderbird amulet and let it swing on her finger. "Well, this may be something else." Angelos examined the turquoise bird and glanced up. "This is beautiful. It's Native American!" He folded his arms on his chest. "I haven't met any Native Americans. My knowledge comes from the cowboy and Indian TV westerns I saw at home. The TV Indians had black hair, skin darker than any Greek, and rather long noses." He paused and cleared his throat. "You don't look like the TV Indians."

Katherine knew the stereotypes. She grew up with her neighborhood boys playing cowboys and Indians. Not until she turned seven did she even realize her Native

American ancestry. Before then, she'd just been another blonde American girl. "I have an eighth Chippewa blood. My great-grandmother on my mother's side was Chippewa. She married a French fur trapper. So, their daughter, my grandmother, was half Chippewa and half French. She married a French man. And I am German on my father's side. That's why I have blonde hair and green eyes. I look like an all-American girl. My outer shell doesn't tell my whole story."

"Is that like your saying . . . 'Don't judge a book by its cover?'"

The Greek waiter reached over to put the glass of ouzo in front of Katherine.

Angelos lifted his glass to Katherine. "Ya mas." Katherine took a sip and grazed her tongue over her lips. "Yes, to your health too." Angelos winked. "How much Greek can you speak?"

"Just what I learned in Greece. Emma Jean and I did our share of drinking. It's always good manners to learn the right toast when you're a guest in another country."

Katherine and Angelos munched on stuffed grape leaves, steaming saganaki, and gyros. In between "opas" and ouzos, Katherine's eyes moved from left to right. She rubbed her forehead to stop the spinning sensations. To keep herself in control, she pushed herself against the back of the chair and smiled between bites and sips.

Like a whirlwind, Katherine's head spun. She lost her balance and tipped toward the window. Her foot kicked *To Kill a Mockingbird*. It flew under the next table and landed on a dining patron's foot. A rosy-faced Greek woman leaned to retrieve the book and shouted something in Greek. A red-faced Angelos rushed to her table and thanked her (at least Katherine thought his Greek sounded polite). The woman waved her hands in the air and shoved the book in Angelos' hand.

Angelos walked back to their table and gave Katherine a reassuring grin. "I apologize for the quantity of ouzo. We Greek's try to welcome guests, and sometimes we overdo it."

Katherine put her hands to her mouth to hold back a hiccup. "I went way past my limit, but the more ouzo I drank, the better the food tasted. I got carried away." She smiled and reached for the book. "That's the book I wanted to loan you. When we talked at the Playboy kitchen, you mentioned you wanted to learn more about the United States and our culture." She caught her breath and touched the novel. "Well, this book is a best seller and explains our race relations and its effect on our culture."

Angelos flipped through the book. "Thank you. When I see Americans, most of them are white. I don't see many dark-skinned people. I guess that's because Chicago is one of the most segregated cities in the United States." He gave Katherine a half grin. "When I first spotted you at the Playboy party, you were trying to get away from that Italian guy." He stopped and laughed. "I thought you didn't like him because his skin was dark. Then you talked to me. You were polite and courteous. Even in Greece, we pick the blonde beauties. Our dark Greek ladies are our second choice."

"If I my skin were darker, would you like me? Would you have liked me in the first place?"

"Maybe, but I like you as you are." He reached for a bag under the table and put a jar of olives on the table. "It's time for more fun. You brought the book; we Greeks always bring gifts too. These are my father's Kalamata olives."

"Cosmos Country Olives! I'm impressed. This your family business.?"

Angelos sheepishly bowed his head. "Yes, my family has an olive business in Greece."

Katherine smiled. "That's wonderful. I bet I ate these

olives in Greece." She looked at her watch. "Gosh, how did we get to 1:30 so soon? I need to be back in time to help my roommate move. She's moving into the Playboy Mansion. Oh, you may know her, Charlotte Delaney?"

"Yeah. Everyone at the club likes Charlotte. She's good-looking, but she's also polite and funny. I don't want you to get in trouble with Charlotte. You better go."

Still feeling the effects of too much ouzo, Katherine pushed too hard on the chair. It tumbled on its side, and she slipped to the floor. She wanted to hide under the table. She took a deep breath and looked up to discover Angelos' outstretched hand. She grabbed it and laughed. "Shh, please keep this a secret. Tipping over chairs isn't the way I behave."

Angelos laughed and put his finger to his lips. He helped Katherine to her feet and escorted her through the restaurant. Katherine's face changed from light pink to scarlet red as they passed the silent, gawking lunch crowd.

Outside in the bright sunlight, Katherine stood tall and steady. "I'm sorry for embarrassing you in front of your relatives, but I enjoyed myself." She walked away and waved. "Thanks again."

Angelos smiled. "I had fun. I'll call you. You passed the ouzo test."

As Katherine wobbled toward the L station, she kept turning over Angelos' parting comment. *You passed the ouzo test. Hm, I wanted to share our different cultures and be polite. I didn't expect an ouzo drinking test.*

13

KATHERINE HOPPED ON THE Brown Line to head downtown. She liked to pretend each journey on the train was
a magic carpet ride to new places and experiences. The L
train's wheels rushed over the tracks and zipped by offices on
the Chicago Loop, a blurry sea of windows, brick, and gro-
tesque gargoyles on centuries-old buildings. These moving
images mirrored her thoughts. They were moving too fast.
She couldn't grab ahold of them. As soon as she caught one,
it vanished. The real became the imaginary, like the light
dimmed by the shadow.

Hanging Cloud's lyrical voice hummed in her heart and
calmed her. Katherine closed her eyes and let her mind focus
on her vision. "Aponi." Hanging Cloud used Katherine's
secret name; only the two of them knew it. Her parents had
named her Katherine Oriel Roebling. She never told people
her middle name, except for legal necessity. Aponi was a better
name. It meant butterfly. Freedom. Joy. Transformation.

The Lake Street L arrived at Katherine's stop, and she
hopped off. She appreciated the decaying city dirt and the

pigeons wandering around Randolph Street. The rock doves made her want to grow wings and soar. Katherine spoke to a friendly bird eating stale popcorn off the sidewalk. Great thinkers say that ideas come when a person's mind wanders to a simple, unrelated activity. Katherine agreed. She continued walking toward the library with a rush of adrenaline. Okay, I'll take a half hour and still get home to help Charlotte. I have to follow my muse's guidance. I don't know where it will take me, but I have to go with the flow.

She sighed at the entrance to the majestic Central Library. She glanced up at the high dome and the Tiffany lamps. She spent lots of hours in this place immersed in the books. After the 1871 Chicago Fire, the city of Chicago had requested book donations to the library. Responses came from other municipalities and countries, and they delivered their best books. Some came from private donors such as Queen Victoria, Lord Tennyson, and Robert Browning. She wondered how to find enough time to read and get the answers to her questions. Knowledge is an endless thread. Answers only lead to more questions. Now that I'm almost finished with my Northwestern class, I can focus on my paper. I can't believe that Professor Kingsley left me go for two years. When I told her I was leaving college to become a stewardess, I can still see her finger pointing at me and her command, 'I'll give you a two-year leave to finish the paper you owe me.' For now, I have to find answers for that paper. My one class at Northwestern University got me into a study groove again, but the city campus isn't the same as the Beloit's traditional campus. At least I'll get a course credit that Beloit will accept. *She looked up to the ceiling and whispered, "Please direct me to a way to complete my unfinished paper and get it accepted."*

As she walked along the rows housing books about ancient Greece, her mind nudged her. What about the Lost

Tribe of Israel? She sighed. *What?* She told herself to expand her mind, explore, travel, and meet new people. That's what she'd said she wanted at her stewardess interview, and she knew that's what every woman told them. But when she reflected on her lame, clichéd reason, she bowed her head and looked at her feet. If she dug deeper, she would find that her actual quest was to find the real Katherine. She realized that her quest for self-knowledge came in messages from other people. She wondered if she was like Emma Jean's mama, who took in stray puppies. But then she remembered a quote from one her favorite authors, Emerson: "What you are comes to you."

She rubbed her brow. How to begin her research? Should she ask a librarian or let serendipity help? Her thoughts crystallized with a clear message: forget the Greeks. How do I explain that I am looking for a mysterious connection between Native Americans and the Lost Tribe of Israel? I'll find the right research since it was a coincidence that it came up during my dinner with Adam and his friends. It must be a message that I must follow.

Katherine moved her finger across the spines of the books. She closed her eyes and waited for one to spark at her touch. A true scholar applies an organized approach to research, but Katherine wanted a magic guide to help her.

A spry, wiry-haired librarian touched her shoulder. "Miss, are you looking for a particular book?"

"No. I found the right book. Thanks so much. I'm okay."

"If you need me, I'll be over at the reference desk."

Katherine looked at the tome she'd grabbed off the shelf and examined the brown leather cover: *World Heritage Encyclopedia*. Flipping through the pages, she ran her fingers along the black thread of words in the index. Tapping from one foot to the other, Katherine bounced her way to a comfy corner armchair in the back of the library's top floor.

After zooming past topics, her finger stopped at "Lost Tribe, 17th–20th Centuries, Theories."

Is this fate's finger pointing to the prophecy I received at the Oracle of Delphi that I would help a great nation? Is this the reason for Adam and me to be friends? Israel could be that nation.

Her heart pounded like a snare drum against her chest as she read:

THE UNITED STATES, AMERICAN INDIANS

In 1650, a British divine named Thomas Thorowgood, who was a preacher in Norfolk, published a book entitled Jews in America or Probabilities That the Americans Are of That Race, which he had prepared for the New England missionary society. Tudor Parfitt writes, "The community was active in trying to convert the Indians but suspected that they might be Jews and realized they better be prepared for an arduous task. Thorowgood's tract argued that the native populations of North America were descendants of the Ten Lost Tribes."

Katherine gulped, and a gentle breeze ruffled the pages as a bright brown feather with an ivory tip landed on the library table. Katherine gazed at it. She placed it against the book's one-foot-long binder. The glossy plume met end to end with the book's cover. With a magnetic force, it slid toward Katherine, and she retrieved it. Her hands shook. She looked around the library. She and silence were alone with the sacred eagle feather. *What does this mean?*

The giant white clock's numbers glared 3:00 p.m. Katherine's throat tightened. She envisioned Charlotte calling Emma Jean to tell her that Katherine lacked dependability and how Katherine had left her to move by herself to the

Playboy Mansion. But that didn't matter. A powerful force held her. She couldn't move. Soft Native American flute music waltzed around her mind with peace. The odor of cedar lulled her into a trance. Eyes closed, she tipped forward until her face landed on the library table. A feather whisked across the back of her neck.

Katherine didn't move. Visions and voices beckoned to take her on a journey to the time when she and her father stood in the woods behind their home in Chippewa Falls, Wisconsin. His hand caressed a bright brown feather. The sun's rays made it glisten. Her father's cupped hands protected the feather from the wind. His rough hand looked small compared to the length of the bright feather. "Katherine, have you ever seen a feather similar to this one?" he asked.

She gazed at the quill then raised her eyes to her father. She nodded. Awakening her mind was the image of the glossy plume on display at the Chippewa Falls Logging Museum. It was on an elementary class trip, but Katherine sensed the importance of the feather.

Katherine and her father sat on a log and he placed his arm around her shoulder. "This belongs to one of my clients. Because of attorney-client privilege, I won't show their name or any details. It's a bald eagle feather sacred to Native Americans."

"Yes," Katherine said, "the sacred eagle feather awards honor to my Native Americans. The Creator chose this majestic bird as the master of the skies. The eagle flies higher than most other birds. I want to fly high just like the eagle sometime. The eagle soars the highest." Katherine paused and touched the feather.

"You're right; they're very significant. We'll take it the National Eagle Repository. My client received a bald eagle feather as part of a bequest from their aunt's estate. She did nothing with it, and now I have a major entanglement to unravel. Do you know what happens to anyone who keeps an eagle feather?"

"The guide at the museum told us it comes with a $100,000 fine and imprisonment."

The vision of her father and her younger self vanished into the mist, and she awoke in the library. She heard a soft voice chanting over the wind instrumental music. "Hold this feather in your hand. It means trust, honor, strength, wisdom, power, and freedom. We choose you to receive this feather. It's from the Great Spirit. You have done a brave deed."

A shrill voice awakened Katherine. "That's her. She's got the feather."

Katherine jerked her head and opened her eyes. She released her clenched fist and spied a lustrous brown eagle feather slip from her clutched fist.

A weathered, hairy hand grabbed the feather and waved it in front of Katherine's face. "Okay, miss, can you explain this? You better have a good one too. You committed a federal offense, and I'll have to report you. What do you have to say in your defense?"

Katherine felt as though she'd entered into another dimension. She stared up at a fat man with a dark blue uniform with badge-embellished lapels. She couldn't speak.

"I'm Tom O'Leary, head of library security. Miss Polkas alerted me to check on you."

"Remember," the wiry-haired librarian said, "I offered help over there by those shelves. You looked confused. Now I understand. You wanted to hide that feather." She stopped and took in a breath. "You made me suspicious. Just by chance, I had a picture of eagle feathers on my desk. You should be so ashamed of yourself. And furthermore—"

The official-looking O'Leary raised his finger to his lips. "Helen, we must let her tell her side of the story. Miss, gather up your things and come with me."

Katherine's face turned white. Her lips trembled as she mumbled to herself. "I don't have $100,000, and why should I spend the rest of my life in prison for something I didn't do? What can I say? That my great-grandmother's friend and dead shaman Soaring Eagle slipped the feather to me while I slept?"

Katherine walked behind the librarian with the feather. The plume waved and moved against its captivity in her arthritis-twisted hand. Katherine could only hope Soaring Eagle would come to her rescue.

14

DANNY O'BRIEN WALKED into the St. Andrews boys'
locker room after an hour-long boxing workout. He nudged
his young Chicago Boys Club trainee. "Hey, Luther. You
looked like Ali today! You deserve an ice cream cone, but
only one. You're in training for the Silver Gloves!"

Luther gave Danny a high five. "I want a chocolate
fudge Sunday with lots of nuts."

"How about this: If you let me take you to the library,
I'll get you a triple scoop sundae."

Luther shrugged. "Can't I have the ice cream without
the books?"

Danny ruffled Luther's curly black locks. "When we
cruised past Lakeshore Drive's tall luxury high-rises, you
asked me how you could live in one of the sky mansions."

Luther smirked. "Yeah. But my people never leave the
hood. Why should I bother?"

Danny motioned to the exit of the exercise room. "Let's
go, kid. I'm giving you a ticket out of the ghetto. If you want
it, walk out this door and follow me."

Danny and Luther sauntered to the Fastback. Danny beamed when he saw Luther's eyes pop at the sight of his red Mustang.

"Don't you want a hot ride of your own, some day?" Danny asked.

"Right on."

Danny started the motor and glanced back to check traffic. "If that's what you want, then keep boxing for concentration and body building for strength and read books for your move up and out to the stars or wherever you want to go. And you can buy nice rags for yourself, your mother, and your whole family."

Luther stared out the window. "You're a white guy. That works for you."

"Skin color is a cover for the real person. The person's insides—their mind and character—are the hardware that drives dreams. When you read lots of books, you'll find heaps of guys with dark skin who made it. You ever heard of George Washington Carver?"

"Maybe. So, what?"

Danny cleared his throat. "He was born into slavery and became a world-famous scientist and inventor. Education," he said, "is the key to unlocking the golden door of freedom."

Luther bit his bottom lip. "Sure. He's one guy."

"Holy moly. Where's that street fighter who told me nothing could stop him?"

Luther jerked away from Danny. Danny shivered when he glanced out the corner of his eye, and a sunbeam reflected on a glimmer of a tear flowing over Luther's cheek.

Danny opened the car window and cranked up the radio volume. The spring breeze and the lyrics from Music Explosion filled the car as they drifted along Lake Michigan: "Now when you're feelin' low and the fish won't bite.

You need a little bit o' soul to put you right." Danny swayed with the music while Luther snapped his fingers and glided his shoulders in sync with the beat. A smile slipped across Luther's face.

"I drove past ice cream," Danny said. "Here's the library on the corner."

Luther slammed a high five on Danny's hand. "I'm cool."

Climbing the circular stairs to the children's book section, Danny scratched his head, put his hands on his hips, and wondered out loud, "What are your interests? Have you read any comic books?"

"I read when I have to. Hey, anything with books is creepy."

Danny jabbed him. "Remember? What is reading?" Danny paused to let Luther respond.

Luther smiled and returned a jab to Danny, "Reading is the ticket to a high-rise on Lakeshore Drive and a fast, cool car?"

"Good kid. But you have to act on that thought. Don't just parrot what I said. Live it. Why not try and read three books in the next six months?" Danny paused and searched for help.

A reference librarian raised her eyes from her papers and smiled at the two lost souls. Danny smiled, since he'd found the best person to help them—a kind, young hippie with round wire-rimmed glasses and long, curly hair. Danny waved at the beacon of aid and guided Luther to her book-laden desk. "Hi, I'm Danny O'Brien. This is my friend Luther Williams. Luther has dreams and places to go, so we're looking for a reading program that will make him a champ. Isn't that right, Luther?"

Luther lowered his head to avoid eye contact with Danny or the librarian. Luther coughed and mumbled, "Yes, sir."

She leaned down to look at Luther. Her peace necklace dangled in front of Luther's eyes. "Hello, young man, you're in the right place. I'm just the lady to guide you on your road to wonder."

Danny coughed to stop a laugh at the librarian's comment. He knew what Luther was thinking: *Wonder? Yuk. Let's halt the babble and give me those books so I can get my ice cream.*"

Turning to Danny, she asked, "Are you his guardian?"

"No, I'm his boxing coach. He's ten years old and goes to Richard R. Byrd Community Academy. I haven't talked to his teachers, so I don't know his reading skills."

She smiled. "Well, I bet I can give him suggestions for books. Let's try Huckleberry Finn. After you've read a couple of chapters, tell your friend what you learned from the book."

The three of them walked over to the shelves. Grabbing a well-worn book, the young woman leaned toward Luther's face. Her sapphire blue eyes beamed into his chocolate brown eyes. Neither one of them moved or blinked. She reached for Luther's hands and placed the ominous looking tome in his strong boxer hands. "Here ya go, young man."

Luther took a step and gulped. "How long do I keep this book?"

"You can check it out for three weeks. If no else requests the book, you can renew it." Luther jerked. With a quick pass, he dropped it in Danny's hands. "Yikes. One day is enough for me." He smiled at Danny. "You can keep it longer. Not me."

Danny laughed. "Don't speak too fast. Once you dive into those pages to other worlds, we won't be able to get the book away from you."

The young librarian confirmed Danny. "He's right. Now you better check it out, so you can get started."

Danny smiled. "Thanks. I bet he reads the whole thing and wants more books."

Luther shrugged.

Danny put his hand on Luther's shoulder. "Okay, guy, let's get this book checked out so you can have your ice cream."

On the way to the checkout desk, Danny bumped into Tom O'Leary. O'Leary was Danny's neighbor on the Chicago Southside.

"Hey, Tom, how ya doin'?" Danny waved, and then he noticed Katherine walking with O'Leary and the librarian. Danny's mouth dropped open. He coughed to cover his reaction. Katherine's face glowed like Christmas as she lifted the *World Heritage Encyclopedia* over her face. Her eyes moved from side to side.

"Hey, Danny boy. Do you know this woman?" O'Leary asked.

Danny had to tell at least half the truth. O'Leary's years as a Chicago cop made him better than a lie detector. "Well, I don't know her, but I met her at a party once."

O'Leary glanced at Katherine and motioned to her to follow him as he tossed Danny a parting comment. "Keep your mother happy and give her my best when you talk to her."

Luther cocked his head toward Danny with eyes fixed on this mysterious woman.

Danny pulled up the image of Katherine at the Playboy party. To him, she'd glowed with innocence in the midst of the wild partygoers. He leaned toward Luther's ear and whispered. "She's a beautiful girl who must have got in with the wrong people."

15

CHARLOTTE STOMPED AROUND the apartment, dashing from her former bedroom to the living room. She looked nervously at her watch and whispered, "Now what? It's 4:30. Kate is one and a half hours late. She's usually an on-time fanatic."

Charlotte searched for answers. Looking for Emma Jean's phone number, her fingers flipped through Kate's phone book. Emma Jean's sweet southern charm made Charlotte want to vomit. *Maybe I'm jealous of their friendship. I knew Kate first. Now I'm just her old friend from home and her former roommate. But I could still use her help.*

"Hello." Emma Jean's charm oozed through the receiver.

Charlotte breathed deeply. "Hi, Emma Jean, it's Charlotte. Do you know where Kate is?"

Charlotte waited for Emma Jean to respond. All she heard was Emma Jean's fingernails tapping on a table like rain hitting the roof.

Then, in her usual southern way, Emma Jean blurted, "Well, shut my mouth. I told that girl to forget that guy. I gave her good advice, too, that she should learn how to play the piano and read poetry. Katherine didn't even want to go shopping with me at Bonwit Teller. What real lady rejects a fantastic experience at the poshest store in town to take a book to a dead-end guy? Could he be a kidnapper?"

Charlotte's heart pounded. "What do you mean?"

Emma Jean released a sigh. "Well, Darlin', after our morning coffee and sweets, your dear roommate left me to go take a book to that Angelos fellow. I warned her about foreign men. Who knows what he'd do with a girl that brings him a stupid book. Do you think men want women to bring them books?"

"Where did Katherine go to meet him?"

"Oh Darlin', what a dreadful situation. To that strange place called Greek Town. Athens was fine, but this Greek Town must be in a bad part of Chicago. I never leave the Gold Coast. My Heavens." Emma Jean sighed. "Once a policeman friend told me that I had to be careful in some areas of Chicago. He said women had been kidnapped and used as sex slaves. That silly girl left me on the corner of Dearborn and Rush Street at 11:00 a.m. I had my hair appointment at 11:15. I hurried to get there on time. Now I'm mad at myself. Have you ever seen Katherine's look that shows when her feelings are hurt? Like, the one where she wrinkles her brow and her lips quiver. She refused to go to Bonwit Teller with me and chose that silly idea to take the book to the Greek guy. You know she's almost too kind-hearted for her own good. I worried that her eagerness to help every manner of person would get her in trouble sometimes. Bless her heart!"

Charlotte took a deep breath and remained calm, even if she wanted to slam the receiver in the cradle and scream for help. "Oh, Emma Jean, what if she's dead or captured? She is the most conscientious person I know. Something terrible must have happened to her. Maybe kidnapping. If she was hurt, the police would have called me by now."

Emma Jean squealed. "Oh, Darlin', I can call my dear policeman friend. He can help us find her. I'll call him right now. We can't lose her."

Charlotte's stomach twisted, surveying Katherine's neat and organized side of the room. She clutched Katherine's stewardess pin on the dresser. The sun slipped away as it made room for early evening skies. A dark shadow covered Katherine's furry white throw rug.

Charlotte stared at the clock. She thought the hands on the clock had stopped when the phone rang. Her heart thumped. That must be her calling. "Hi, Kate, where are you?"

"Huh? I'm Adam Goldstein, Katherine's friend. I am at Palmer House. "I'm checking to see if Katherine can go to dinner tonight."

"Oh, I'm sorry, Adam. Kate is missing. I thought you might be her calling.'

"Missing? Why?"

"Her good friend Emma Jean has an idea that this Greek man might have done something with her."

Adam shouted, "A Greek man. Who is he? Where did Katherine meet him? What gave Emma Jean the idea he might harm Katherine?"

Breathless, Charlotte threw words out like a pitcher at batting practice. "Katherine met him at a Playboy party. He and Katherine talked about her interest in learning more about Greek culture. Emma Jean last saw her this morning for coffee. Then Katherine didn't go to Bonwit Teller with Emma Jean. Instead, she took a book to this guy. It gets worse since Katherine's airline asked her to represent them as hostess for its sponsored event with the Chicago sports teams. It sounded fantastic with the team members coming to autograph stuff and raise money for a Native American school. She never showed up. That's not like her. She has a giant calendar with every day's activities listed. That's her airline training to get everywhere right on time. Not a second late."

Adam exhaled. "Okay, Charlotte, let's not rush to conclusions. I agree she is dependable, but Katherine is also a free spirit with a dash of spontaneity. I'll grab a cab and be right over to help."

"That's wonderful if it's not too much trouble. Should we call Katherine's parents?"

"Let's hope that Kate will be there when I arrive, so let's wait to call her parents. We don't want to alarm them yet. I'm sure she's okay . . . except for this Greek guy."

Charlotte hung up the phone and sighed. She remembered the time Adam had come to take Katherine to dinner. He was a smart guy. She'd been very attracted to him. To relieve her guilt, Charlotte told herself that Katherine might have just gone off somewhere with the Greek and planned to dump Adam. *That girl does some off-the-wall things when she gets mad.*

Adam hung up the phone and hit his fist on the desk. *She made me think she might even move to New York. And my friends loved her!* He told himself that Katherine should use her common sense and not run off with a Greek man. He decided that Charlotte, a Playboy Bunny, might be his best revenge.

16

OLD MUSTY BOOKS STACKED on steel gray filing cabinets lined one wall of Security Officer O'Leary's office. The only view out of the window was a brick wall. *All this place needs are iron bars on the window,* Katherine thought as cotton filled her mouth with fear. She knew the seriousness of the federal laws for illegal possession of a bald eagle feather. Katherine tugged at the zipper of her purse. Her sweaty hands kept slipping. She dug deep and pulled her calendar from her bag.

"Oh, no, I had two appointments. I missed them both. Charlotte and the St. Joseph—" Katherine's adrenaline bubbled. She smiled. The St. Joseph Indian School benefit dinner, she thought, could be a great explanation. *I'll tell them my airline wanted me to donate the feather to the tribe, and I need to deliver the extraordinary feather before the dinner starts tonight.*

Katherine twisted her jacket's belt and listened to O'Leary's speakerphone conversation with a Fish and Wildlife official. Katherine's heart leaped to her throat. Her ears muffled his words. Her sweaty palms swiped and saturated her paisley mini skirt. She knew too well the federal penalty for stealing an eagle feather.

Red-faced, O'Leary slammed the phone in the cradle. "Well, young lady, you better have a good story or you'll be in the hoosegow. My shift ends in thirty minutes. I want this wrapped up now."

Katherine quivered a smile at the librarian and then nodded toward the security officer. "I can explain everything. I'm one-eighth Chippewa, but that's not why I have the bald eagle feather. Could I see my eagle feather again? I need it for my explanation."

The woman searched around her. Then with a white face and shaky voice, she released a whisper, "I don't think I have it."

O'Leary helped her move chairs, his desk, and bookshelves to find the missing feather.

"You idiot," he yelled at the frazzled librarian. "You lost it. And now we don't have the evidence. How can we prove her guilty?"

The librarian scowled and pointed at Katherine. "You're a witch. Stay away from me."

Hm, Soaring Eagle delivered a bald eagle feather to me, and then it disappeared? Was this the work of a shape shifter? Katherine wondered.

"Look," O'Leary said, "get out of my sight right now. We'll forget the whole thing."

Dashing out of the security officer's office, she noticed a man leaning on the wall across from the officer's door. In her rush, she almost knocked him down. Breathless, Katherine sprinted down the library's spiral staircase and flew out the front door.

Her mind rushed with a rambling list of questions. *Will Charlotte forgive me? Will I get fired for missing the Indian School benefit dinner? Will my life ever be normal again?*

17

KATHERINE'S HEART POUNDED in sync with her feet rushing away from the library. She had to get home, but there wasn't a taxi or bus in sight. Chicago at rush hour seemed like the Indianapolis 500 racetrack. Her breathing roared faster than jet engines. Like a searchlight, her eyes darted from left to right until they fell upon a pay phone.

Katherine fumbled a quarter in the slot. The phone rang and rang. At the last ring, someone answered. "Hello," Adam said.

Katherine opened her mouth, but only puffs of air floated out from her quivering lips.

"Hello? Hello?"

Katherine gasped. "Adam? What are you doing at my apartment?"

"That doesn't matter right now. Are you okay? Should we rescue you or call the police?"

"Why? I only had a minor incident with an eagle feather in the library."

"An eagle feather? What happened with the Greek?"

Katherine wrinkled her brow. "Yes, an eagle feather. I don't have time to tell you now. How do you know about the Greek? Is Charlotte there?"

Adam cleared his throat. "Is the Greek guy a long story too? Your friend Emma Jean worried that he kidnapped you."

Speechless, Katherine slipped the phone in the cradle to disconnect it.

Adam wasn't a boyfriend, but she considered him a trusted friend. Charlotte and Adam had betrayed her. And worse they misjudged her. *What are they thinking? What made them think Angelos was some derelict?*

She took a deep breath and repeated her mantra: "Stay calm and breathe in peace." She dropped another quarter in the slot and dialed again.

"Kate? Why did you just hang up on Adam? Where are you? What happened to you? I guess you didn't get kidnapped, but you're late for everything. Your supervisor called to say that you missed that special event for the Native American School. You need to call her first thing tomorrow morning. She sounded pissed. I won't be here when you come home, since Adam will help me move the rest of my stuff to the mansion. You'll have to come and see my new digs."

Katherine stared at a line of twenty-five cars weaving along Michigan Ave. while Charlotte finished her breathless monologue. "Okay." *Maybe you should stop talking and let your throat rest.* "Have fun tonight. Bye."

Katherine's chest tightened. Her stomach rumbled and struggled to puke. She held the receiver in her hand and pondered what to do with it. Should she toss it in the air? Should she slam it the phone cradle? She didn't know if she should scream or cry. She wanted to talk to a friend. She needed support and understanding from Emma Jean.

Katherine enjoyed visiting Emma Jean's neighborhood. It was two blocks away from Wrigley Field. The Chicago Cubs lived in her father's heart, and she'd inherited his love of the worst team in history. The smell of baseball season with hot dogs, popcorn, and beer mixing with the scent of spring grape hyacinths made Katherine forget her problems. She'd lost two friends and, possibly, her job.

She cherished Emma Jean's friendship and needed her reassuring support. Emma Jean would forever remember Katherine's way of introducing her to new adventures and pushing her to go new places that took her out of comfort areas. But this was one of the first times in their friendship when she needed her friend's sympathetic ear.

Katherine climbed three flights of stairs to Emma Jean's walk-up in the vintage-era building. Katherine could still hear Emma Jean's stories of Charleston's history dating back to 1670. She liked vintage walk-ups since these buildings were as close to old Charleston as she could get in Chicago. And Emma Jean loved talking about Charleston whenever she could. Katherine preferred her high-rise apartment. For Katherine, visiting Emma Jean was a refreshing visit to a friend and a cultural experience.

Katherine knocked on the brass doorknocker. Emma Jean threw open the door and grabbed her friend. "Oh, Darlin', Charlotte and I fretted for you. Come in and tell me what happened!" Emma Jean had never hugged her so tight; her best friend had apparently imagined the worse. She collapsed on Emma Jean's rosy velvet loveseat.

"Oh, Emma Jean. My life is falling apart. I'm getting fired. I was a no show for a big airline PR assignment for a Native American School. I should just go jump in Lake

Michigan right now. My friends betrayed me and I got caught with an illegal possession of an eagle feather in Chicago's Public Library."

Emma Jean relaxed on her grandmother's historic Charleston wing chairs. "Can I get you something to drink? Coffee, tea, or water? Oh, I didn't know what to do after I talked with Charlotte. We didn't know what to do to find you. Did that exotic man hurt you?"

Katherine scrutinized her friend's face to understand the misguided perceptions that her friends held of Angelos. He was from a country and culture that they didn't know, so Charlotte and Adam created false ideas and opinions without knowing the real man.

"No. I'm not thirsty." Katherine paused. "Emma Jean, where did you ladies come up with the idea that Angelos kidnapped me?"

Katherine waited for her answer as she watched her friend glance around the room.

Emma Jean coughed. "Oh Darlin', I started it when I said I thought that Angelos fellow must have done something with you. I'm sorry." She paused and stared at her friend.

Katherine waved her hand in the air. "Oh, we all make snap judgments. I've done the same thing. Let's move on." She paused and smiled at her friend and pointed to a gold-embossed copy of Omar Khayyam's The Rubaiyat on the marble coffee table. "Oh, there's that book that you're always quoting."

Emma Jean nodded. "It's my prized possession. My beautiful aunt Millie gave it to me. She told me always to stay romantic. And Darlin', she is right. There isn't enough romance in the world. My dream man must be an ardent gentleman. Real men should give us roses."

Katherine strolled over, turned to the bookmarked page, and read Emma Jean's favorite verse. "'A Book of Verses underneath the Bough, A Jug of Wine, a Loaf of Bread—and Thou, beside me singing in the Wilderness—, Oh, Wilderness were Paradise now!'" Katherine closed the treasured book and looked at her friend. "This is your life and love quote. And it reminds me of you."

Emma smiled. "Yes, it's my favorite." She paused and nodded. "Darlin', you have an enchanting voice. I never heard it read with such emotion."

Katherine sighed. She sat motionless, except for her eyes. They darted from the book to her friend, who never read books. She loved her friend but didn't place much credit in her intellect. I value my friendship with Emma Jean. Katherine's way of life and people insights helped Emma understand other parts of the United States. That was one reason she appreciated being a stewardess. If she'd stayed in Wisconsin, her life might be like a flat sheet of white paper— empty and boring. "Yeah, I surprised myself. That quote has power. It's amazing a message made by a poet who lived in the eleventh century still is still relevant for us today."

"But you've never read his poetry. How do you know when he lived?"

Katherine rushed over the details of her day at the library and her eagle feather incident. She wondered if she could ever explain the eagle feather willing itself to disappear. Someday she could tell her parents. "Well, at the library today, I researched the Lost Tribe of Israel. And the Omar Khayyam book was lying on the library table." Katherine stopped and chuckled. "It made me think that I was getting a message from you."

"Darlin', I said read poetry and play the piano. You didn't have to take me so seriously."

"I never take you that seriously. I was just curious to see about my Native American connection with ancient Israel."

Emma Jean furrowed her brow and stared at Katherine. "Israel? What does that country have to do with you? My heavens, first you ran off with that unromantic book to give to the Greek man. Now you mention Israel in the same breath." Emma Jean paused and shook her head. "What can I do to talk sense into you? Why don't you just have fun and enjoy being a young woman living a life that most young women would love to have?"

Katherine nibbled her thumbnail. Why didn't I just keep quiet? How could she even be a friend with Emma Jean? I wish I could share my inner self. And my unique gift of the prophecy at the Oracle of Delphi. I can never tell Emma Jean the message I received.

Katherine gulped and took the safe road by switching to "man" talk. "Israel? Oh, Adam mentioned going there."

"Adam!" Emma Jean slapped her lap. "'Darlin', he's out with your friend right now."

"So I went to the library this afternoon to do some research?" Katherine shrugged and went on, "I had no clue that you'd create an uproar that caused my friends to betray me."

Emma Jean sighed. "Oh, Darlin', we all care about you and didn't want anything to happen to you. I would never do anything to harm you. " She walked over to her friend and patted her shoulder. "Do you like Adam? Is he Jewish?"

Katherine shook her head. "He was a special friend and shared lot of good times together. I'm finding my path and I want true friends along the way. That's where we're different. I can visit in his world, and I may never stay there. My dad advised me to spend time and understand other people and their cultures. He said dig into another person's culture, and it helps you discover yourself."

Emma Jean shrugged. "Well, if I want to figure out drug dealers, I don't want to be one. Should I hang out with them, so I can find my true southern self in a better light?"

The veins in Katherine's neck bulged. She glared at Emma Jean. "I thought you'd be the one person to understand."

Emma Jean offered a small southern smile. "Oh, bless your heart, you remind me of my mama. Your heart's so big; it's like a bus that fills up with people needing help. You are a rare and precious soul. Remember, I'm always ready to listen and sip sweet tea with you."

Katherine waved at the top of the three flights of stairs. "Well, I better get home."

Emma Jean smiled. "See you soon. Be careful."

Even though she was a free spirit, Katherine turned and gave her friend a longing gaze. She didn't want to leave the friendship that they'd shared for two past years. Katherine sensed the river of life moving her away to new waters. Having Charlotte as her roommate felt as if part of Chippewa Falls lived with her. But Emma Jean's southern ways were a constant culture lesson. Her stomach twisted in sync with her thoughts that spun like a descending anchor.

18

KATHERINE LOOKED OUT THE CTA bus window as it wove along Lakeshore Drive. Lake Michigan was like a graceful dancer; the waves of the massive body moved in rhythm and never lost a beat. The undulating waters mesmerized Katherine. Tight knots wrapped around her neck melted. Water always soothed her.

I hope Charlotte is gone, so I'll have the apartment all to myself, she thought. *I'm not ready to see her. And Adam? He's a drag. Who needs him? The eagle feather vision popped into her mind. That plume caused my life to change. I want to forget about that mystery feather and Adam and Charlotte's act of treason.*

Katherine's mood changed as she gazed at the impressive sight of Michigan Avenue's lights, which sparkled and brightened in the early evening sky. Their glow waved a magic wand of joy over Katherine. Then a weary gray-haired man with an overpowering salami scent plopped next to her. His world-weary brow dripped with sweat. "Woo, what a hot night. My dogs are tired." He bent down and untied his shoelaces.

Katherine smiled, "Is your day almost over?"

"Yeah, I've been up since 6:00 a.m. at my deli stand. Can't wait to get home."

Katherine nodded and offered a pursed smile before she returned to glancing out the bus window to watch the night traffic zoom past the bus.

Something tickled Katherine's wrist. "Excuse me, miss," the older man said. "Is this feather yours? It was on my seat!"

Katherine didn't need to examine it. It was the eagle feather. *Should I claim the feather? What if this man is a fish and wildlife expert? What if he's a retired police officer? What if I get arrested?* Katherine kept her silence.

The man shrugged. "Must be from someone's hat. Do you want it?"

Katherine's heart raced. She told herself to act nonchalant. "Oh, I have an aunt who wears old hats. Maybe she could use it."

"Fine." The older man handed Katherine the cherished eagle feather. "Oh, here's my stop." He bent down and tied his tennis shoes. "Now I'm almost home. Be careful, sweetie."

Katherine waved the feather at the man and smiled. "Thank you," she said. "Have a good night." Katherine watched the man leave the bus. She clutched the feather and glimpsed around her before she dropped it in her purse. *I hope no one saw that.* Katherine slouched in her seat, her heart pounding. It felt like someone was watching her.

Katherine pretended to cough. She took a Kleenex from her handbag and dropped it on the floor. Stooping to retrieve the tissue, she bowed her head and lifted one eye to look at the back of the bus. Her eyes narrowed in on a man with bushy eyebrows hanging over squinty eyes that set off his contorted face. His leather jacket opened to a white satin shirt unbuttoned down to his navel to display a hoard of gold chains hanging down his chest. She couldn't believe it! *I might be wrong, but I think that's the guy from the library. He was outside O'Leary's office.* Katherine's hands got sweaty. *I remember he stepped back from the door when I ran out of O'Leary's office. He was listening at the door.* Katherine covered her mouth to stop a scream when she glimpsed the scar across his cheek and the toothpick hanging from his cracked lips.

What's he doing on this bus?

19

THE BUS JERKED TO a stop. Katherine wiped her sweaty palms inside her jacket pockets and rushed off the bus three blocks earlier than her usual stop. Like a warrior ready for battle, her shoulders tightened; her legs prepared to dash. Stealing a glance back, Katherine couldn't see anyone following her. What did that man want? If he was the guy at the library, then he was trailing her. Why? What did he want with her? *Maybe Dominick sent him. But why would he have done that? He must be with that woman Debbie now anyway. Who else would be stalking me? And why? Maybe he's just a nut.*

One block and she'd be at her apartment. On a spring night, she loved to stay outside and walk with friends. Her mind tussled with how much difference one day could make in a person's life.

Today had started with a happy, chatty talk with Emma Jean while they'd munched on flaky croissants smothered in strawberry preserves. Then, with the best of intentions, she'd taken *To Kill a Mockingbird* to Angelos. What a muddled day.

She'd shared an inspirational story about the harm caused by prejudice, and then a real-life discrimination experience had hit her hard as a cold wind. What would cause Adam and Charlotte, even Emma Jean, to conjure such a ridiculous idea that Angelos kidnapped her? And then there was the eagle feather's strange appearance and its shamanistic vanishing act. What was happening?

Katherine smiled. *I'm becoming a character in* One Thousand and One Arabian Nights. *When I talk to Emma Jean, I'll tell her I'm learning how to be Scheherazade.*

Footsteps pounded behind her like thunder. The sound of heavy breathing flowed through the quiet spring night. The hair on the back of her neck bristled. Her Native American instincts warned her of danger: a mugger, a rapist, that jerk on the bus.

Like a frightened deer running in Wisconsin's Northwoods, she dashed to her apartment, her heart pounding to the rhythm of the clunk of her feet on the sidewalk.

When she reached safety, Fred, her building doorman stood guard outside. He whistled and gazed at the stars. "Hey, Miss Katherine, what's your rush? I love these warm spring nights. Summer's just around the corner. Charlotte just left, and I have a note for you."

After her last call with Charlotte, Katherine didn't care to get a note from her. She just wanted to get inside and upstairs to her locked apartment. "Thanks." She paused. "Oh, Fred, if anyone comes asking for me, please say you don't know me and, whatever you do, don't give them entry to the apartments. Call the police if you have any trouble."

Fred nodded. "Okay, Miss Kate. Protecting the tenants is my job."

Katherine closed her eyes and nodded. "Thank you, Fred." She paused and admired his shoulders, which rested on a body-builder physique. Just like a knight protecting the entrance to her castle. She patted his strong shoulders. "You're the best. Have a good night."

Tonight, the elevator ride to her fifteenth-floor apartment was like a cross-country flight. Katherine longed to retreat from the world to clear her mind and catch her breath. *I can't wait to lock the door and never open it again—at least, until daylight.*

When the elevator door opened in front of 15B, she dug into her purse with shaking hands, searching for her apartment key. Her hand touched every corner and side pocket of the bag but found only the lone eagle feather. Katherine pounded on her apartment door, but no one came to the door. None of her neighbors opened their doors to see what the hallway raucous was. She lifted her purse and shook the contents on the floor. Still no keys. She kicked the apartment door and stamped her feet. She wanted to use every curse word that her mother had washed out of her mouth.

The elevator door opened, and Fred walked over to her. "Hey, Miss Kate, are you looking for your keys? A strange gentleman brought these to me. He said he found them on the bus. What a scary guy. He held his chin down and looked up from under his hat brim for just a second. And he wore sunglasses at night. It's dark as molasses out there."

Her knees shook like cymbals slamming together. Her stomach knotted. Her chest tightened with fear. What's the matter with me. I'm safe now. Fred is here and stands guard downstairs to stop any strangers. Now why did I think about that terrible mass murder Richard Speck's hiding under those nurse beds to kill them? She squeezed the apartment key so hard, a trickle of blood dropped on the floor. She looked at Fred with a glassy stare. "Thanks. I'll be okay."

He put his hand on her shoulder. "Miss Kate, please let me help you into your apartment. Your roommate moved her things today; you'll be all alone in there." He touched her squeezed hand and worked to release her hold on her keys. "You looked frazzled."

Katherine lifted one finger at a time to open her palm. A key imprint rested in the middle of her hand. Her body sagged; going loose like leaves ready to fall to the ground. Her day had begun with hope and joy and had ended in a gray haze of confusion. With a quiver in her voice, she sighed. "Oh, Fred, I need your help."

Fred helped Katherine gather up her belongings from the floor. "Is that guy a threat? I can call the police for you. He sure looked creepy. I don't mean to get involved, but you don't need that kinda guy."

Before Fred could notice, Katherine slipped the eagle feather into her purse. The quill rubbed her hand. Katherine wrinkled her nose and scratched her forehead. Her mind raced like a greyhound dog chasing the mechanical hare around the racetrack. A flash of questions darted like a rapid-firing gun clicking in her mind. *Who was that guy? Why did he follow me? How did he find where I live?* Glancing to the right and left, twisting her purse's handle, Katherine swallowed before responding. "I don't know that man."

20

KATHERINE JOSTLED WITH HER blanket and twisted on the living room sofa until daybreak. Sunlight infused the living room with a glow. Don McNeill's Breakfast Club replaced Dick Biondi, the Wild Italian's Midnight Radio show.

Katherine, fatigued from the sleepless night, lingered. The phone, hidden under a crumpled lavender quilt resting on the floor next to her, let out a muffled ring.

Charlotte's soft voice increased an octave with each word. "Kate. Are you okay? I called you every ten minutes until nine last night. Adam and I even went to Emma Jean's place to check on you."

Katherine held the receiver against her chest and bit her lips. She wasn't ready to talk to her. Charlotte's words—"Adam, and I"—bounced around her stomach. *I can't trash a lifelong friend. And Adam, well, he was just a friend. So, two of my friends went to dinner? So what?* Bigger problems glared in her thoughts like a burning sun: meeting her supervisor to fix the charity event issue and finding an explanation for last night's frightening experience with the stranger and her keys.

Katherine scanned the bedroom, now empty of Charlotte's belonging. She needed to sit with her friend and tell her everything. The two girls from Chippewa Falls had shared their entire lives, from their first kindergarten nap to their last time together in this apartment.

"Hey. Did you read my note? Nothing happened with Adam. We just freaked out. We thought that Greek had kidnapped you."

Katherine's stomach quivered. *What happened to her and Adam doesn't matter, but I want the truth.* "Okay, I better get moving. I'll call you."

Charlotte responded with a muffled good-bye.

Katherine dropped the receiver in the phone's cradle. She'd get to Charlotte's note, but right now she needed a good long bath.

Jungle Gardenia bubble bath swirled in the tub like the rush of a fresh stream running to unite with a river. The scent elevated and revived her spirits and calmed her heart.

Katherine's mind drifted to the lesson her mother had shared with her when she was only six years old. Her mother had always avoided discussing her Native American heritage unless she wanted to teach Katherine. To help her learn how to live, her mother explained the remarkable aspects of being Native American.

One day, when Katherine ran outside to avoid taking a bath, her mother dashed after her and sprinted alongside her. When weariness overcame them, they stopped by a pond. Her mother wiped her brow and smiled at Katherine. "Sweetheart, I hated to take baths once upon a time too. Then my grandmother and your great-grandmother, beautiful Hanging Cloud, told me an important characteristic of our ancestors, the Chippewa. Native American's valued their hygiene and daily bathing. They bathed in the waters of nearby rivers." She paused and glowed at Katherine, who shivered and wrapped her arms around herself. "Yep, even on frigid winter days. Now, we have warm water and luxurious bubble bath. And you know, when you have a cold, a nice warm bath always helps you get well. That's what our ancestors did. In times of sickness, they searched for healing springs. Even when you're not sick, a good bath gives you extra energy and joy."

Her mother's words drifted to her as she whisked the soothing bubbles around her. Katherine remembered one time, fifteen years ago, when she'd been worried, she'd never talk to Charlotte again after an argument. "Best friends are like diamonds, precious and rare," her mother had said. "False friends are like leaves, found everywhere."

Katherine gazed in the bathroom mirror. "Mirror, mirror, who are my real friends?"

Before she got an answer, the phone rang. *It must be my loyal friend or Mom.*

"Hi, Katherine," Angelos said on the other end. "How are you? I wanted to thank you for the fantastic book, *To Killing a Mockingbird*. I tried to call last night."

Katherine slumped on her bed and wished she'd never answered the phone. She didn't want to talk to anyone right now, but her stewardess good nature won out. "Oh, Angelos, you're welcome. I hope you found it interesting. All my teachers told me that this book will be a classic since it shows some serious issues in our country's cultural history. Hey, right now, I'm running late for work."

"Oh, okay. Would you like to go out for dinner next week?"

Katherine believed that every person that wandered into her life had a message. Some have lifelong messages, and some are little reminders and warnings. There's also Aesop's quote, "No act of kindness, no matter how small, is ever wasted." And Angelos was on her "Good Deed" list. She tried to have at least three people at all times on this list—friendly, kind individuals who had crossed her path and would only be in her life for a short period. Her mother had told her to do kind acts for a stranger or people who couldn't repay her. "Okay. Can you call tomorrow?"

"I'll call in the afternoon. Good-bye."

"Bye," Katherine said.

Katherine rubbed her hands over her brow. She turned and noticed Charlotte's Chanel-scented note crumpled on her bed. *It can wait until I've had breakfast.*

21

ON THE WAY TO THE Third Coast Coffee Shop, Katherine stopped at the local drugstore to buy a new journal. *The Diary of Anaïs Nin* had inspired Katherine's journal writing. Like the eleven-year-old Anaïs Nin, who began writing in her dairy as a letter to her father, Katherine, an archer, wrote notes in her journal to Artemis, the goddess of hunting. *I've neglected my best friend,* she thought. *And I'm disconnected from my thoughts. I need to reconnect. Life moved me along, and I need to pull out snippets one at a time. Each bit forms a tapestry. Each piece calls out and begs a place in a completely woven message.*

With a steaming cup of coffee, Katherine pulled out the new journal and wondered how to start. Why did I share *To Kill a Mockingbird* with Angelos? After a long gulp of coffee, Katherine rubbed her cheeks. Her eyes riveted on the blank page, she rubbed her forehead and took in a deep breath. Prejudice and injustice: that's what she'd been thinking. Slavery was part of our history. Why hadn't she gone further back to the United States first act of prejudice toward Native

Americans? Katherine wiped her hand over her face to stop the stream of tears. There was too much to tell, from losing their land through broken treaties to the false images today of Native Americans as savages.

A picture of her parents slipped out of her wallet and rested on the table.

"Hey, Katherine. Are these your parents?" Neal asked.

Katherine looked up and saw Neal, a friend of Charlotte's. She wrinkled her brow and nodded. Neal was one guy Katherine would like to date, but alas she thought he was interested in her charming roommate, even though he and Charlotte had not been on an actual date. He spent many nights visiting in the young women's apartment. His blond hair and bronze tan framed cosmetically whitened teeth. Katherine liked his square-jawed good looks. "Hi, Neal. It must be photo shoot time for you."

Neal plopped in the chair across from her. "No. I just got back from one. It was a commercial sunrise shoot on Oak Street Beach. Sunrise on Lake Michigan lets off the best light. The air is fresh, and the waves just swish on the shore. What else do I need? Hey, I talked to Charlotte last night. She's concerned you got kidnapped, or worse."

Katherine took in a deep breath and burst out, "Kidnapped, or worse!"

"Yep. Charlotte asked me to check in on you."

"Check in on me?" Katherine's body tightened. Her face turned red. She grabbed her purse and her notebook.

Neal reached out and touched her hand. "Hey, lady. Charlotte is your best friend. You should feel good that someone cares that you're safe. Now cool it. Please sit and chat. Let's have one of those wonderful sugar and spice muffins and a cup of coffee. Okay?"

Katherine gazed at Neal's cobalt blue eyes; his touch made

her knees weak. No wonder Charlotte liked this guy. A rush of devil-may-care thoughts abounded. *Maybe Neal and I could go to dinner like Charlotte and Adam. Hmm*, she thought, and her eyes twinkled. *I need to talk with a good and understanding listener.*

"Well, I'm bummed. When did you talk to Charlotte? Before she went out with Adam?"

Neal's face turned red; his brow wrinkled. "That guy that she was with? Is he your friend?"

Katherine cocked her head. "Yeah. Did you see them?"

"Well, I thought Charlotte might want to go for a drink. Her phone was busy. So I walked over to ask her out. Just as I got inside your apartment lobby, Charlotte and your friend came into the entrance. Charlotte slumped into a chair and burst into tears. In between gulps, she gave me the story about you. Your friend, Adam, asked if I wanted to join them."

Neal leaned forward and stared into Katherine's eyes. "I went to McGuire's and had a couple of beers with them. You were the topic of our conversation. They admire you. So, I decided to find out what had happened to you. I stopped at your apartment; the doorman said you'd left for coffee."

Katherine threw her head back and laughed. "As Alice said, this gets 'curiouser and curiouser!'" Katherine filled Neal in on Angelos, Charlotte, and Adam. She ended with a smile. "People and their heads! I took a book to an interested young man from Greece, and you'd think I became a war prisoner or something."

Neal shook his head and nodded. "People are too lazy to discover the truth. They don't bother to find out the facts. I guess that's why I'm going to law school. People will never stop jumping to conclusions and make poor decisions. That's employment security for me."

Katherine's heart leaped. A lawyer? "You're going to law school?"

Neal smiled. "Yep. I'm in my last year. I never mentioned it to Charlotte. Since she liked Neal the model, I left the law school part out. You know, I remember you with your nose in textbooks when I visited Charlotte at your apartment. You surprised me with all the knowledge and wisdom that you expressed. Are you a stew in school?"

Katherine howled and patted his hands. "Yes. I'm a stew who's on a sabbatical of sorts from school. Two years ago, when I left Beloit College to become a stewardess, my professor agreed to give me an incomplete." She paused and looked up at the ceiling and smiled at Neal. "I got hooked on my travels and life in Chicago; the time stretched to over two years. Now I have had the drive to get back on track. The past couple of weeks were wild."

Neal's grin widened like a hound dog with a steak bone. "Hey, I saw you at the Playboy press party a couple of weeks ago. First, it seemed like a Mafioso guy had you in a locked embrace, and then a mysterious knight in shining armor rescued you from a tumble. And then there was Bunny Katherine. You made the most incredible vision." Neal chuckled.

Katherine's face turned red. She cleared her throat. "I did that to help me write my article covering the Mansion and the party."

"Yeah, Charlotte said you'd be taking notes or mingling for your 'fake' article."

Katherine slammed her notebook on the table. Charlotte's unread letter flew out and touched Neal's elbow. "She didn't even need to bring it up. I'm not a journalism student; I'm majoring in anthropology with a focus on archeology. She only told the Playboy party coordinator that I was a student who wanted to write an article as a ruse to get me an invitation. As far I know, the publicity lady never asked to see any fake story. I forgot about it since I didn't have to write anything. It did help me get away from that gangster guy."

Neal sat back and picked up Charlotte's note. "Jungle Gardenia," he said. "Charlotte's trademark. Is this for me?" He paused and laughed. "Is this a Dear John letter?"

Katherine snatched the note from Neal's clutched hand. "It's a letter from Charlotte to me. I couldn't bring myself to read it, but now that I know what happened with you and her last night in the lobby, I bet she wrote and asked me to tell you to stay away from her."

Neal laughed. "You look like a hit squad recruit. You did hang out with that gangster."

"Yeah. I'm on the payroll as a spy or mole," Katherine shot back.

Neal smiled. "You're interesting. And I thought you were another fly girl, a step above a Playboy Bunny."

Katherine glanced at Charlotte's note but didn't read it. She closed her notebook and did everything possible not to look at Neal. This sort of thing didn't happen to her. It did to Emma Jean, but not to her. She wondered if he'd come on to Charlotte the same way. Her body temperature surged. *He's just another scoundrel. He's just another hunk who wants every chick who crosses his path.* "Well, when I see Charlotte, I'll tell her I had coffee with you."

Neal leaned forward and pulled Katherine across the table toward his face. He leaned in and whispered in Katherine's ear. "Stay calm. I noticed a creepy guy at the back table. His eyes have stayed glued on us the whole time. I know a stalker when I see one. Play it cool. Give me a kiss and hold my hand."

Katherine's muscles tightened. Her heart thumped. Was this a trick? No, she remembered that creep who had followed her on the street last night and had her keys. She gave him a smile that melted into his warm kiss. She felt safe with him and thought. *Wow. Is this how bodyguards do their job?*

Neal rested his elbows on the table and looked into Katherine's eyes. His eyes shined with concern for her. He didn't act like a guy who'd made another conquest. "Katherine, are you and that gangster guy an item?"

Katherine swallowed in an attempt to calm her stomach. She wanted to scream but took control of her emotions. "No. I barely know him!"

Neal grabbed Katherine's notebook for a piece of paper. He grabbed Katherine's pen and wrote: *Then why is that guy tailing you? He may have other accomplices also checking us. If you want to talk more, we should leave this joint. Let's go over to the zoo. We can speak in private.*"

Katherine read it and nodded. In a rush, she gathered up her notebook and purse, and Charlotte's letter dropped to the floor. A cold sweat surged over her when she picked up the note. When her sweating hands grabbed Charlotte's note she spied the stranger glaring at her. *Yikes, that's the snake, the one on the bus, the one who followed me on the street, and the one from the library. What does he want with me?*

"Darlin' Katherine!" Emma Jean squealed, rushing up to them outside Third Coast. She hugged Katherine and waved her hand through the air to reach out for Neal's hand. "Are you two going somewhere or can you come back in and have a cup of espresso with lil ol' me?"

Katherine sensed Emma Jean itching to pull her away to get the details on this handsome man, but the thought of the stalker made her feel queasy. "I'll have to call you later. Neal and I have an appointment."

He gave an impatient nod. "Yes, we're late now. It was a pleasure meeting you."

Emma Jean eyeballed the couple and raised her eyebrows. "Oh, my. I don't want you to miss an appointment." She turned to Katherine and gave her a look that sent thrills through Katherine's veins. "Call me when you have time."

She watched her best friend disappear into the Third Coast restaurant. Katherine sensed time and events moving her on to new things. Katherine wiped her brow and lifted her head with the support of a quote from W. Somerset Maugham from *Of Human Bondage*, "The secret of life is meaningless unless you discover it."

Neal turned and touched her shoulder. "Hey, I don't want to interfere with you and your friend. I'd say go after her, but you have something threatening in your life right now."

Katherine twisted her love beads and frowned. "Yeah. I honestly don't know why."

Neal smiled at her and grabbed her hand. "The polar bears are waiting for us. They'll have an answer for you."

Katherine nodded. "I sure hope so. I'm on a ship that's lost its rudder."

Neal's eyes swept around Dearborn Street. He shrugged. "Sure appears like the same street I've walked thousands of time. I can't see a lick of water."

Katherine wondered why Neal was here. And she wondered how to share things with him. He was Charlotte's friend, almost a stranger. Right then, she wanted her happy, carefree self to return, but a frightened, weepy person had taken her place. She turned away and wiped a tear from her eye.

Neal put his hands on her shoulders and turned her toward him. "Hey. I might be wrong, and that guy isn't stalking you. Maybe I made it up, so I could kiss you. And it worked."

She tucked her hand under his arm and motioned toward Lincoln Park. When she needed a place to connect with nature and quiet herself, Lincoln Park and the zoo gave her strength. The park took the place of her Wisconsin meadows and became her secret sanctuary.

Abraham Lincoln's statue towered at the entrance to Chicago's landmark park. Katherine turned to Neal. "Good Ol' Abraham. This statue is one of my favorite places in the park. When I want inspiration, I walk over and visit Abe and walk over to the Chicago Historical Museum."

"Abe is my hero, and I'm a history buff too," Neal said. "He inspired me to become a lawyer."

Katherine smiled. "My father's a lawyer. He keeps a statue of Abe on his desk to guide him."

Neal raised his eyebrows. "Yeah?"

Katherine wanted to run up to Abe and give him a hug. A soft place in her heart told her she could tell Neal everything, and he'd understand. *Yep. Abe's his hero too.*

22

THE SUMMER SUN'S GLOW moved toward the west as Katherine bounded through the lobby of her building, head held high and a twinkle in her eyes. "Greetings, Fred. Isn't this a super day?"

"Your shining personality makes it a super day. Did something special happen to you? You have a grin that won't stop. Did you find that strange man? Is that problem solved?"

While the mysterious, sinister man was still a stalker, Neal made her fear manageable. For the first time, another person was giving her strength.

"That menacing evil man . . . I may have a solution for him after all," she said before going up to her apartment.

When she'd left in the morning for breakfast, she'd wanted to be alone, but Neal had appeared like someone from the mist. *Doors open, doors close, and then a magic haze floated around me. I didn't even tighten my seat belt for the magic carpet ride with Neal. I drifted with ease.* Katherine and Neal had never made it to the zoo since Abe Lincoln's statue had beckoned them to pause on their walk. Sitting at the base of Abe Lincoln's statue, they'd talked and talked. Katherine breathed in the sense of peace and calm. Everything seemed aligned in its right place.

After her few hours with Neal, she'd realized that she'd faked her liberation. She depended on Charlotte for security and comfort, and she relied on Emma Jean for the lighter side of life. She'd never thought on her own. She'd told Neal every detail of her past two weeks. When she talked with him, it was like talking to herself. Before Neal, she'd needed Charlotte and Emma Jean to give support. Neal filled her world. Now she *wanted* Neal. She wondered how one person could give out so much confidence. *Is Neal a passing fling? His magic mist is there to give me the push I need to grow.* Katherine laughed. *And he will help keep me safe from my evil stalker.*

The phone interrupted her reflections.

"Hello, Katherine," Angelos said. "How about a dinner in Greek Town tonight?"

Katherine put her hands on her face. *He is my good deed. I have to keep my good intentions. Maybe I can find another way.* "Oh, Angelos. I have plans. Another time?"

"Okay. I'll call next week."

"Thanks for understanding. Bye."

Katherine's shoulders tightened. Neal had mentioned Angelos when they sat at Abe Lincoln's feet. She remembered his words.

"Hey," he said, "remember that Greek guy I saw helping you at the Playboy party?"

"Yes. Angelos. Do you know him?"

"No, but I ran into a couple of Playboy Bunnies at Mr. Kelly's a few nights ago, and they mentioned him. I asked about life at the Playboy Mansion, and they brought him up. Half the Bunnies at the mansion have a crush on him. They told me fascinating tales about Bunnies fighting over him with knockout battles and hair pulling. Did he hit on you?" *I didn't lie to Neal. Angelos didn't hit on me. We shared an interest in each other's culture.* Katherine grabbed her stomach to stop the pain. *Neal might agree with Emma Jean that I like to save puppies. But is Angelos a lost puppy? No, he's not lost. He's not a lost foreigner in a new land. What was I thinking?* Then she thought of Charlotte's note. *Maybe Charlotte's correspondence has new roommate news for me.*

Katherine dug through her purse for the note and reclined on the long green sofa. *Golly, Charlotte's letter. I guess I should read it. That's the reality, but with all the changes it might as well be years.* Katherine held the letter in her hand like it was an old discovery from a lost treasure chest. Katherine sighed and wiped a solitary tear from her cheek.

My dear friend,

When you read this, I'll be in my new home. Here are a few things you need to know.

First: Anita will not be able to be your new roommate. She got married, and her supervisor made her quit flying last week. She called from her honeymoon in Cancun. She's pretty nervous to leave you with an empty apartment. She did say she'd try to find someone to take her place. You'll find a message from her in your mailbox at the airport with more information. You're okay with the rent for the rest of this month. Then, you're stuck. I'd move back, but I can't. I'll ask the Bunnies at the mansion. Maybe someone here would like a change from the mansion to an apartment. Second: Neal has a thing for you. I'll give you the details when I see you. Third: You're cool with your supervisor. I told her you got kidnapped. I saved your neck and your job. When I told her you got kidnapped, she gasped, and she cried for you. Fourth: Now, you have to save my job and make that fake article about the Playboy party a real story. Our PR coordinator keeps asking me about it. I fibbed again and told her that the airlines sent you to work for two months in Hawaii. That's it. You have to get something done before two months, my friend.

Got to run now. Sorry, we missed each other. I still love you. Char XO, XO

Katherine laid the paper aside. A single black crow feather floated and stalled mid-air in her living room before it drifted down to land on the letter. Katherine leaned back on the sofa and wrapped her hands behind her head. She picked up the feather and held it close to her chest. *Everything will be fine. Something will change, so I won't need to write that silly Playboy party article. After all, I'm going to be a great scholar writing about ancient civilizations, not this wild sexual revolution.*

23

GETTING READY FOR HER overnight layover in Portland, Katherine tossed her suitcase on the bed. A haunting echo bounced around the room when the bag hit the bed. Katherine sighed. Slumping onto her bed, Katherine picked up the picture of her and Charlotte and smiled with misty eyes. *Char, I'll miss you, but we both have new paths to take. I apologize for my reaction to you and Adam. You both care for me, and I overreacted. Our friendship is like an evergreen tree. It weathers storms and keeps growing greener.* She placed the photo on the nightstand and glanced around the room. She felt like she'd already left this place. Her only company was her memories. She smiled and took in a deep breath. *Okay, girl, it's time for an adventure in Portland, the City of Roses, and a trip with Emma Jean. Should be fun!*

After tossing in her civilian clothes, her regulation flight manual, and her serving smock, she checked her toiletry bag. *Dang, toothpaste tube empty, no deodorant! Well, I have time to walk to Big Apple; I'll need some groceries for when I get home.*

Strolling down North State Parkway to her apartment with her small bag of groceries, Katherine pondered. *I wish I could stay home today, and that Neal would call. But maybe I'll never hear from him again. Did he feel the same connection as I did yesterday?*

At the entrance to her apartment lobby, Katherine looked around for Fred, the doorman, but he'd stepped away. She wanted to let him know that she'd be without a roommate for a while. Mom and Dad were going to worry. It would help if she could tell them that Fred was watching out for her.

Katherine stopped at her mailbox before heading to the elevator and sensed another person standing near her. She turned around, expecting to see another tenant waiting to get to their mailbox, but the person was nowhere in sight. She shrugged.

Katherine pushed the elevator button while she flipped through her mail. When the elevator opened, Katherine kept reading a letter from her mother. She didn't notice the man slip in behind her.

The odor of sweat and tobacco filled the small elevator box. Katherine's nose twitched, and her fear antenna rose. *He's breathing down my back. I've got two more floors to go then I'll run, rush into my apartment, and lock the door.*

When the elevator stopped at the fifteenth floor, Katherine jumped out.

The man coughed and mumbled "Hello, Katherine."

His raspy voice startled Katherine. She froze. She hadn't looked at her elevator partner on the trip up to the fifteenth floor. She turned and screamed. It was the stalker from the library, the CTA bus, and the Third Coast Coffee House. Her finger shook as she pointed at him. Her voice quaked.

"You, you've been following me." Her shoulders tightened, and her breathing rushed in and out like a rapidly firing rifle.

He glared at her and walked closer to her. "Yes, I need to talk with you. You have something that doesn't belong to you."

"I don't have anything that doesn't belong to me. If you don't leave me alone, I'll call the cops." Katherine kept talking and moving backward toward her apartment.

"Go ahead and call the police. Those lawmen will agree with me that you're a thief. You know. You stole that eagle feather in the library. And I'm here to recover it."

"Eagle feather?"

Katherine's heart pounded, and her mind rushed with conflicting thoughts. *Should I talk with him? If he knows about the eagle feather, he may want to sell it on the black market. He looks like a crook. Do I run? Yes.*

Katherine reached in the grocery bag and grabbed a couple of tomatoes. Wham. The first tomato slammed into his right eye. The second hit his nose to create a red clown look. He shouted. "Shit! Woman."

Katherine ran to her apartment door. She struggled to unzip her purse to retrieve her key. Before she could open her purse, the stalker charged up behind her.

He grabbed her arm. "Look, you're making this difficult. I have a job to do, and you better comply with me."

What do I do? He might molest me if we stay out here. What do I do? A flash of inspiration charged her into action. She had her best protection waiting for her in her bedroom. *I can take care of myself.* "Okay. Come in."

He smiled. "Great. Once you give me the eagle feather, you won't be on the Fed's wanted list."

Katherine unlocked the door. Right inside the door in the hallway, she motioned for the man to wait there. To keep him calm and give her time. She smiled and whispered.

"I need to pee. Give me a second and I'll be right back with the feather."

Katherine held her breath. *At least he won't follow me to the john. Thank goodness I loaded my Crow Bow for my practice at the archery range.*

Katherine's Crow Bow stood in the ready position. It almost jumped into Katherine's hand when she flew into her bedroom.

An adrenaline rush fortified her. She rubbed her Thunderbird necklace. She grabbed the Crow Bow. A blessing of courage filled her with power as she dashed down her hall with the Crow Bow in hand. Four feet from the man, she faced him at a 45-degree angle. Holding the bow gently, Katherine stood with both feet pointing toward him. "If you don't leave now, I'll be forced to defend myself."

Drops of sweat flowed from his forehead. His hands shook as he raised them over his head. "Hey, I don't want to harm you. I only want you to give me the eagle feather. It's a federal offense to keep eagle feathers." He reached into his jacket and pulled out identification. "I'm an undercover agent for the federal government. I was a thief just like you. The Feds hired me after I did my time for stealing and fencing artwork. Now they hired me to return eagle feathers to Native Americans. When the library security officer called the Fish and Wildlife Office, my contact at the federal office called me. I rushed over and started to track you down. Since you're a stewardess, it made sense that you planned to sell the eagle feather. I figured that you would fly out of town and sell the feather in some distant place. I wanted to catch you before you ran off to Timbuktu with the feather."

Katherine dropped the bow and laughed. "I agree with you that an eagle feather belongs to the Native Americans. Do you agree that when a Native American receives an eagle feather, it is an honor to the recipient and has a special meaning to that person?"

He nodded. "But this doesn't give you a right to have the feather."

Katherine smiled and lifted her Thunderbird necklace out and held it up. "This is a special gift from my great-grandmother Hanging Cloud, a member of the Chippewa tribe. She gave it to me for protection. If you know anything about Native Americans, you know about the Thunderbird."

"You're a tall, beautiful blonde. I don't see an ounce of Injun in you."

Katherine sighed. "My father is German. I have one-eighth Chippewa in me."

He released a breath and glanced down at her Crow Bow. "You held that bow like you're an expert archer and that Thunderbird necklace makes me think you might have Native American blood in you. I don't need to see any more evidence." He ran his fingers through his hair. "Yeah, and O'Leary told me that you made the eagle feather turn into a mouse—something like shape shifting. Yikes!" The man jumped. "What the hell?" He shook his leg and out popped a mouse. It ran over his shoes and disappeared out the open front door.

He shook his head and walked over to Katherine. He extended his shaking hand. "I apologize for bothering you, miss. I'll write up a report that you have a legal right to the eagle feather."

Katherine smiled. "Thank you. And I apologize for throwing tomatoes at you. But I didn't know what you planned to do to me."

He laughed. "Well, I do come on like a thug, but in my business, I run into a lot of real criminals who make lots of money from selling Native American artifacts. In business, people are guilty until proven innocent." He gave her a smile and said, "But you, my lady, are an innocent and must have a sacred mission if you received an eagle feather. But be careful what you do with this gift. If you mishandle the possession of the feather, you may be breaking the law."

24

NEAL CRAWLED OUT OF bed and dashed to get ready for an action-packed day. The shower water flowed in sync with his review of the day: a morning photo shoot at Wrigley Field and a contract law class in the afternoon. With a quick wash and shave, he barely had enough time to run his hands through his thick, blond hair. Leaping over his dirty jeans and shirts strewn over his bedroom floor, he landed on his bed and dialed the Playboy Mansion. "May I speak with Charlotte Delaney? Neal Meyer is calling."

Debbie giggled. "I'll get Charlotte. She's getting ready to have breakfast. Oh, and next time, you can call and ask for Debbie."

Neal sighed. "Yeah. Thanks."

Before Charlotte came to the phone, Neal reviewed his fantastic day with Katherine. The times he had called to speak to Charlotte and Katherine had answered the phone were so different than this conversation with Debbie. Katherine would say hello and get Charlotte. But every time he'd called, he'd wanted to talk to Katherine. *Are all stewardesses different from Playboy Bunnies? No. Katherine is different. That's why she intrigues me.*

"Hi, Neal," Charlotte said, "it's good to hear from you."

"Sorry to interrupt your breakfast."

"Neal, you never interrupt. How's everything? I let Katherine know you're interested. I put it in my last note to her. I haven't talked to her yet. What's up?"

"I found her at the Third Coast Coffee Shop. I kidded with her. So, I wanted to let you know before you talk to her., I told her I wanted to deck her friend Adam when I saw you with him last night. She thinks you and Adam have a thing now. Hope you don't mind. But if you could help me out—"

"Adam and I, well, I'm going to New York next week. He wants to take me to the Hamptons. I was trying to remember that quote from that Thoreau guy. You know the one that Adam said describes Katherine. It started, 'A different drummer,' I think."

Neal laughed. "That's my favorite quote too: 'If a man does not keep pace with his companions, perhaps it is because he hears a different drummer. Let him step to the music which he hears, however measured or far away.' Good luck with Adam. Thanks, Charlotte, you're a smart lady."

"And good luck with Katherine."

"Sorry to keep you, but one more thing? Is Katherine involved with any mafia guys?"

"Are you crazy? Her dad's a lawyer who practiced law in Chicago and warned Katherine before she could say Mama and Dada to never talk to the Chicago mob guys. Long before she ever dreamed of living in Chicago." Charlotte sighed. "Where did you dig up that idea?"

"This strange guy stalked her when I met her at the Third Coast, and she told me he's the same jerk that followed her home last night. It's a long story, but he found her keys on the bus and somehow knew where she lived. I thought he might work for the mob."

"Katherine's straight and narrow. I don't want anyone to hurt her. I have to run, but I will talk with the Playboy security guy, Danny O'Brien. He knows most of the cops in town and his brother is a criminal lawyer."

"Thanks, Charlotte."

Neal leaped into his khaki pants and slipped on his white polo shirt. He jammed his feet into his well-worn Weejuns. The sunshine brightened everything in sight as he walked to catch the Red Line to Addison for his Wrigley Field photo shoot. He reviewed all the conversations he'd had with Katherine. He wanted to share everything with her. When would he tell Katherine that he was Jewish?

25

CHARLOTTE RUSHED PAST THE brownstones that lined
State Parkway. Her heart pounded with the adrenaline rush
and her concern for her friend. Danny O'Brien approached
the Playboy Mansion entrance, he spotted Charlotte and
smiled, "Good afternoon, Bunny Charlotte."

"Hey, Danny. You can forget all the Bunny stuff outside the mansion." Charlotte peeked at her watch. "I've got
five minutes before I get into my Bunny suit. Do you have a
couple of minutes?"

Danny slipped his hands into his pockets. He recalled
his brother's warning to stay away from any involvement
with the Bunnies. So far, he'd continued on the straight and
narrow, but Charlotte was a sweet girl. He noticed her hands
wringing and her blinking eyes. All clues said this was no
casual meeting. He recognized a frightened woman.

"Sure, let's step over here." He motioned for them to
walk to the corner next to the Ambassador Hotel. "It's better
to talk away from the mansion entrance."

"It's not me," Charlotte said once they were out of ear-shot. "I need you to help my old roommate."

"Your old roommate?"

"Here's a picture of her from a couple of years ago when she attended Beloit College. She's even better looking today."

Danny examined the photo and gasped. "I recognize her."

Charlotte cocked her head. "You've met?"

Danny took in a deep breath. "I encountered her twice: at the Playboy party and then again at the public library, a couple of days ago."

"Katherine is the sweetest, most charming lady. At the party, she ran into this guy." She had to stop and catch her breath before she could continue. "He was on one of her flights to Las Vegas. She was just polite to passengers, but he misunderstood her friendliness." Charlotte paused for a moment. "The public library? What was she doing there?" She paused and rubbed her brow. "Oh, she said something about an eagle feather. Does that mean anything?"

Danny shrugged. "I don't know. I wouldn't be concerned. I'll see what I can rake up."

Charlotte glanced at her watch. "Yikes! I should be in my Bunny costume right now." She gave Danny half a hug. "Thanks, big guy. Please take care of my friend."

Danny's knees buckled, and he moved back and smiled. "Hey, no problem. Glad I can help. I'll keep you updated."

Danny scratched his head as he watched Charlotte stride away. *Something happened there. She's not a damsel in distress; this is something different.* Danny cocked his head and smiled. *I hope I see her at the club.*

Danny dropped a quarter into the slot of the Ambassador's pay phone to call his brother. "Hey, guy," he said. "Can you meet at McGuires after work? I need your help."

"Does it involve a woman?

"Yeah."

"Is she in trouble?"

"That's for us to find out."

Danny hung up and gaped around the Ambassador. *Wow. I'm, in the classic hotel where I saw Cary Grant appear in Hitchcock's* North by Northwest, *a real thriller. Is Katherine involved in a real life thriller?*

26

KATHERINE STOOD IN FRONT of the mailbox at the airport before her flight to Portland with Emma Jean. Legs tingling and chest tight, Katherine tugged the bright blue stationery from her box. The note from Anita, her almost roommate, tumbled out of the box. She wanted to wait to deal with her apartment problem until she got back from her flight. Her father's favorite quote from Sophocles, "Quick decisions are risky decisions," kept her from making some big mistakes.

Katherine leaned against her mailbox and read the letter.

Dear Katherine:

I'm so sorry I didn't have time to talk to you before my life got upended. Things happened fast, and I had little time to decide. Does that ever happen to you? When you read this, I'll already be living my new life. So here's what happened.

Dave, my boyfriend, and I lived together. We wanted to get married next fall. I thought the supervisors were spying on us because we lived together. You know they fire stews for living with a man. Well, that's why I wanted it to look like I had you as my roommate. I planned to pay part of the rent, and you'd have the apartment all to yourself.

Well, before my flight two weeks ago, a supervisor met my flight and escorted me to her office. I didn't even get to pass go; it was like going to jail. She sat me down and said I'd violated airline policy because I'd gotten married. I don't know how they knew.

Boy, was I stunned. And we weren't even married yet. So Dave and I decided that we should get married. I am pregnant, so I would have quit anyway.

When I talked with your roommate, I didn't think of this idea, but I'm wondering if Dave and I could take over your lease? I didn't mean to leave you in the lurch, and you only have a couple of weeks before the rent's due.

I'll be back from my honeymoon in Cancun on July 15. I'll call you.

Anita

Katherine shook her head. *I can live alone and take care of myself. If I can afford rent, I'll forget about finding a roommate. How would I replace Charlotte, a lifelong friend, who was like living with a family member?*

Katherine folded the letter and stuffed it into her purse. The situation made her think of Mr. Albert Einstein advice: "Life is like riding a bicycle. To keep your balance, you must keep moving." With a laugh, she whispered, "For me, I change it to a horse, and now I better trot over to check-in."

Soaring to 30,000 feet, the DC-8 glided into the bright sunlight painting the underlying clouds. Katherine appreciated the golden glow that illuminated the pages of *The Diary of Anaïs Nin*. She loved this time before they reached cruising altitude when the passengers sat locked in their seats and waited for the captain to turn off the No Smoking sign. Katherine wished the captain could leave the No Smoking sign on the whole flight.

Glancing at the sea of humanity, Katherine wondered who they were, where were they going, and what waited for them at the end of their journeys. Anaïs Nin's words flowed off the page: "We don't see things as they are, we see them as we are." *Oh my, this fits me,* Katherine, thought. *I've rushed through life and didn't take the time to examine people and things in my life. Do they fit? Each person, each experience is like a headlight or guidepost leading us.*

"Hey, Darlin'," Emma Jean said, waving her hand in Katherine's face. "The captain turned off the No Smoking and Seat Belt signs. It's time for us to be our charming hostess selves."

Katherine smiled and snapped her seat belt open. "Let's go girl; it's show time."

After stuffing the last meal tray in the galley, Katherine untied her apron and sighed. *Another pleasant meal service with pleased and resting passengers. How many more flights will I take before I move on? Could this be one of my last ones? I should savor each trip because we never know when life takes away. Don't take anything for granted.*

Katherine stretched back on the jump seat and closed her eyes. "At the hotel, I'll take a warm bath." She turned to Emma Jean and smiled. "Do you want to walk down to Barbary, the old pirate section of Portland, or take a tour of the Pittock Mansion? It's haunted."

Emma Jean rolled her eyes and sighed.

Katherine grabbed her friend's arm. "Don't you want an adventure?"

"Remember: you're the adventurer. I'm just the ever-charming romantic. Give me a tall, dark, handsome man and roses and a candlelight dinner at the best restaurant town."

Katherine gave her friend a big grin. "Well, then—"

"We hope all you back there enjoyed your flight," the captain's cheery voice interrupted. "We're approaching the beautiful City of Roses. The weather is perfect, and we're even arriving five minutes ahead of time. Just buckle your seat belts and relax."

Climbing the lush red carpet to the lobby of the Benson Hotel, Katherine paused to take in the grand crystal chandelier, the English wingback chairs, and the grand piano in the corner of the landmark Portland hotel. "I can't believe that the airlines use this great hotel for a layover! I feel like a rock star."

Emma Jean squealed. "Oh, my heavens look at those great mahogany pillars. They must be over 100 feet fall. This lobby reaches to the sky." Emma Jean raised her chest and tipped her chin toward the ceiling, pretending to be a wealthy Portland socialite.

Katherine shrugged. *Once a Southern belle, always a Southern belle.* Every time Emma Jean's real southern character shined, Katherine felt more lost. *What is my way? How do I find the actual Katherine hiding behind all these masks?*

After checking in, Emma Jean glanced toward the gift shop. "Look at that shop. It must be full of gorgeous clothes. Let's go and take a peek inside."

The young women split ways in the store, heading toward their separate interests: Katherine to a fake fur vest and Emma Jean to the mod dresses.

As usual, Katherine made a free choice and went to pay for her vest. True to her nature Emma Jean admired herself in the mirror with every possible dress on the rack. Katherine said yes to every dress. She knew better than to tell her friend her real opinion. Out of the corner of her eye, she noticed a tall young Japanese man lost in a trance watching her southern friend.

With ease, the dark, handsome stranger strolled over to Emma Jean and gave a slight bow. "Please excuse me, but may I give my opinion? The red dress is the one you should buy."

Emma Jean angled her head slightly, trying to look innocent. "Oh my, I did need your help. Do you think this is right for me?"

"Of course," he said. "And if you buy this dress, I'd be pleased if you'd wear it as my dinner guest this evening."

Emma Jean turned toward Katherine, who'd already walked halfway to the shop door. "Oh, Katherine, wait." She paused and turned to the stranger. "Can my friend join us?"

Katherine shivered. "Thanks, Emma Jean, but I'm meeting friends."

Emma Jean's brow wrinkled as if to say, *What friends?* Then a flash of recollection: their silent language for I'm bowing out, you have fun. "Oh, that's right." She paused and, with composure, said to the young man. "I don't go out with strangers. I only go out with gentlemen."

Katherine giggled as she walked out the door. *That woman should win every acting award in the book.* Katherine knew her friend had already sized up his income and social status.

This man had all the qualities on Emma Jean's check-list for acceptable men: money and station wrapped up in a perfect gentleman.

As the elevator door opened, Katherine felt a tug on her sleeve. "Hey, Darlin', you didn't even wait for me."

"Well, you and that guy hit it off, and I didn't want to crowd in."

"He's nice, *and* he said he could find a date for you, so you can join us."

Katherine's neck rushed with heat. "I can find my partners without your help."

"He said you're beautiful and could find any man you want. He was just thoughtful."

"I appreciate his thoughts, but you know me, I can always find something to do."

As the elevator door opened to the tenth floor, Emma Jean turned and laughed. "Oh, I forgot, you want to visit the pirate haunts or that Pick Mansion."

"It's called Pittock Mansion," Katherine said as she entered the room. "We'll both have our fun tonight, right?"

Emma Jean opened her shopping bag and held her new red dress up to show Katherine. "Do you think I bought the right dress?"

"You mean did *he* buy the right dress, don't you?"

Emma Jean giggled then glanced at Katherine's hip hugger pants and fringe suede vest. "*You*, on the other hand, must find something else to wear if you want to go with us, Darlin'."

"I can decide what to wear. You'll have a grand time without me. Besides, I've planned an excursion. First, I'll have dinner at the Barbary Coast where I might meet a swashbuckler. Then I'm going to an after-dinner tour of the Pittock Mansion, the best time to see ghosts lurking in corners." Katherine shook her hands in the air and rolled her eyes in search of spooks.

Emma Jean lifted her eyes and shrugged. "Oh, my. Something might happen to you."

Katherine fanned herself. Pirates intrigued her. They had a code similar to the Chippewa warriors who'd ruled the Great Lakes to conqueror the wilderness. These warriors were real men. Katherine secretly imagined having a pirate as her lover. He'd sail the seven seas to find diamonds, rubies, and sapphires to bring home to her. *Hey, girl, what are you thinking? Pirates were murdering thieves. Is Dominick like a pirate? Is there something in me that is attracted him? No, I'm just a good girl from Wisconsin, and good girls from Wisconsin aren't attracted to Chicago mobsters. It's just my romantic imagination running wild.*

Emma Jean's vision of roses, poetry, and sweet tea couldn't compare to her dream: a conqueror, brave and genuine. Katherine looked up and grinned. "I suppose something could happen." She watched as Emma Jean primped and groomed for her dinner date. "What's this guy's name, by the way?"

"Yuki. Happiness, he told me, in Japanese." Emma Jean dabbed Jungle Gardenia under her ear lobes. "Isn't that lovely?"

"I don't mean to be a nudge," Katherine said, "but remember you're looking for a southern gentleman."

Emma Jean turned and rolled her eyes, "Oh Darlin', this is just a nice dinner with a tall, dark stranger." She put her finger to her cheek. "Don't you have a friendship with a foreign man? That Angelos?"

"I'd call him an acquaintance. I enjoy meeting new people from other cultures and learning their ways. It's the same as traveling; the more you see of other places and individuals, the more you learn about yourself." She paused. "I'm trying to find myself right now, anyway."

"Yourself? All we women need to know is how to look ravishing, stay poised, and be gracious at all times, and never let the man know what you're thinking." Emma Jean grabbed her Gucci handbag. "That's it, Darlin'. Be careful tonight." She threw Katherine a kiss on the way out.

Katherine walked over to the window. The sun setting on majestic Mt. Hood—a mixture of lavender, pink, and gold surrounding its snowcap—took Katherine to another place. She was a warrior just like Hanging Cloud, and she wanted to travel to places where she could bring home treasures. No gold, jewels, or rare art that others would covet; rather, a gem of hope for others, the tribe that ran through her blood even though her skin and hair belied the Chippewa blood that roared beneath it. The world saw her as a wholesome all-American girl who loved life and laughter, but she was much more: a warrior woman fighting for the rights of those who needed her help. *Hey, didn't I just chase off that federal agent?*

Katherine slipped into her hip huggers, flung the fringe vest over her T-shirt, painted her face with a fresh coat of Bonnie Bell powder and rouge, and went down to the Benson Hotel lobby with her head held high. She felt heads turning, eyes taking in her majestic presence. Something special swarmed inside her, ready to emerge and meet the world.

27

KATHERINE TUSSLED WITH her twisted blanket to reach for the ringing phone. The pink Bulova clock radio's alarm numbers blazed bigger and brighter than she wanted. 7:30. *Geez, I need more sleep.* Getting home at 1:30 a.m. from her Portland flight had depleted her sleep bank.

"Hello, Katherine Roebling?" a voice said on the other end. "I'm Danny O'Brien, the bouncer at the Playboy Mansion. Our paths crossed at the press party last month. Then I saw you at the public library a few days ago. Sorry for calling so early, but your friend Charlotte Delaney asked me for help. Do you remember me?"

Katherine bolted up from her reclining position, shoulders tightening, and moisture forming around her lips. "Charlotte? Did something happen to her?"

"No. Charlotte asked me to help you. It concerns a strange man stalking you. Could we meet this morning?"

Katherine pursed her lips. *Hm, how did Charlotte get involved with this non-issue? Why is this Danny guy involved? I want to tell Charlotte first that the problem is solved.* "Thanks, but I'd like to talk to Charlotte beforehand."

"Sure, I understand. You're smart to check me out." Danny paused. "I'll have Charlotte call you."

Katherine nearly gasped. "Okay. I'll wait here for Charlotte's call."

"Thank you. Please call me right back. And don't worry, you'll be safe."

Katherine held the pink princess phone receiver next to her chest and dropped it into the cradle. The ticking of the bedroom clock broke the silence. Katherine thumped her fingers on the nightstand. Her mind shuffled back to her unpleasant meetings with Danny O'Brien. *He must think that I'm a real mess. Well, that's old news.*

Katherine stretched her back and spread her arms wide.

The phone rang again. "Charlotte?"

"Yeah, it's me. Danny is the nicest of guys. Do you know how much effort he and his brother put into helping you? They called in a favor from the top detective in the Bureau of Investigative Services to take your case. Lots of resources and time went into helping you."

Hm, did he find out something that I don't know? I'll play along for now. I don't have time to give Charlotte the whole story. I'll tell her later. I'm curious to see what this Danny person found.

Katherine smiled. "Well, I wanted to check with you first since you asked Danny to help. I'll tell you the whole story when I see you."

Charlotte's voice softened. "Oh, you're right. I don't blame you. You are the smarter one. Good news. Danny found the sleaze bag. How did you get into this predicament in the first place?" Charlotte sighed. "Don't tell me now. Call Danny right back!"

Katherine sipped on her cappuccino as she tapped her fingers on the table. After scanning the empty Third Coast Coffee Shop, she looked at her watch. *After this last sip, I'm leaving. Fifteen minutes is long enough!* Katherine savored the last drop of warm espresso and pushed away from the table , stood up, and started to walk out.

"Katherine?" a man with a deep voice said behind her.

Katherine turned to the square-jawed, blue-eyed strong man standing next to her. *Wow, my vibes are speaking. He might be the right man for Charlotte.* "Danny?"

"I apologize for being late. I had to hunt for a parking place and found one in my usual spot at the mansion. Hef stopped me for a second. He's the boss after all."

He slipped Katherine's chair back and stood. "Thanks for meeting me."

"Danny, thanks for looking into this for me. I hope it didn't become a wild goose chase. I mentioned him in passing to Charlotte. She's super, but she overreacts sometimes."

Danny put his elbows on the table and leaned forward. "Well, when Charlotte first asked me to help you, I was skeptical. You seemed like a nice girl, but a little flaky. The kind that's good but falls into sticky situations."

Katherine's face burned crimson. She pushed away from the table. "Hey, Mr. O'Brien, you've said enough." She pulled money from her purse to pay for her coffee.

Danny raised his hand. "Please sit. I understand, but you didn't let me finish. I jumped to a conclusion, but when I dug deeper, I found something different. You're a fantastic woman who's smart and knows how to handle herself in difficult situations. So please accept my apology for my first impression."

Katherine shrugged and slipped back into her seat. *Let's see what he knows.* "Okay. I accept your apology, but you better have a good story to tell me. I'll give you ten minutes."

Danny smiled. "That's what I mean. You're a lady who knows when and where to throw her punches." Danny cleared his throat. "Anyway, I talked with Debbie, the one you traded uniforms with to escape that Dominick guy." Danny paused and shrugged his shoulders. "I was off base on that one. I thought you had a relationship with him. And I hate to say it, but I grew up thinking that women involved with mafia guys were scum. But then I realized you weren't actually with him. You ladies have a more dangerous job than all the Bunnies in Hef's harem."

Katherine winked and kidded Danny. "Yep, our blue uniforms are magnets to men. And don't you agree that men dislike those curvy, busty Bunnies?"

Danny shrugged and joked. "Well, most men like their curves, but I can't stand my job with those Bunnies swarming around the club. They're so needy and helpless. But it's a job." Danny raised his hands. "Enough of this. I don't want to waste your ten minutes. Let's get to the real and most important reason for our meeting." He paused, looked around the coffee shop, and moved his chair around the table to sit next to Katherine.

Katherine's brow furrowed.

"Don't worry. I want no one to hear what I've got to say. It concerns the eagle feather O'Leary found you with the day I saw you at the library. He told me the whole story. He thinks you must be a witch, but I know you're not. Charlotte gave me details on your Native American ancestry, and how unusual stuff happens to you sometimes, that crow feathers appear around you. She doesn't recall any eagle feathers, though. She told me about the trip you two took in the sixth grade to a Native American museum and your interest in the sacred eagle feather. Do you remember this field trip?"

Katherine reclined against the wooden chair and nodded. "Yes. It popped into my mind the day I was at the library. Promise me you won't tell anyone what happened to me with the eagle father in the library."

Danny smiled. "I won't. It's an extraordinary story, but please listen to my story first. My friend found the guy. He's an undercover agent for the Feds. He could have done you serious harm, life-threatening damage if we hadn't found him in time."

Katherine feigned a gasp. "What do you mean?"

"Well, my brother's P.I. checked with the doorman in your building. He told him that the guy followed you to your apartment and gave the doorman your apartment keys. They verified his ID. He confirmed that the culprit had stood outside O'Leary's office. The Fish and Wildlife folks tipped him off about you and the feather. He's a shifty guy with a small crime background, which makes him the right man for the dirty job he does for the Feds. He tracks down criminals like himself who steal Native American artifacts." Danny pointed to his head. "He can think like they do, and he has a super record for returning stolen Native American goods." Danny cleared his throat. "Since he's a former con man, he used the same modus operandi on you."

He must not have the latest news. But he's a swell guy; I'll see what else he knows.

Katherine commented. "How ridiculous, since I received the eagle feather. Like magic, it appeared before me. The librarian thought I was a thief. Like magic, again, it disappeared when I left the library. And then the sacred feather returned when I was on the bus. Now, once again, the mystical feather is gone. You can search my apartment."

Danny interrupted. "I know you're innocent, and you don't have the eagle feather. I won't pretend to understand this Native American stuff. I know criminals; you're not one of those." He pulled a photo from his coat pocket and handed it to Katherine. "Is this the man that's stalking you?"

Katherine dropped the photo on the table. "Yes, that's the guy that I almost shot with my bow and arrow."

Danny put both hands on the table and leaned toward Katherine. "What? Did he try to molest you? Did he try to harm you?"

Katherine sat up and lifted her chest. "No. I think I scared him. He knew I could handle the bow like a warrior, so he backed down and quivered until he said 'uncle.'"

Danny leaned back. His eyes widened like round circles. He shook his head. "You're an extraordinary woman. So what happened after he peed in his pants?"

"Well, since my encounter happened before my Portland trip, yesterday, his report may not be in the official records yet. I convinced him that I had Native American blood and received the eagle feather as a sacred gift. He accepted my evidence and agreed that I was innocent. He said that he'd file a report to remove me from the 'most wanted' list." Katherine chuckled. "In a week or so, do you have a way to check the records to make sure that I'm not on the dangerous criminal list?"

"Certainly. My brother is the lawyer who helped me. He can check the records. I bet he filed the report like a speed demon after his experience with you."

Katherine clapped her hands and cheered. "Thank you. I appreciate your efforts. And thank your brother. If I can do something for you, let me know."

Danny's eyes twinkled. "Well, you can put in a good word for me with Charlotte."

"Charlotte needs a guy like you. I'll be thrilled to help you two. Have you asked her out?"

"I want to ask her to go with me to watch a youth Silver Gloves boxing event. I mentor an outstanding young man from the projects. I thought it would be a low-key first date."

Katherine envisioned the time that she and Charlotte spent the summer tutoring the Chippewa tribe's kindergarteners. Charlotte had gotten bummed out when the summer was over. Charlotte and Danny would be a good match. "Yep, she'll love it. You'll hit a home run."

Hmm, Danny and Charlotte? My intuition tells me there may be a wedding in their future.

28

KATHERINE STROKED THE MAJESTIC brown and white feather. Reverence filled her. Gazing around her bedroom, she breathed in slowly, feeling a sacred peace with the magical return of the eagle feather. Katherine savored the aura of security and safety with no roommate to discover her with this secret treasure, the miraculous artistry that only the grandest of creators can design. The crisp white plumage surrounding chocolate brown feathers was an invitation to cherish it.

Katherine placed the feather on the bedroom dresser near the photo of her parents and rubbed her hands together as she asked the photo, "Mom, Dad, what should I do? How do I explain the feather's mysterious appearances? Why is it here?"

She looked up, hoping to get a response. Before an answer came, the phone rang and prompted Katherine back to everyday life.

"Hi, Katherine. Are you okay?" Neal asked.

"Yeah, sure." She cleared her throat. "How are you?"

"I was wondering if you want to talk."

"Is something wrong?"

"I thought you might want to share your experience with Charlotte's bouncer friend."

How does he know about Danny? Of course, Charlotte and Neal, my friends, helped me. "Well, I could use a Lincoln Park Zoo fix."

"Hey, that's cool. We didn't make it there the other day. Can you be ready by two?"

"Sure. See you. Bye."

"Bye."

Katherine stretched her arms to the ceiling and moved them from side to side. Her meeting with Danny had turned out super. *Neal must have been involved with Charlotte's contacting Danny, which means Neal wants to take care of me, to protect me. Maybe, I'll just tell him the happy ending that I'm innocent. Not the details. Does he need to know that I can take care of myself?*

She slipped into her fitted jeans. They reminded her of her horseback riding days on the Hay Meadow Trail at home in Chippewa Falls. A black Jefferson Airplane T-shirt and paisley headband topped off her look. A tab of light red rouge and a swipe a lipstick to refresh her lips and she was ready to go.

Katherine dashed down to the lobby to open her soul to her special friend. Her heart felt heavy carrying all the changes in life, but her spirit told her to go for it. *You don't understand where you may land. It might be a new paradise created with a deep conversation underneath the surface.* The sunlight became a spotlight on Katherine's exit from the apartment lobby. Her calm attitude made Neal's face brighten.

"Wow," Neal said when he saw her. "Wait until those zoo tigers see you."

After visiting every zoo site from the sea lion pool to the lion house, the happy couple paused for a Coke at the zoo refreshment stand across from the lions' caves.

"Would you like to visit my favorite place in the zoo?" Katherine asked.

Neal took her hand in his hand and smiled. "Let's go."

"Can you lead the way to waterfowl lagoon?"

"Nope. Today is my first time to see every place in the zoo."

"I guarantee you'll find the lagoon a calming place like Walden Pond. It's peaceful. Look around at all the skyscrapers, and here we are nestled in this sanctuary of nature. Something special happens when I jaunt past the swans floating on the lagoon and the brood of Mallard ducks drifting on the pond. A magic biosphere surrounds me and fills me with bubbles of joy. It's a perfect place to ponder the questions of the universe."

Neal's eyes sparkled. "Let's go. I'm ready for a new adventure."

As they walked toward the lagoon, Katherine's mind darted from one point to the next. She looked up and a bright, warm spark sent her a message. It was time to share this part of her. Yes, Neal was her true Niwiijiwaagan. Katherine jerked back. She closed her eyes and smiled. *I've never used that Chippewa word for a friend, but he is my best pal.*

Katherine squeezed Neal's hand and pointed to a bench at the edge of the lagoon. "Let's sit over there. I hope you don't mind if I spill my secrets."

Neal put his arm around her and looked into her eyes. "That's why we're here. Charlotte and I thought you needed to talk. She called and told me you'd met with a guy she knows with police contacts." He paused and motioned for her to sit on the bench.

Katherine searched Neal's eyes and smiled "Thank you. Thank you. I was in real danger. I got warnings, but I didn't take the time to figure out what they meant."

Neal narrowed his eyes. "Warnings?"

Katherine glanced around and leaned toward Neal. "Yes. They're very extraordinary. I never tell people when I get these warnings, except for my closest friends and family who understand the nature of Native American mystical ways."

Neal leaned in and gazed at Katherine. "Tell me."

Katherine sat up straight and tilted her chin. "When you look at me, you see a tall blonde woman, thanks to my father's side. I'm German from him. But on my mother's side, I'm French Canadian and Chippewa Native American. I hope you can understand it, but that part of me is speaking out with signs and warnings."

Katherine sensed Neal's understanding. He gave her a welcoming ear. She reached inside her T-shirt and pulled out her Thunderbird amulet. "As you know, this necklace has a special meaning for me. My great-grandmother saved it for me. She was from the Chippewa tribe." Katherine cleared her throat. "There's so much more to tell you. I'm confusing you. You wanted to know what happened with that stalker." Katherine explained that the stalker was really a government agent who ordered Katherine to return the eagle feather. She gave Neal the stellar highpoints of her reasons that convinced the agent that she should keep the feather.

After she relayed the details of the feather's appearance, Neal rubbed his chin. "Okay. All the eagle feather stuff is where my story requires you to suspend judgment. I did not steal the eagle feather. It came to me, and I still have it."

"You mean on a magic carpet?" Neal laughed.

"You're a lawyer in training and a logical thinker. I ask you to open your mind to another realm where magical and mystical things are real, maybe more real than your logic."

Neal nodded. "Okay. I'll try, but I'm not really into that sort of stuff."

"These are my particular Chippewa ways I carry with me. I hope you don't think I'm weird."

Neal turned to Katherine, placed his hands on her shoulders, and leaned close enough to touch her nose. "You're the most wonderful woman I've met. You have more to teach me. Stuff I never studied in my world."

Her Native American blood flowed in her veins and guided her forward.

"Neal, the fact that an eagle feather landed in my hands at the Chicago Public Library made my Native American part real. It might be magical and mystical. I must take care of this sacred possession, but I'm not sure what to do." Katherine stared into Neal's eyes, and a light flashed from his eyes to hers like a lightning bolt.

Neal held her hands in his. "You have the answer, don't you?"

Katherine sprang from the bench and pulled Neal up to kiss him. "Yes! Thank you. I have a solution and action plan for the eagle feather."

Neal smiled and kissed her again. "Whatever. I'll take your kisses for now. But don't keep me in suspense about your mysterious plan."

29

"YOU'D MAKE AN EXCELLENT Rudolph the Reindeer," Neal said, laughing.

"What do you mean?" Katherine asked.

Neal took his napkin and wiped the tomato sauce from Katherine's nose. "I'm sorry, but it was too funny. I couldn't resist the fun. You're cute whatever you wear."

Katherine picked up another piece of the Numero Uno pizza and chewed for a long time. She gave Neal a fake scowl.

"I'm sorry," Neal said. "I just discovered the sensitive side of you."

Katherine put her fork down and smiled a wide-mouthed grin. "And don't forget it!" She took her fork to a piece of pizza with pepperoni, onion, mushroom, sausage, and pepper. "I forgive you only because this super dish pizza is the ultimate. Thanks for bringing me here."

"Yeah, this is the only place for pizza. I come here only on special occasions."

"Special occasions?"

"Yep. Our visit to the zoo, and you sharing so much with me. Isn't that worth celebrating?" He leaned closer and smiled. "And the biggest thing," he paused and lifted his hands to make finger quotes. "You decided how to solve the 'eagle feather gift'."

Katherine folded her arms across her chest and grumbled. "You missed the whole point. To me, a Native American, receiving an eagle feather is the highest honor, and it's only the way it came to me."

Neal coughed. "Oh, Katherine, me and my clumsy mouth. You and your situation did impact me on many levels. I'm too much of a pragmatist since I can't understand mystical things like magical eagle feathers. Tell me, what's your decision about the eagle feather?"

"Before we went to the zoo, my mind was a mess. And I was terrified. I pondered and pondered the right way to return an eagle feather, especially a sacred eagle feather that I never took. Even though the Fed's undercover agent said I'm innocent, he warned me to be careful with the gift and not break the law. I had a scary experience with my supposed breaking of the law. I don't want to get into that mess again."

"Yeah, you even got Charlotte and me in a steam pot of worry."

"And I realize that. My situation did affect others, and I don't want to have that happen again. The idea came to me when I looked in your eyes. Remember, I'm half through my major in anthropology from Beloit College?"

"Do you plan to escape to academia and finish your degree?"

Katherine's eyes flashed with anger. "You're making fun of me. I devised a real plan." She coughed. "I'll take the feather to my Beloit College advisor. Since she's a mystical thinker with extensive knowledge of Native American culture, she'll understand my situation."

"Even if your professor swallows your story and takes the feather, won't she have the same possession problem?"

"When an Indian receives a feather, it's an individual honor. It can't be put away; it must be on display. My professor's focus is Native North American people and their culture. The feather can be displayed in an exhibit."

"That's brilliant, but why are you still in school?"

"I completed two years at Beloit and started to wonder where I could find a job after spending all my dad's money on tuition. After all, women are raised to be nurses, teachers, and stewardesses. Then they're told to get married and stay home and raise kids. But I'm an adventurer. I loved anthropology; I wanted to understand humanity." Katherine paused, cleared her throat. "Women are waking up. I'm reading Betty Friedan's *The Feminine Mystique;* she's my guru and says things that I already thought, like 'Women who "adjust" as housewives, who grow up wanting to be "just a housewife," are in as much danger as the millions who walked to their own death in the concentration camps . . . they are suffering a slow death of mind and spirit.'"

Neal interrupted. "Being a stewardess is a great place to study men." He chuckled. "I mean mankind. And you can be a modern-day spinster and not be a victim of the living death of marriage."

Should I say that love and marriage work if there's freedom to let a woman be her own person? No, I'll give him a challenge. "I've learned more than you know, but I won't bother telling you now. I'm going to keep working on my degree. I have been fortunate to have an understanding faculty who let me take two years off to complete one open course. Now I'll have to figure out how to finish my degree." Katherine thumped her fingers on the table and smiled. "Zap. Like Eureka, I received a plan. It's been tumbling around in my head. I'm going to talk with my professor about writing a paper, which she made me promise that I would finish when I left to be a stewardess."

Neal stared at Katherine "Hey, wait a minute. You left Beloit College two years ago. You must be a genius for her to give that must leeway. What's the topic? Are you going to leave the high-flying glamor of being a stewardess and return to the active student life?"

Katherine gave him a soft kick to the shin. "Of course not, but there's something exciting peeking around the corner waiting for me."

Neal took a gulp of his draft. "Do you have the right man in mind?"

"Not a man but helping mankind! Someday, women will run the world."

Neal reached over and touched Katherine's hand. "And I believe you are the woman for the job. I hope to be around to see it."

Katherine turned her head and fluttered her eyelashes. "Well, if you prove worthy, you may be the fortunate person to see me make history."

Neal lifted his beer mug to click Katherine's mug. "Here's to Katherine Roebling conquering and saving the world."

"You're on," Katherine said with a thumbs-up. "I'm going up to Beloit tomorrow. How about coming with me? You can explore the campus—a seems like a traditional New England university—and the Indian mounds are extraordinary."

Neal rubbed his face. "Tomorrow. I have my Moot Court oral argument. It's a big show, and the last time we law students can impress the faculty. For sure, the Indian mounds are worth a future trip up there with you."

"I'd like that. We both have important things for tomorrow. We'd better head home."

When they left the restaurant, a light breeze floated around them. The breeze stopped, and a long black crow feather drifted and landed at Katherine's feet.

She picked it up and smiled at Neal. "This will give you good luck and protection. Would you like this one?"

30

BACK IN HER APARTMENT, Katherine danced from room to room. During her visit to deliver the eagle feather to Beloit College, Katherine had found direction for her unfinished assignment. Katherine turned the pages of Cyrus Thomas' book, *Wisconsin Mounds.*

She heard an echo from her friends that called her the Turtle Mounds lady. When she'd walked around campus, she'd imagined what Roy Chapman Andrews, the famous Beloit College explorer and adventurer, thought as he wandered around the campus. Did he imagine becoming a famous anthropologist and explorer? Katherine couldn't remember what she'd thought. She did know that those mounds nestled around the campus beckoned her to visit them. *Is this my inspiration?*

Or was it the photo of Roy Chapman Andrews adorning her advisor's office wall? His quote posted under his photo stirred Katherine's mind. Were these words entwined with her dreams? "I wanted to go everywhere. I would have started on a day's notice for the North Pole or the South, to the jungle or the desert. It made not the slightest difference to me."

At the start of her stewardess career, when the airline reserve desk supervisor called her to takes trips to Reno and Omaha, she'd felt like an adventurer. Now her adventurer/explorer spirit propelled her on an unknown path. *I can't wait.*

Her chest felt like a giant balloon filled with excitement. The air to float her came when her professor glowed about Katherine's notes about Native American burial mounds and the various theories of their origin, including the Lost Tribes of Israel theory. Katherine rubbed her brow and shrugged. She could breathe easy now that the eagle feather had a home at the Logan Anthropology Museum. She couldn't wait to bring Neal to see it.

The mysterious conveyance to her of the eagle feather, what did it mean? Katherine looked at the ceiling. *I'm not that special. What does Soaring Eagle want from me? I'm a regular American girl with a drop of Chippewa blood. What about my German blood? What about my French blood? All these streams flow through my body.* Scrutinizing the veins on her hand puzzled her. *Is one race's blood different than another's? No.* The Native American part shouted out for attention. Everyone appreciates white Caucasians, but the Native American inside her offered much to share with the world.

With her index finger in mid-air ready to dial Neal's number, the phone yelled out. Katherine jerked and lifted the receiver. "Oh, Neal. You beat me to it."

"Neal? I'm your mother, dear. Who's Neal?"

Katherine sighed. "Oh. Hi, Mom. Neal's a law student. Charlotte's friend." Katherine's heart pounded in rhythm with her thoughts. *Should I tell Mom that I went to Beloit College yesterday? Mom keeps a hidden crystal ball, so why hold back?* "Hey, yesterday, I went to Beloit College to visit my anthropology advisor."

"Oh, did you enjoy it? Your father will applaud you. He

wants you to continue your studies when you're ready to quit flying and leave your glamorous life."

"I'll finish the incomplete term paper. My advisor is super to keep me in good standing with my incomplete record for over two years. And she was pleased that I did take that one class a Northwestern." Katherine paused and smiled. "And I got extra points when I told her that I liked Beloit College better."

"Katherine, you're lucky to receive such support. That's a sign. Keep learning. You can tell us all your plans when your father and I visit next week. I assume you'll be home. We'll be in town next Thursday through Sunday. You father serves on a Chicago Bar Association Committee for Native American civil rights. I'm thrilled that they awarded me an art booth at the Old Town Art Fair."

"Wow! The Old Town Art Fair is one of the highest rated juried art fairs in the country. You didn't even tell me you'd applied. And yes, I'll be home then. My next trip is a San Mateo layover, and I get home late Thursday night, but I'll be home until Monday morning. What's your hotel?"

"The Drake, of course. Would your father stay anywhere else? Let's plan dinner on Friday night. How about meeting us at six at the hotel?"

"Super. See you next week. I love you."

"Love you too. Behave yourself."

<hr/>

The summer ritual began with Chicago's high-rise cliff dwellers strolling on the warm sand as they savored the mild Lake Michigan waves. Katherine relished her strolls on Oak Street Beach's sand. The hot sand soothed the soles of her feet to calm and ground her while she gazed at the lake's waves, swelled in rhythm with earth's heartbeat. The lake and beach were Katherine's world, a magical place where she could put her thoughts on hold and lift them to the sky gods to arrange for her. Katherine scanned the luxury high-rise condos lining Lakeshore Drive and admired Lake Michigan's undulating waves. Like a lighthouse, Oak Street's sights beamed light on her course.

Katherine wondered if she should go back to school full time. What would she do with a degree?

She could work as a stewardess until she was thirty-two, but where did she go after that? *I'll find new horizons, since women are opening new doors. It'll be exciting to see what's ahead for me.*

A familiar voice shouted, "Katherine! Katherine!"

She turned to see Neal approaching. "Hey, I called you, and you didn't answer. I took a wild guess and came here. What happened at Beloit?"

"Oh, Neal. My trip was so helpful and inspiring. Let's grab a drink at McGuire's."

Neal wrapped his arms around her. "Super idea. After my long day of legal beagle stuff, I need a drink." He pulled Katherine to him and gave her a long kiss. "And I have something to ask you."

Katherine touched her throat. Her pulse thumped against her fingers, and her thoughts flipped in her mind like shuffling playing cards. *What could he want to ask me? We've been friends for maybe a month. We're not lovers.*

Katherine didn't talk as the couple meandered by Hermes window and Marilyn Migin's makeup shop. Katherine picked up her step and grabbed Neal's hand. "Let's get moving!"

Neal squeezed Katherine's hand as the couple laughed and strolled around Rush Street to the corner of Division Street. Chicago's early summer sun blended with the humidity. After a walk on Oak Street Beach, her insides simmered like the Sahara Desert. Her tie-dyed T-shirt clung like a wet noodle. Visions of the refreshing draft beer shouted to her.

Butch McGuire's was whimsical and magical with its leprechaun-painted beer mugs and the variety of lucky creatures hanging above the bar. Neal ordered two cold draft beers and led them to an open table at the back of the bar.

Katherine hopped on the soft cushion barstool and immediately guzzled five fingers of the golden brew. She licked her lips. "I'm sorry, I'm thirsty."

Neal snatched his mug and chugged half of his brew. "Yep, but I'm thirstier than you." He laughed and continued. "So, my question. I've created a cool idea for us." He paused and then leaned forward. "Katherine, would you move in with me? When you were out of town yesterday, I worried about you. What if that federal agent guy had been a real thug stalking you? And then, my mind nagged me. What if someone followed you on the bus to Beloit? You are alone in that apartment, and you need a safe place to stay. Since I'm a gentleman with two bedrooms, I plan to give you your own room." He stopped and looked down.

Neal sat back, took another sip of his beer, and waited for Katherine's answer.

Katherine grimaced and gulped a long swig of Guinness. Her hands shook as she sat the chilled mug on the bar. She rubbed her chin and waited for her mind and heart to find a response for Neal.

31

KATHERINE'S CHIN RESTED ON her thumbs as she scanned her journal's "What Next?" list:

1. Neal. Give him an answer. Should I move in with him?
2. Live alone or find a roommate?
3. Spend another two years as a stewardess or have the guts to charge forward?
4. If I charge forward, where will I go? What do I do? Go home and live with Mom and Dad? Go back to Beloit College? Go to a Greek island and learn to paint?
5. What is the meaning of Israel to me? To find out if Native Americans are the Lost Tribe of Israel?
6. Could I be part of the Lost Tribe?
7. Will I find out why the eagle feather came?
8. Read poetry and take Emma Jean's advice.

What to put as the next item on her list stumped Katherine. In twenty-two years, Katherine had lived, learned, and enjoyed the journey. What next? Anaïs Nin had the answer: "Throw your dreams into space like a kite, and you do not know what it will bring back, a new life, a new friend, a new love, a new country."

Katherine vaulted from her desk. Her powder blue provincial chair tipped. Katherine flipped the chair back on its feet and told herself to breathe out worry and be patient. "Stay calm."

Katherine examined herself in the full-length mirror. She glowed in her pink and turquoise mod dress, which was her mother's cherished "Twiggy" look. And the final touch, broad striped pink and green stockings slipped on her feet and into beige-and-white Mary Quaint Mary Janes. She was ready to stride along Michigan Avenue to the Drake Hotel.

Katherine reached the top of the stairs, admiring the fresh white lilies in the lobby's cobalt vase. The floral arrangement meshed well on the American Chippendale table. Katherine drew a fresh breath and walked toward the front desk to call her parents' room.

"Kate!" her mother squealed across the lobby.

Katherine spun around and was embraced by her mother. "Mom, I'm so happy you're here tonight!"

Katherine inspected her stylish mother in a black-and-white Guy Laroche dress. It made a decorative frame for her olive skin. Her dark hair was swept away from her face to showcase her high cheekbones. Katherine shared her mother's perfect cheekbones, but she'd always wished she had her mother's onyx hair. Maybe it was the Chippewa part yearning for freedom.

Rene Roebling's eyes glowed like evening stars when she held her daughter. She gazed into Katherine's green eyes.

"Where's Dad?"

Her mother pointed toward the cocktail lounge. "He's meeting with the ABA committee."

Katherine and her mother settled in two classic club chairs. The waiter joined them and smiled. "What's your cocktail choice?"

Katherine's mother ordered a gin and tonic.

Katherine never drank alcohol in public with her parents. They had wine with dinner at home, but now she wanted something that fit her style. "I'll have a gin gimlet."

Her mother didn't blink.

"My dear, your father and I are always with you. You know that, don't you?"

Katherine's heart's charged messages to her bustling mind, processing her mother's comment. Katherine nodded and smiled. "Sure, Mom."

"Before your father gets here, we need to talk. For the past month, I know you've had extraordinary events in your life." Her mother paused while the waiter served their drinks.

Katherine bowed her head and took a sip of her gimlet. "Mom, you remind me of one of those whales who always knows what their babies are doing. Your radar stays charged. Yes. I guess you could say that my life has had a few hairy events. I planned to tell you and Dad the details."

"Don't tell your father your stories until I censor it. You know his hot-tempered side."

Katherine shuddered when she envisioned her father's reaction to the eagle feather. *He flat out won't believe that the feather swooped by magic into my life.* Both women appreciated his solid, logical mind, which left no room for wonder and magic. Katherine contemplated her mother's mystical wisdom with her dark eyes beaming a signal. Katherine discerned her mother's insight, and her heart whispered: *Dear Mom knows everything about you.*

Katherine smiled. "You're right. He won't understand my eagle feather experience." Katherine paused and leaned close. "Did your third eye observe the whole story?"

"Of course, dear. Your mother always knows."

"Yeah, I know, but Mom, your depth of knowledge of my life isn't the same as most parents. Can I ever hide secrets from you?"

Rene laughed. "Of course, you can. I see significant events. Not everything."

Katherine put her palms on her lap and squeezed her eyes closed. "Wait. Don't tell me you saw the disappearance of the eagle feather at the library?"

Rene stood. "Relax. It's a gift to help you not hurt you. If I saw danger in your path, I'd do everything in my power to save you."

"Mom, why didn't you call, warn me, and help me?"

Rene sipped on the gin and tonic. "Kate, dear, mother eagles know when to release their young so they can learn to soar. I hope I'm as wise as you." She reached over and touched her daughter's hand. "You soared with this experience, and now you're ready to fly. And I don't mean on those jetliners you trek on around the country."

Katherine closed her eyes and sighed. She wanted to shout, "Thank you," to the universe for giving her the most spectacular mother. Katherine's inner strength climbed from her stomach to the top of her head to float over her life like a beam of light. She wanted to fly higher. "Okay, Mom, let's go on to the neat stuff. Tell me what you'll be showing at the art fair."

Her mother glanced at her watch, "It's almost six. Your father should—"

"Hello, beautiful ladies."

Katherine leaped from her chair and smacked a big kiss on her father's cheek. "Dad, you made it!"

He beamed and shouted. "Goldie. Wow. You're beautiful."

Her father was the only person who used this nickname, which came from Oriel, her middle name, which meant gold. Katherine liked her nickname, but the name her great-grandmother had given her in secret, Aponi, had more influence. Katherine had researched the meaning of Aponi and had found that it meant *butterfly*. People with this name were supposed to have a profound inner need for quiet and a desire to understand and analyze the world they live in, to learn the deeper truths.

The description fit her so well that she had written the full definition in her diary: "People with this name tend to initiate events, to be leaders rather than followers, with influential personalities. They tend to be focused on specific goals, experience a wealth of creative new ideas, and have the ability to implement these ideas with efficiency and determination. They tend to be courageous and sometimes aggressive. As unique, creative individuals, they tend to resent authority and are sometimes stubborn, proud, and impatient."

Katherine hugged her father. "Dad, I missed you. I can't wait for our catch-up talk."

"Me too. Right now, I'm thirsty. What are you two drinking?"

Before they could answer, the server approached them. "Good evening, sir. Are you joining the ladies? Can I get you something to drink?"

Without hesitation, Hans Roebling responded, "Bring me a Jack Daniels," and settled on a chair next to his wife. He loosened his tie and stretched. "Boy, did we get a bucket load of drafting done."

"Mom said you were doing something with Native American rights."

"A draft for a proposed law for Native American civil rights. I got roped in because of my so-called civil rights work. The Chippewa tribe came to me and asked me to work on the committee." He turned to his wife. "Of course, your mother gave me a gentle push." He patted his wife on the knee and turned to Katherine. "Enough dry stuff. Your mother and I need an update on Katherine Roebling's life!"

Katherine's mind rushed around, sorting out what to tell Dad and what to save Dad from knowing. He didn't need to know about the eagle feather saga or the stalker, but she could tell him about the trip to Beloit College. He'd cheer the idea of her working on her degree. Her mind decided, but her stomach flipped and flopped, sending a message to make her hands fidget. She picked up her glass to take a sip of encouragement before she spoke. "Where do I begin?"

"Oh, Hans," her mother said, "let's get to dinner. These drinks are going to my head."

"Golly, you're right." He looked at his watch. "We've got ten minutes to make our reservations."

Italian Village's dark red and walnut panels wrapped their arms of comfort around Katherine as she and her parents sipped Chianti and caught up.

Katherine had loved her time growing up in Chippewa Falls. E. E. Cummings burst into her thoughts: "It takes courage to grow up and become your true self." The warmth and the glow of the Chianti became happiness inside Katherine. Her past, present, and future became one.

Before her thoughts could take a journey to tomorrow land, her father's voice aborted her musings. "Goldie, we'd love to hear about your exciting adventures."

Katherine smiled and studied her mother, who gave her a wink. "I visited Beloit College the other day, and I've got an idea for a research paper, so I can finish my course."

Her father beamed. "Your course? Oh, the one that the great professor who gave you time to that finished paper as an incentive to get to finish your education." He paused and winked. "And I didn't even have to bribe her." He sat back and sighed. "It's still amazing that she gave you that much time. It's pretty unusual."

Katherine smiled. "Yep, my professor and I are good friends. We kept in touch when I left to become a stewardess. And she kept hounding me about her promise to keep my course records." Katherine giggled. "And once she kidded me that she'd give up teaching if I didn't come back and finish my coursework."

"I'm sure it's because you were her star student. Was it good to be back on campus?"

Katherine sighed and nodded. "And I have a plan. I'm going to research the theory of the Lost Tribe of Israel. I am the perfect person, with my Chippewa blood, and I have Jewish friends, so I'd like to do something to help Israel."

Her mother gasped. "Israel?"

Her father stiffened and assumed his logical way. "Your Jewish friends? Are you in love with a Jewish man? Of course, your mother and I are fine with your choice."

Katherine laughed. "Oh, no. I'm not in love with anyone. I just want to do something that helps others. Dad, isn't that how you live and what you want me to do with my life?"

"Kate, your dad and I always support you, but I have something exciting to share with you."

Her father raised his eyebrows, folded his hands, and sat back.

"I'm open to your thoughts, Mom. Fire away."

Her mother looked at her watch. "It's getting late, and your father and I both have to get up early. Could you meet us at the Old Town Art Fair at lunchtime? We can have coffee at this wonderful concession stand and chat then. Okay?"

32

NORTH STATE PARKWAY'S summer crowd headed for late night watering holes at the Division and Rush Bars. Glancing at her watch, Katherine turned to go inside the apartment lobby and slammed into a man. She screamed and started to push the man away before realizing who it was. "Neal! Geez, you hit my scare meter over the top. You're lucky I'm unarmed. What are you doing here? It's late."

"Nice to see you too," Neal snickered.

Katherine hugged him. "I'm sorry, but I didn't expect you, at least not this late."

"I got done with the legal brief for my torts class, and my body said, 'I need fresh air,' and my feet led me here. Plus, I have in my possession a limited special offer: a member's key to the Gaslight Club. Just for tonight. The lawyer who teaches my torts class is a member and thinks I spend too much time studying. So the gold key called out, 'See if Katherine's home yet and if she's up for a visit to the club that inspired the Playboy empire.'"

Katherine squished her eyebrows. *What's his real motive? It's 10:30. He didn't bother to ask me out. He appeared unannounced.* She rubbed her Thunderbird necklace and waited for an answer.

Neal put his hands in his pockets and rocked back on his heels. "Hey, I know it's late, and I didn't call you ahead of time. I apologize, but the gold key made me do it. Do you work tomorrow? If not, you can sleep in. Right?"

"I have three days off, but I'm meeting my mother at the Old Town Art Fair for lunch."

A couple walked by Katherine. "Go for it," they said. "He's a good man."

Neal waved at them. "Thanks." He smiled at Katherine and laughed. "I remembered that your parents are here." He paused and offered an extended appealing stare and then he tapped her nose with a kiss. "I wanted to see you."

Katherine giggled and twined her left foot behind her right foot. "Well, okay."

Neal smiled and put his arm around her waist. "Fab, let's head to the Ambassador Hotel and grab a cab."

Katherine fought the urge to take Neal's hand and stroll along North State Parkway's esplanade. Life and its mysteries intrigued her; she'd always believed in magic, mystery, and destiny. And being with Neal right then was one of the most magical things that had happened to her in Chicago. It was mysterious because she didn't know the source of her new feelings. Glancing at Neal prompted Anaïs Nin's quote to dance across her heart: "You don't find love, it finds you. It has to do with destiny, fate, and what's written in the stars."

Neal squeezed her hand, "You're busting with happiness. I bet you had a good time with your parents."

"Sure did. I hope you can meet Mom and Pop sometime." Katherine gulped after the words slipped out. *Hey, I've never asked a guy to meet my parents. What's come over me?*

"Sounds great. If those two people created you, they must be out of this world." He paused and motioned Katherine to head to the cab at the Ambassador Hotel. "Hop in."

Neal leaned over and told the cab driver, "13 East Huron Street."

"Oh, that place—you're my fifth customer tonight."

Neal looked at Katherine. "Now you know I only take you where it's happening."

Katherine laughed. "The Gaslight Club intrigues me. Charlotte and her friends explained that Hugh Hefner got his idea for the Playboy Bunny from it. Charlotte said the Gaslight Girls sing and dance. She's happy that Hef didn't steal that part since she can't sing or dance. Thanks for the invite."

Neal touched her knee and squeezed it.

Katherine's stomach floated and fluttered, but she wasn't sure that Neal felt the same. Her self-defensiveness reacted. Katherine jerked back and glared at his hand. "It's a little soon for that, don't you think? I'm not a Playboy Bunny."

Neal pulled his hand away. "I know that. I didn't ask you along because of your looks. I'm thrilled for you, the whole Katherine, to join me. You're the whole package, and I feel so lucky to have you right here with me." He paused and smiled. "And you're an adventurous person."

Katherine's eye widened when the cab stopped at the magnificent Queen Anne mansion. "You know me. I bet this place will outshine the Playboy Mansion."

Neal paid the taxi driver and clasped Katherine's arm. "Like Helen Keller, you think, 'Life is a daring adventure or nothing at all.'"

A tuxedo-clad host opened the wood carved doors of the mansion and greeted Katherine with a deep European accent. The door was dark mahogany with red velvet, and it opened to a room with a long, handsome bar and a crystal chandelier shining over patrons socializing at small tables centered around a stage. The stage pulsated with the song of glamorous, curvaceous Gaslight Girls dressed in a fringe-trimmed, sequined costume—the inspiration for the Playboy Bunnies sans tail, rabbit ears, and bow tie. The atmosphere transported Katherine to a scene in *Casino Royale*.

Like a butler from the House of Windsor, the host bowed and greeted Neal and Katherine. "Welcome to the Gaslight Club. May I please see your key?"

Neal held out the gold key, which resembled a three-leaf clover. "This is our first visit."

"Wonderful. Let me give you a brief review of your rooms." The gracious host first pointed to the plushy carpeted room. "This is the Paris Room. You may stay and enjoy cocktails while our talented Gaslight Girls serenade you."

He directed Katherine and Neal to a hand-carved grand staircase. "If you want a quiet place to sit in comfy chairs, sip cocktails, and listen to our classical pianist create a romantic mood, please head upstairs to the Library. The Gourmet Room, at the top of the stairs, is closed since it is after the dinner hour."

"Let's try the Library." Neal turned to Katherine. "Is that okay with you?"

Katherine's chest floated with bubbles of joy. Katherine smiled and felt herself blush. "Sure."

The host raised his hand toward the grand stairway. "Just take this stairway to the top. The Library is the first room on your right. You can't miss it." He cleared his throat. "After the Library, you might try the Speakeasy. It's outside the hall to the left of the Library. It's bustling with Dixieland jazz and Gaslight Girls who dance on the stage. They wear long beaded necklaces that they swing around their necks in time with the music. They keep twisting and turning until the beads land around their pumps. The best of all is the girls dancing Ballin' the Jack and maybe the Charleston. Knock on the door and tell a Gaslight Girl that Joe sent you. We close at two." He waved them up the stairs. "Please enjoy yourselves."

Katherine fought the urge to take two steps at a time up the long stairway. Neal followed on her heels. "This is cool. Thank for taking me along with you to this unique place."

"Hey, this is more fun than meeting Ernie Banks and Ron Santo."

At the top of the stairs, Katherine turned and gave Neal a shoulder nudge. "You're a Cubs fan? Your ratings moved up the scale."

Neal escorted her into the Library and guided her to a quiet corner. The plush dark green Chesterfield chairs reflected comfort and a place to relax. They settled in comfy chairs, and a Gaslight Girl in a floor-length black evening gown accented with white beads greeted them.

"Good evening, may I see your key, sir?" the Gaslight Girl asked.

Neal, like a seasoned key holder, slipped the golden ticket on her black onyx board. "Sure. Please bring us a bottle of champagne. Do you have Dom Pérignon?"

"Excellent choice, sir." She smiled and walked away.

"Are we celebrating?" Katherine asked.

Neal lounged in the comfy chair while he tapped his fingers on his thighs. The gleam in his eyes shot off a beam of joy. "We are. You didn't notice my heart beating off the chart tonight? The cab ride, the host tour, and the stairs created a delayed volcano inside me. I have news." He paused and smiled. "I'm the first guy in my law school class to get a job. I'm packing for my new life as a Justice Department attorney in Washington D.C."

Katherine squealed and leaned forward to give Neal a hug. "That's fabulous. And I'm honored to be the first on your list to hear the good news."

Neal beamed. "I got the news this afternoon and knew that you were out with your parents. I couldn't wait until tomorrow. And I fibbed that my professor loaned me the key." He pursed his lips. "It's my key, and you get to be with me for my inaugural use of it. My dad and mom sent it to me and told me not to use it until I could celebrate something special with someone special."

Katherine threw her shoulders back, smiled, and winked when the chilled champagne arrived. The Gaslight Girl filled their flutes with the sweet bubbly.

Lifting a glass, she offered a toast, "To you, Neal, and your new career and adventure. I wish you tremendous success."

They clinked their glasses and sipped.

Neal sat back in his chair and sipped half his glass before speaking.

Katherine savored the silent time and waited to let Neal talk.

"There's one more thing for you to answer."

Katherine sighed and sat back in the chair. She knew the question. *Am I moving in with him? No. I thought maybe he'd changed his mind now that he's leaving for Washington D.C. in a couple of months. That's it! He has a dog that he wants me to take in.* "Oh, your dog. What's his or her name?"

Neal wrinkled his brow, "My dog's name? I don't have a dog."

Katherine gulped. "Oh, I thought you had a dog and wanted me to take it for you."

Neal leaned in, took Katherine's hands, and stared into her eyes. "At McGuire's last week, I asked you to move in with me. Now you're alone in the apartment. It's safer to have a roommate. Last night I fretted, imagining you in the flat alone. And I have a lease until the end of July. You can stay until then and maybe you'll be ready to come to D.C." He squeezed her hands. "I promise to be a gentleman."

Katherine glanced away from Neal's blazing stare. She blinked and slumped back in the plush chair, rubbing her temples as if her fingers could sort out the thoughts jetting in her mind and zooming straight to the hollow of her stomach. Temptation came first. *Wow.* Her emotions danced on their toes right now. *What does that mean? We've only known each other for less than a month. But if you love someone, it's not the length of knowing, but the heart's knowing.*

Katherine's mind calmed, her heart bounced, and her spirit took a flight to give her the words of strength. "Neal, my heart says yes. You fill me with calm feelings. My mind says, well, yes and no: yes, because you're a gentleman for sure and no, because my parents would say no. My spirit says no. No, because I'm standing at many intersections and new roads. I need to determine the path before I can commit." Katherine paused. "You tell me that you're asking as a good friend for me to move for my safety. Here's my rebuttal to you, from a woman's point of view. To share a place with a man to me means more than just safety. It could just become wild sex, even if that wasn't the original plan; it could be real love that grows, or it could just go bad." Katherine paused. "My conclusion, I don't want to ruin the beauty of our relationship right now."

33

OLD TOWN BUSTLED WITH artists from around the country preparing their exhibits. In Katherine's opinion, her mother eclipsed them all with her modern Native American art. Katherine's mom's artistry inspired Katherine. Katherine never dreamed of the artist life for herself. When she was six, she'd spent half a day in her mother's studio watching her paint brush dip into yellows, blues, greens, and blacks. With the twist of her mother's hand, the colors would glide on the canvas to create real pictures. Katherine fell in love with her mother's art. She still remembered her mother's anger when she saw Katherine's small hand dip into the black paint to add her touch to her mother's masterpiece. Her backside had hurt more than her pride. Artistry and painting were not Katherine's destiny, but an appreciation of good art never left her. She dreamed of her home with original art lining the walls in every room of her house, even the bathrooms.

Katherine's toes rose over the cobblestones as she advanced on her mother, who waved her over and hugged her for a long time. "There's my gorgeous daughter. You got to bed early, right?"

Katherine nodded.

She smiled. "A good night's sleep is a woman's beauty secret."

Katherine curbed the burst of thrills flowing in and out of her. Her feelings floated on the surface just like the thousands of dandelion seeds that soar into a million places on a summer's day. Being enthralled, she pinched her lips to tie in the Cheshire cat grin struggling for freedom. Katherine was there to hear her mother's mystical and mysterious message. Neal could wait. "I'm so hyped to see you! Are you ready for lunch?"

Her mother gazed over her shoulder. "Hm, oh there he is. Your father is my relief to man the booth. I don't want to miss any sales."

Katherine's father gave her a peck on her cheek. "Hello, Goldie. Grand time last night." He turned to Katherine's mother and glanced at his watch. "Okay, my next committee meeting is at 3:00 p.m. You two go have a lady chat."

Katherine and her mother had a special bond even if they were poles apart. Her mother, the artist, spent quiet time alone while Katherine, the curious, wanted to talk and learn from others. *An in-depth mother-daughter talk is monumental. Mom and I never have "lady chats." Maybe when I was twelve, she stumbled with the "becoming a woman" talk. Do I want to "talk" with her?*

Her mother touched her arm and a chill bolted through Katherine. "Don't worry. It's good! Let's have those sticky ribs." Her mother threw a kiss to her husband and put her hand on Katherine's arm to guide her toward a tangy barbecue aroma.

Katherine's nose twitched with the enticing scent of hickory smoke, brown sugar, and secret sauce. The desire to eat was more fundamental than any problem or issue her mother's talk presented. *What's my problem? My mom loves me. We had a great time last night. She didn't send me any signs that something was wrong in her world.*

"Boy, Mom, how do you work with these delicious scents floating around the exhibitors' booth? My breakfast vanished, and my stomach is shouting for those ribs."

Her mother laughed. "If you smell it every day, you never want to come near a roast pig."

Both munched on their sourdough buns stuffed with pork smothered in hickory sauce.

"How's your job? Are you getting restless for something new?"

Is this lady talk? "Well, maybe. I love the benefits: travel, time off, and money. What else could I need, at least for now? But do I want to do this for another five to ten years? I've been a stewardess for two and half years. I could get married, but I don't want to find someone to marry right now."

Sitting straight like a gracious statue, her mother nodded and listened. Katherine recognized the demeanor. Behind the tranquility of those dark eyes and finely chiseled cheeks lurked a mind buzzing with ideas. Katherine sensed well-oiled thoughts organized and ready for delivery to her beloved daughter. Like a spark emerging from the flares of Prometheus, a profound revelation flowed from her dark red lips like an arrow aimed straight toward Katherine. "As the wise Hopi say, 'Wisdom comes when you stop looking for it and start living the life the Creator intended for you.'"

Her mother placed her hands on her lap, smiled, and waited for Katherine's response.

She had visions of her feather signs, her great-grandmother's visits, Soaring Eagle, the message she heard at the Oracle of Delphi, and the eagle feather. Like a neon sign, they were giving her one message. Her mother had birthed her twice, first as a baby and now as her destiny guide. And now she'd settled on a topic for her anthology research: Native Americans as the Lost Tribe of Israel. Katherine gazed up at the sky, paused, and opened her eyes to her mother. For the first time, harmony circled her, and she and her mother breathed the same air and shared a single transmission. "Mom, you're guiding me on my Vision Quest, aren't you?"

Her mother nodded and retold the legend of Hanging Cloud. "Hanging Cloud," she said, "'Goes Across the Sky Woman,' *Aazhawigiizhigokwe*. She was the only woman full warrior among her people. She wore war paint, carried full battle weapons, and was a deadly fighter. As a fighter, she took part in battles, raids, hunting parties, and sporting events reserved for heroes. She was a full member of the war council, performed war dances, and took part in warrior ceremonies."

The sounds of the rock band playing in the background melded with Katherine's inner musical thoughts. Like a jet engine humming at cruising altitude, her mind followed her journey from Beloit College to the life of a sophisticated stewardess. She was on a sojourn wandering through a wilderness. Now she saw the thread of protection that circled from Soaring Eagle's feather messages and warnings, her great-grandmother, whom everyone called Hanging Cloud, journeying with her.

Diamonds of moisture flowed from the corners of her eyes. "Yes, Mom, Grandmother told me the legend and why her mother was like Hanging Cloud, Chippewa warrior woman. How my great-grandmother, pregnant with my grandmother, journeyed from her tribe to help save her life. She struggled to escape her tribe's smallpox demons. After riding horseback, she made it home to Chicago and stayed with a friendly medicine tribe on Green Bay Road." Katherine paused, and half smiled. "I found out that Clark Street was Green Bay Road. Goosebumps pop up every time I walk down Clark Street."

Her mother raised her hand to motion for Katherine to stop. "I have to get back to my booth. Your father has to prepare his report for the committee meeting. So please listen carefully. My message concerns your Rite of Passage on the Vision Quest. That Thunderbird around your neck, the one that my mother, your grandmother, bestowed on you, is a constant reminder of your destiny."

Katherine touched the turquoise Thunderbird. "I thought it offered protection."

"Yes, it does that. Those individual tests that you encountered with fears, weaknesses, and uncertainties can disappear now. Your future will open to a new horizon with a realm that brings magical and transformational worlds. Your path waits out there for you." Her mother paused. "You are to help our tribe, the Chippewa nation." Her mother leaned over Katherine and kissed her cheek. "Now go and reflect on our chat. The rest is in your hands. Find your kismet and watch for it to uncork its secrets."

34

TWO DAYS BEFORE HER next flight, Katherine walked between two worlds. Her life as a stewardess faded away to her new future. Her eyes gleamed, and her feet floated across Old Town to stroll along Clark Street. Katherine paused to rub her feet on the sidewalk. Flashing images of Native Americans following the same path she walked circled her mind. *My ancestors walked on this spot on the earth. For them, it was the Green Bay Trail that took them to Green Bay, Wisconsin. Today, for me, the name is Clark Street.*

Their mother-daughter talk had produced an exciting struggle with her inner world of mixed feeling and thoughts. Her heart pounded and demanded that she be alone while electrical jolts of excitement rumbled in her stomach for action. Indeed, like reinforced bolts, her mind was locked on her new destination. Feathers and visions like pebbles blended in the sand to present hidden clues to her destined life path. Now she had so much to learn concerning her tribe and its blood that flowed through her body. Anaïs Nin had the answer for her feelings: "The possession of knowledge does not kill the sense of wonder and mystery. There is always more mystery around the bend."

Yes, her mother's ancestral announcement had hit a bull's eye on her truth meter. Her mother had gifted her with a future like a great block of variegated marble. Now Katherine's mind and heart became chisels to sculpt her new life. When she envisioned the significant, overwhelming size of the marble, she looked up for invisible guidance. Becoming a stewardess had been simple: she won an interview and got hired for a job that many young women envied and that made her a woman that many men salivated to know. Katherine, too, savored her privileged life.

Katherine's heart sunk but then rose with the thoughts of unexpected adventures. She had to earn a living even if she wanted to be a modern Hanging Cloud warrior for her people. She saw roadblocks to her dreams in men's view of women and their belief that women didn't have abilities beyond smiling, serving, and following. What if she finished her degree and published her paper on the Lost Tribe of Israel, then what? *The same dilemma that prompted me to fly away and become a stewardess stares me in the face. What shape will my destiny take? I won't get dropped in a box of acceptability. I'll kick the can beyond Sacajawea and Annie Oakley. I'll make my place.*

Instead of going home to live with this intense battle, Katherine turned toward LaSalle Street and Lincoln Park. She yearned for calm. Lincoln Park offered a new venture into a faraway world of Alaskan polar bears and African penguins. On her path to Lake Michigan, she waved at the lions lounging in the sun at the Kovler Lion House. Lake Michigan's blue water fed Katherine with balance. It cleared a path for her to focus. Right then, she wanted to find Neal and walk with him along the lake. But she needed time alone and a place to find the new Katherine. *Will others perceive the new me? No makeup changes, but when a person's inner-self changes, does it show on the outside?*

She remembered the days when her spirits soared, and she got more winks and whistles than on the days when she dipped into a dark funk. A comfortable rock on the edge of Diversey Harbor beckoned to her to come to the perfect place near the water to clear the mind and find answers. Katherine plunked on her white Rivera sunglasses and reclined on her comfortable, solid rock.

Splashing waves and the golden orange setting sun invited Katherine's battling emotions to find a quiet, calm space for dreams to open with a journey back to her happy horseback riding days at Chippewa Falls' Hay Meadow Trail. The memory of the power of her horse, Shining Star, beneath her seemed like a jet-propelled engine moving her forward. A sense of freedom enlivened her muscles, mind, and heart. On her mighty steed, she'd had a place to discover in herself the qualities to help her become a better human being. She longed to become a great person. The wind blew in her hair, and she became one with nature's freshness—the smell of the air, foliage, and soil atop Shining Star. Power and control over a 1000-pound majestic creature had given her confidence. Katherine wanted nothing more than to put on war paint and ride to victory. She stretched her hands to the sky and rose back into a walk. Calmness and knowledge to stay the course flowed from her. She needed patience and time to see it appear.

Katherine entered Diversey Harbor. There, right in front of her like a neon sign, stood a bronze statue of a Sioux chief on horseback, Indian Signal of Peace, 1890.

As she stepped away from the magnificent statue, she jumped at a tap on her shoulder. "Are you following me or are you visiting one of your relatives?" Neal laughed.

Katherine squealed. Neal, a delightful vision, casual in his beige Bermuda shorts, white T-shirt, and Dockers, dropped a small sailing duffle bag. "Neal! What are you doing here?"

"I was helping the crew on my friend's sailboat." He stopped and hugged her. "Whatever brought you here, I'm grateful. I planned to call you when I got home. How are Mom and Pop?"

Katherine's hands tingled. She tipped her head back and smiled at the sky. "It was the best. Better than just a regular visit."

Neal's eyes scanned Katherine's face like a professional photographer looking for the best shot. "Wow, you look fantastic. I dig that red and black spiral tie-dye. You're super, man." He squeezed her. "Hey, let's go to the Diversey Bar and grab a chilled brew."

Katherine's heart fluttered and commanded her adrenaline to charge around her body like an Olympic runner. Her chance meeting with Neal confirmed it. She thanked her inner-self for doing serious beauty work. She gave him a hug and grabbed his hand. "Let's go."

The couple strolled up to the Diversey Yacht Club. "Hey, Neal," a man yelled from a crowded table, "come on and join us."

Neal waved his hand and shouted to his friends, "Another time." And guided Katherine to the harbor bar. "This is great we have the place to ourselves. Right now I love a quiet place, without my rowdy crowd. You can tell me what's making you look so exhilarated."

Katherine smiled at the crowd at the outside bar. "This is fine. We can always go out later and join them. Right?"

"Sure."

"So. You're a sailor."

"I guess I was sailing on Lake Washington while you rode horses and shot bows and arrows in Chippewa Falls. I knew we had lots in common." He laughed and ordered their draft beers. "Now it's your turn. I shared my good news with you the other night." He paused and put his finger to his chin and gazed at Katherine. "I can tell that you're like a helium balloon ready to take flight. Shoot. I'm right?"

"Yep, you're right on." Katherine's breathing increased, and her words flew out of her mouth like moths flying from the dark to a bright light. "Here's the short of it. I'm going to help my tribe, the Chippewa. My dad helps the tribe with his volunteer civil rights law. My mother creates Native American modern art. I must help too."

"That's great. But do you have a particular plan?"

"Ray Bradbury says, 'Jump, and your wings will unfold as you fall.'" Katherine pointed her thumbs to her chest. "That's my plan."

35

KATHERINE GOT TO THE check-in desk with five minutes to spare before her 1:00 p.m. flight to LAX. There he was, the crew desk guy who had given her the Las Vegas junket. *Oh dear. I don't have his autograph from the Copa Girls. How can I give him that signed photo with jam smeared on it? Do I tell him the truth or fib?* Katherine leaned over the sign-in desk, hoping he'd forgotten.

"There's my Vegas girl," he said with a smile. "Where's my Copa Girls' photo?"

Katherine sighed. "I'm so sorry, but I didn't go to the Copa show since I couldn't stay up late because of my 6:00 a.m. check-in."

"That's a good girl. I was just joshing you. I knew you had an early check-in. If you'd gone, I'd think you were violating the 8-24 drinking rule. Now, where are you headed?"

"Flight 210 to LAX."

"Okay. You're checked in, but you have an appearance check with a supervisor." He paused, stood up, and leaned over the counter to give her a quick review. He gave her a peace sign. "You look fantastic. Have a safe trip."

Katherine released her breath. "Thanks. See you soon."

On the way to her supervisor's office, Katherine trod on the opposite side of the weigh-in scale. She slipped two fingers inside her skirt waistline and sighed. *I'm okay with my weight.* Regulation hair length, nails painted, uniform neat, girdle on, hose check, and shoes polished. Katherine sighed. *I should pass with flying colors.* Katherine stopped outside the supervisor's office, waiting for her to look up from the papers on her desk.

Like a master drill sergeant, the supervisor stood aloof and curled her upper lip as she surveyed Katherine. With a casual hand wave, she lifted her head and walked over for a closer review. "Please stand and turn around." Katherine turned and smiled.

The supervisor nodded. "Well, you're okay with the regulation appearance stuff. And I don't think you need a weight check. You look fantastic. Sign my review report. And please sit."

Katherine sat across from the supervisor to sign the report.

"What's that?" the supervisor asked, pointing at her wings.

Katherine reached up and touched her wings and exclaimed. "My stewardess wings."

"No, no. Something is sticking out from behind your wings under your blouse. Let me see it."

Katherine's body chilled. Her hands shook. *I can't show my precious Thunderbird. It's not regulation. I don't want to get busted.* She rubbed her wings. "It must be a reflection. There's nothing there."

Her supervisor leaped across her desk, staring right at Katherine's neckline. "You're hiding something. Pull it out."

Katherine tugged at her necklace and took time pulling it up and out from under her wings. The turquoise protector flew over Katherine's blouse neckline and glared at the supervisor.

The supervisor waved her hands toward the amulet. "Take it off right now. You can't work your trip wearing it."

The amulet wasn't just another piece of costume jewelry. This particular necklace united Katherine to everything in her being. Her body quivered, and her voice cracked. "It's a gift from my Chippewa great-grandmother. I've worn it on every flight. It gives me protection. No one sees it."

The supervisor's face went from porcelain to crimson. Her voiced lifted to the ceiling. "No one *sees it*. I saw it." She pounded her hand on her desk. "You know the rules. No crosses, no Star of David, and no lucky charms such as yours."

Turning points in one's life appear out of nowhere. After the signs and her mother's message, Katherine knew at this moment; she had to stand for her destiny. Being a stewardess was a grand tour on the way to her true calling. Katherine leaned forward, inches away from her supervisor's dark accusing eyes. "If I don't take it off, what will happen?"

The supervisor leaned back, straightened her back, and shuffled papers. "You will be given two weeks off without pay. And when you return, you can't wear that necklace."

Katherine's mind rushed, and her heart pounded. She saw two streams flowing in opposite directions. One stream rushed into a lush green meadow that had no end. The other drifted over dry, barren soil. "Okay. I'll take the two weeks with no pay."

Her supervisor pursed her lips. "And you'll return to work without that necklace?"

Katherine looked up at the ceiling and returned to give her supervisor a forceful stare. "I'll take the two weeks to think about it."

36

FREEDOM PRANCED IN THE AIR. A canopy rainbow glowed. Imaginary rose petals surrounded Katherine's mind as she walked from the supervisor's office to the O'Hare Airport shuttle bus. Today, it was her chariot with twelve white horses instead of a big tin can full of people. Katherine fought the urge to take off her hat and throw it in the air. The test had appeared—her necklace—and Katherine hadn't backed down. Soaring Eagle and his partners had cleared a path for her. Someone always told her that you'd know when things were right.

Is this my last journey on the expressway as a stewardess? She wondered. *What roads will I take? And where will they lead me?*

"Katherine!" Emma Jean squealed from her seat two rows back. "Darlin', what's up with you?" E. J. patted Katherine's hand. "This must be kismet. I wanted to call you when I got home." Emma Jean held her hands in fists in front of her and produced a closed-mouth smile that looked like she had a world of words to spell out. Then, she thrust her left hand in front of Katherine's nose. A diamond as big as the end of Katherine's nose glowed. "I'm getting married!"

Katherine paused to breathe. What news to share. Emma Jean had been her best friend since she'd started flying out of Chicago. Now her friend was moving on. Just like her. "Wow. I'm thrilled for you." Pausing again to gather her thoughts, Katherine turned and hugged her friend. "I want to know all about him and your wedding plans."

"Can we meet tomorrow morning at the Third Coast? I'll tell you then! Okay?"

"I won't sleep tonight. Can't you tell me anything right now?"

Emma Jean stretched and sat with a smile that looked like Katherine's imaginary rainbow. "No, you must hear the story in one sitting.."

"Oh, I'm so excited for you. Only my Emma Jean deserves a fairy-tale romance." Katherine decided not to tell Emma Jean about her two weeks off. "I have some news to share with you too. Mine's not a fairy tale, but for me, it's just as thrilling."

Emma Jean turned toward Katherine, smiled at her face, and surveyed it for clues. And then she lifted Katherine's left hand. "Well, Darlin', what else is there *but* fairy tales?"

"Oh, golly, there's a lot out there. And I'm ready for it."

Waiting for Emma Jean, Katherine contemplated the Third Coast and its crowd. Stale mustiness filled the air. Nothing in this place had changed in the two years since she and Emma Jean had started their friendship. This coffee shop was where they met and shared their life adventures. As rookie stewardesses on their first flights out of stewardess school, they'd bonded like a perfect yin and yang: Katherine a freedom horse running with the wind, Emma Jean an elegant swan floating on a lily pond. The past two years gave Katherine a friendship with favor, love, and adventure in a new world. Anaïs Nin's words on friendship fit Katherine's magical journey: "Each friend represents the world in us, a world possibly not born until they arrive, and it is only by this meeting that a new world is born."

A flood of memories prompted a sliver of a tear to slip down Katherine's cheeks. A familiar laugh jolted her. Emma Jean stood at her table and placed a pink floral gift-wrapped package on the table in front of Katherine.

Katherine bolted up. "Boy, am I going to miss my sweet southern lady."

Emma Jean kept her friend close. "Oh, Darlin', I already bawled my heart out. Please come and visit Andrew and me in Charleston."

Katherine pulled back from her friend to admire her glow. She motioned for her friend sit down. "Now you, I can't wait to know all about Andrew from Charleston."

Emma Jean leaned back and held her head high. "Oh, my dream came true all in one person. Mama asked me to visit home for her Charleston Garden Club show. I think I told you about Mama's love of gardening. That's the week you had a different line of flying. I tried to call you, but you were never home." She winked at Katherine. "Is it that fella I saw you with on the street a while ago? I almost wrote you a note to ask you if he was your special man."

Katherine leaned forward. "We'll talk about that later. Tell me all about Andrew!"

"Oh, Darlin', I'll miss your northern impatience. We Southerners go too slow." Emma Jean pointed to the wrapped gift. "Open it!"

"Emma Jean, I didn't know we were exchanging gifts today. I don't have a gift for you."

"I don't expect a gift. You've already blessed me with a new way to look at life. What you gave me was experiences that I will laugh and cry about for many years." She put her fingers to her lips. "One thing, for sure, when you meet Mama and Papa, never mention the Playboy party. Mama will faint. Papa would still horsewhip me."

Katherine laughed and unwrapped the gift. "Okay. My lips are locked, and the key is missing. Don't you remember all our museum tours and art lectures? I'll tell your Mama and Papa all about them." She winked at her friend. "I'm good at writing stories."

Katherine folded the wrapping paper and examined the gift: a gold-engraved, leather-bound, illustrated volume of the *Rubaiyat* by Omar Khayyam. She held the volume to her chest and closed her eyes as memories zoomed past her mind. This book symbolized her friend and their friendship.

"Darlin', this is so you can remember me."

Katherine placed the book on the table and sighed. "Emma Jean, I hope we stay in touch, even after you return to your southern roots. Now, give me the full story about Andrew."

The sparkle in Emma Jean eyes competed with the glow from her four-carat art deco engagement ring. Emma Jean looked at her watch. "This will be the short version since I have a hair appointment at Bonwit in thirty minutes. I went with Mama to the lunch before the garden show where we met a lady friend of hers and her son. That was Andrew. I knew him from other Charleston events, but he's five years older than me. But every time we'd meet, I would talk with him while we sipped delicious Southern Breeze punch. The more we drank, the more my heart flipped.

"Well, he never asked me out since I was too young for him. Now that silly girl little is gone, and Andrew saw me as a woman. He said he'd liked me all these years but wanted to be proper and knew my parents would not approve of him as the older man. But, oh my, it was like the Fourth of July fireworks blast at Patriots Point when we had our first date at the Harbor Club. The electricity between us could have lit up the whole waterfront. After that, we had breakfast, lunch, and dinner together for a week." She paused and smiled. "The final night before I went home, we went back to the Harbor Club. Guess what?" She clapped her hands and dropped them on her lap. "Over she-crab soup, he pulled out his grandma-ma's ring and asked me to put my hand beneath the table, and he slipped this ring on my hand."

Katherine's eyes moistened. "A true romance story. Your dreams come true!"

Emma Jean put her hands to her lips. "Oh, dear, we can talk later. I can't miss my appointment. But I want to thank you for showing me about being more than just a wife. I'm not going to work, but I am going to be a major volunteer for the Charleston Junior League. I'm going to give back to others. And you, my dear friend, inspired me." Emma Jean looked at her watch. "Oh no, I have to go, but you had something to tell me too."

Katherine didn't mind relinquishing her time. Her friend's news meant more to her, and it would take too long to explain her mission to Emma Jean, "Oh, my story can wait. When you have time, I'll catch up with you. Your news is so out of sight and mine is, well, I'll tell you later."

Katherine waved at her friend as she walked out of the Third Coast and on to a new horizon. Would she ever tell Emma Jean about the turns in her life? Probably not, since Emma Jean would only pity her for not getting married and living happily ever after. She just smiled and sighed. *I don't need to give anyone an explanation. I'm the only one who needs to know the truth.*

37

THE SUMMER BREEZE RIPPLED the treetops to create natural air-conditioning at the Ravinia Pavilion where Neal would soon meet her with a picnic. Katherine wondered if she'd get chilled in her spaghetti-strap linen blouse.

Neal greeted her with a big kiss and gave her a hug that warmed her. "I found us a perfect place on the lawn." He took her hand and led her toward to the festive picnic spread. Katherine beamed at the inviting picnic feast: a plaid outdoor mat covered with delectable food, including fried chicken, bean salad, fruit and cheese, and a variety of chocolates. There was also chilled wine, a loaf of bread, and flowers. "How was your flight?"

Katherine coughed and looked away. "Oh, fine."

Katherine didn't want to think about work. Instead, she recalled that last night she'd reread a *Rubaiyat* quote: "A book of verses underneath the bough, a flask of wine, a loaf of bread and thou, beside me singing in the wilderness, O wilderness were paradise now." *I can hear Emma Jean whispering, "Now you know what I meant for you to do with your life."*

Neal guided her next to him on the blanket, poured a glass of wine, and offered a toast to Katherine: "To a fun summer night."

Katherine clicked her glass against his glass. "I love The Associations. Thanks for inviting me."

Neal smiled and gave Katherine a thumbs-up. "Yep, The Associations and The Buckinghams, those are two things that we share." He paused and smiled. "The first time I stopped by to visit Charlotte, you had their song 'Kind of a Drag' playing. And you mentioned that you met Carl Giammarese, their guitarist, at Butch McGuire's." He leaned over and tickled her rib. "I was jealous of Carl."

Katherine's cheeks burst into a red glow. She gave him a wink and lowered her head.

He paused and sipped his wine. "Hey, I'm leaving for D.C. in a few weeks, as soon as I find out that it's a sure thing with the Justice Department. I will miss you. Can you bid flights to D.C.? I hope often."

Katherine wrapped her arms around herself. Her outer chill competed with the arrows bouncing against her stomach. Katherine rubbed her neck and nibbled on a cuticle. *What a coward I am. I couldn't tell Emma Jean or my parents the saga of my two weeks' suspension. Why can't I tell Neal? Will even my parents think I did something wrong?* She wondered. It was her doing. She'd stood up for herself. Now, she may not have a job. If she went back to work and didn't wear her Thunderbird, what would she do? *Maybe Neal will understand.*

"Well, to be honest with you, I might not be a stewardess any longer." She paused and pursed her lips. She saw her younger self reporting to her parents that the principal had sent her home from school for misbehaving. But she hadn't misbehaved; she'd acted with honor and dignity. She told Neal the whole story.

"Wow," he said when she'd finished. "You jumped! Good for you. It won't be long before your wings take you up and away."

Katherine's brow wrinkled. "Sure, it's good, but how will I pay my rent and buy food? It's frightening when reality plopped in my lap. When I was a high-flying stewardess, I could talk big and dream grand, but . . ." She pointed at a dark solo cloud. "Now what?"

Neal smiled. "What happened to that dynamo?" He paused and pretended to look under the blanket. "You know her—the one who's going to help the Chippewa tribe?"

Katherine shrugged. "I took Mom's words as my action plan. My common sense told me that's all I could do. My friend, Emma Jean, is engaged. She had a solid plan. I completed that course at Northwestern and got an A." She paused and smiled.

Neal hugged her. "Congratulations. Maybe you want to transfer from Beloit College and finish at Northwestern?"

Katherine sighed. "Northwestern is an excellent school, but for now I'll finish my long overdue term paper for my anthropology class for my Beloit professor. I'll ace it, and then what?"

"I guess that's your quest, to answer that very question." He rubbed his chin. "Do you expect me to propose to you? Is that why you didn't want to move in with me?"

Katherine rolled her eyes and shook her head. "No! No! I'm just philosophical with the decisions that we make and the results."

"Okay, let's be logical about your decision. First, you have two years of college completed. Right?"

Katherine nodded. "Yes."

"And you'll have two more years to complete to get a degree in anthropology, right?"

Katherine tapped her fingers on the blanket. "Yes, but where will it take me, even if I dig in to finish my studies?

What are my options? Go home and work in Dad's office as his secretary and slink through life?" Her hand trembled as she picked up a chicken leg and nibbled a bite. "Today, I scanned the Help Wanted ads in the *Tribune* for choices listed under women. First time I'd ever looked at the Help Wanted ads. I had no idea they were segregated according to sex. I could apply for a job as a posting machine operator, bookkeeper, or even a bridal consultant. Nothing else." She took another bite of her chicken leg and stared at Neal. "The airlines were the pinnacle of discrimination against women. My dad even laments about their violation of the Civil Rights Act with respect to age discrimination. Don't get me started." Katherine paused and released a big breath. "You're a lawyer, you know about that stuff."

Neal scratched his head and squeezed her hand. "Yeah, but you can overcome that detail. I wonder, where is the real Katherine? The one that's full of dreams, inspiration, and talent." He shrugged for her. "You're a defeatist." He paused, squinted, and peered behind her back. "Yep, I figured as much. No backbone!"

Katherine laughed and rolled over on her back, fighting the urge to fall into his arms. She moved around, clutching at her back. "Guess what. My backbone is stiff and vigorous and ready for action. I needed that elbow nudge. You have a talent for unwinding twisted thoughts." She leaned over and fell into a long kiss and an embrace with Neal.

Neal leaned back and held her shoulders to look right in her face. "It's good to have you back. Now you can make real plans. For starters, think about moving to D.C. with me where you can find the perfect career."

Katherine nodded her head. "Hm, that's what my dad mentioned." She stopped and smiled. "Not moving with you, but going to D.C." She scanned his face and winked. "Destiny has the answers."

38

NIBBLING ON AN ENGLISH muffin covered with butter and honey, Katherine reminisced about her time living with Charlotte. Oh, what changes they'd shared. Katherine, the stewardess, had gained travel, the world, and journeys with interesting people and experiences. Charlotte, the Bunny, had had an opportunity to study art and paint while she earned enough money for designer clothes. Now, Katherine's stewardess uniform hung in the closet. Anaïs Nin's words spoke to her: "Life shrinks or expands in proportion to one's courage."

Courage, that's what flying at 30,000 feet, gave me. I'll remember the times that I could stretch out in a row of seats and gaze out the window after serving meals and chatting with passengers. Through cotton ball clouds, I saw the majestic woven-tapestry pattern of well-organized cities with roads and buildings like children's playthings full of vast natural wonders. Now, on the ground, everything seems less organized, but I have the courage to see through the disorder and discrimination. Maybe there is a plan and order to everything. I'll keep my time at 30,000 feet, where everything had its place, as my most cherished memory.

Katherine wiped the muffin crumbs from her face and sighed. What would she tell her mom and dad? How would she tell them that she might be grounded forever? She knew they wanted her to do something on the ground when she left her high-flying life, but they hoped that it would be on her terms not being forced to quit. Then, she thought what if the airlines still had the *retire at thirty-two requirement.* Yikes. What happened to all those women who retired at thirty-two? If they weren't married, did they have to get jobs for women only? Jobs like posting machine operator, bridal consultant, or accountant. Oh dear, what a dismal destiny after having wings to the world.

Katherine took the last bite of her muffin and jumped up to take her dishes to the sink. As she washed the plate and cup, a smiled flashed over her face. *That's it! I have to be like the woman who headed the airline stewardess union, the one who knocked down the age barrier for a stewardess with her testimony to Congress. If that woman hadn't been a warrior, I'd be doomed to retire at thirty-two. I have to be a fighter too, not as a stewardess but as a hero in the world. I have something to live up to. My sister stewardesses have been fighting for women's rights since the beginning of aviation. I can do the same on the ground. There have been warrior women from the beginning of time in every part of the world. I'm Katherine the warrior woman, breaking false barriers.*

39

THE PHONE SPLINTERED HER musing like a rock through a window.

Katherine jump. She whispered to the walls. *I don't want to talk to anyone right now.*

She mumbled a greeting. "Hello."

Angelos deep voice jolted her. "Hi Katherine, I hope you're doing well."

I'm make this quick. He's a nice guy, but I have to focus on my life transition. "I'm great but I'm weighed down with life stuff like a pack mule."

"Me too. I wanted to call you sooner, but I had piles of work and school. And thank you for the book."

"You're welcome. You have a real American classic to keep in your library. I hope you'll remember me when you look at it, years from now."

"I will." Angelos paused and cleared his throat." I'm also calling for something else.

My cousin from Athens is a curator for the National Archeological Museum of Athens. I thought of you and your love of Greece since she delivered a few select Greek art objects for the United States touring the exhibition. It starts at the Chicago Art Institute with an exclusive member preview tonight. They'll have Greek food, Greek music, and dancing. Doesn't this sound like fun? Can you make it?"

Katherine blinked and smiled. *Wow, I'd like to meet his cousin, a woman who's doing something of meaning. And the call of Greece can't be resisted.* "Well, I'm not flying this week. I have a couple of hours available. Yes. I'd be thrilled to meet your cousin."

"Wonderful, I'll come by, let's say six. What's your address?"

Katherine took in a breath and waved her hands up in the air and rubbed them together. *What an invitation. Something is brewing for me at that Greek event. What about Neal? Will he care if I go? No. We're only at the friend stage*; she lied to herself. *An evening at the Chicago Art Institute is perfect. I need some art and culture right now.*

"My address is 1576 North State Parkway. I'm right next to Lincoln Park."

Like a rapid response, the phone rang as soon as Katherine plopped her pink princess receiver in the cradle. It was her mother.

"Sweetie, you sound like you have a cold."

Talking to her mother right then was not on her list. Katherine pondered telling her mother that she had a severe sore throat and couldn't talk. But the good daughter side won out. She cleared her throat. "No, Mom. I'm great. I just hung up with a friend. He invited me to a special event for Greek art at the Chicago Art Institute."

"What a fun night. That's my kind of affair. Too bad we can't be there. Father and I are going to Washington D.C. tomorrow. Your father has a committee meeting, and I will spend most of my time at the National Gallery. In case you called, I wanted to let you know." She paused. "If you have a few days off, maybe you could join us."

Katherine clenched her fist. *Dang, Mom! You know everything.* "Well, Mom, I do have time off. You were on my list to call. My supervisor gave me two weeks off because I refused to remove my Thunderbird amulet. I've been wearing it for my entire flying career, and no one has ever noticed. But she did. She insisted. When and if I go back to work, I can't wear the necklace."

"When it's time to change, we receive a nudge. You got your marching orders. Now, what do you have planned?"

A grin slipped across Katherine's face to mirror her inner calm. *As usual, I didn't need to tell Mom. She knew. My mother is my protective wing that lifts me higher.* "With my time off, I'll take a standby flight and meet you and Dad in Washington D.C. and go over my plans."

"Wonderful. We're staying at the Mayflower Hotel. We'll make another reservation for you. I have to run now. Call us when have your travel plans. And remember, your heart knows, so stay calm and go ahead. Love you."

"Me too, Mom. Thanks. Talk to you soon."

Time to get moving. Don't think. Just breathe and stay calm. Decide my trip to Washington D.C. Pick clothes for tonight. Katherine stopped and put her hand to her cheek. *What am I doing? Why should I jaunt to D.C. and snuggle with Mom and Dad? My life and my decision are mine alone. Didn't I throw away training wheels when I was five years old? I'll call Mom later and say no thanks. Now, it's up to me to find my new life. And it may begin with my visit to a Greek art exhibit.*

40

A FLOW OF THE ART FUNCTION crowd streamed from the Chicago Art Institute. Media cameras and reporters followed them to get their quotes about the visiting Greek exhibit to publish in the *Chicago Tribune* morning "Art Note". The summer moon provided a glow over the city. Michigan Avenue's warm summer wind flicked Katherine's hair as she strolled toward the front steps. On the way, they passed tons of Greek guests and art lovers flowing out the front doors of the Chicago Art Institute. A mix of Greek and English voices echoed the success of the Greek art exhibition.

Katherine and Angelos separated from the crowd. Katherine strolled over to the art museum's steps and glided to the majestic lion statue. She leaned on the base of the lion's pedestal and giggled. "That was so festive. I loved it with all the art, the ouzo, the hummus, and the Greek people. Greeks make any place exhilarating."

Angelos slipped next to Katherine and gave her a pinch. "And, wow, you know how to dance the Kalamatianos. Since the last time I saw you at my uncle's restaurant, you've become an ouzo aficionado. You might be part Greek, not Native American." He paused. "And my cousin liked you."

Katherine focused on Angelos' dark wavy hair. His image brought back pictures of her and Emma Jean's visit to Greece, and Emma Jean's infatuation with her swarm of Greek gentlemen. By contrast, Katherine's fascination leaned toward the Greek ancients and myths. Rubbing her hand over her heart, Katherine retraced her prophetic visit to the Oracle of Delphi. She closed her eyes and saw the radiant eagle's wings floating over her head as she heard the whispering, *You will help a great nation.*

Was it fate to be at this spectacular event honoring ancient Greeks? She mused, her brow furrowed. She had the urge to stand up and shout, "I am a warrior woman. I am a Chippewa—a great nation." She blinked and smiled. "Oh, yes. Your cousin is a super lady. Don't laugh, but she made me think of the goddess Athena with her knowledge and influence. And she even knows a couple of the faculty in Beloit College's anthropology department." Katherine leaned back and exhaled. "And this Greek atmosphere gave me shivers. It was like being back in Athens."

The crowd passed by the two. The couple didn't notice that the museum was closing or that it was getting darker. Angelos took Katherine's hand. "Have you seen the Playboy Club?"

Katherine's face turned red when he mentioned how they'd met at the Playboy press party. "Oh, yeah. I was hoping you'd forgotten how we met. No, I haven't been to the Playboy Club."

He reached into his pocket and pulled out a silver Playboy Bunny key. "The restaurant manager loaned me his key since I'm going home to Athens. It's his thank-you gift to me. Let's get some food and drinks."

Katherine blinked. She had just visited the Gaslight Club, another member key club, a few days ago with Neal. Was this coincidence or destiny calling?

"What's going on at the Playboy Club tonight?" the taxi driver asked as they pulled up.

Angelos shrugged. "Must be a convention of some sort."

Inside, modern wood-paneled rooms with chrome and leather furniture shouted out, "This is a man's kingdom!" A mass of gray business suits flowed up the circular stairs to the dining room. At the bottom of the stairs, another mass of gray suits intermixed with gorgeous Bunnies leaning over pool tables. The clink of pool cues knocking the balls into the side pockets harmonized with boisterous cheers.

Angelos turned to Katherine and laughed. "Conventioneers."

Katherine's eyes twinkled. She scanned the sea of gray-suited businessmen and turned to the welcome standout sight of Angelos' khaki pants and white-buttoned shirt. *Great look,* she thought. "Yeah, they look like my typical passengers."

He pointed to the bar where Bunnies played pool with the members. "Yeah, this is a real man's paradise where your road warrior travelers come after a long day."

Katherine burst into an uncontrollable giggle. She clutched Angelos' arm when he added his snickers.

A Bunny interrupted their hilarity. "Excuse me, sir, may I see your key?"

"Do you like looking at the Bunnies?" Katherine asked as he handed her the key.

Angelos laughed. "You forget where I work. If you live in a candy store, you get overloaded with sweets. After a while, each white-tailed lady looks the same. Similar to what the gray suits mean to you."

Katherine smiled. "I know. Men in gray suits are a drag. I'll miss working with such boredom." Katherine paused. *That was stupid. I didn't tell him I might lose my wings and my job.*

Angelos raised a brow. "You won't be a stewardess anymore?"

Katherine cocked her head and wrinkled her nose. *Should I tell him the whole story? No. I'll never see him again. He gets the short version.* "My phenomenal two-plus years as a stewardess opened the world to me. Now, it's time for me to do more with my mind and find a career." Katherine paused. *I don't need to mention my mission to help my Chippewa ancestors. He'd be bored with my* real *plans.*

Angelos clapped his hands and smiled. "Wonderful. You know, the Greeks created fate from the Moirai, the goddesses of fate." He sat up and placed his hands on his lap. "See, I invited you to come to the exhibit tonight with, well . . ." He paused and winked at Katherine. "I'm interested in you, but I had another motive." He coughed. "I'm going home to Athens at the end of August. My brother and I are starting a tour business in Athens. With my cousin's connection with the Hellenic Ministry of Culture, we have a solid business plan." He smiled at Katherine. "We will be the biggest tour company in Athens. And you're on an informal job interview tonight."

Katherine raised her hands. "Wait. A job interview?"

"I thought of you right away as our tour coordinator. First, you're a stewardess, you're gorgeous, intelligent, and a traveler. Second, you love Greece and Greek people. Third, the executives from the Ministry of Culture gave you a stamp of approval tonight. We'll pay you well, help you move, and get your work visas. And if you don't like it, we only ask that

you give us six months' notice. You can stay as long you like."
He pulled a color brochure out of his pocket. "Here's a draft
of our tour company. Please take it and look it over. I'll call
you tomorrow, and you can ask me more questions."

Katherine was ready to say no, but the thought of working in Athens piqued her interest. She could work on an
independent ancient Greece exploration project for one of her
anthropology courses. *Well, he might be a fair boss. He has an
excellent professional manner, and he acts like an open and understanding person. But I've never had one boss.* Her hands shook as
she took the crinkled advertisement.

"Okay, I'll look at it and talk to you tomorrow. Thanks
for thinking of me. I have to admit, my interest in fate comes
from my study of Greek mythology. I'm thrilled for you and
your brother."

The Bunny server interrupted the couple again. "Miles
Davis will perform in the library in the next twenty minutes.
It's his last set for the night."

Angelos nodded toward Katherine and smiled. "I'd love
to hear 'Nefertiti.' I have the album. It gets you grooving."

Katherine scanned the room as key holders, and their
guests left for the evening. "Yikes. I have an early morning
tomorrow."

Angelos smiled at the Bunny. "Thank you, but I guess
that's a no. Please bring my check."

41

ANGELOS AND KATHERINE strolled along North State Parkway. Katherine walked in silence and attempted to fathom the evening. What a fantastic night. The ancient Greece exhibition had been unbelievable. And meeting Angelos' cousin had been serendipitous, especially the fact that she knew Katherine's Beloit College faculty advisor in the anthropology department. Did it mean something? What did ancient Greek artifacts mean to the Chippewa tribe? And the job offer. Out of the vastness of the universe had come an intriguing possibility. She could still help her ancestors after a brief detour as a tour guide in Athens. It might be fate's path. It seemed better than her other choices: bookkeeper or postal clerk. *I can't be a stewardess any longer. I won't give in and give up my scared Thunderbird. It's my destiny. Right now, I need a job. Maybe in Athens.*

Angelos broke the silence. "I'll miss Chicago." He paused and pointed back to the Playboy Mansion. "And I was the envy of every guy I knew. They always asked me to sneak them into the mansion. I have a secret. I got my uncle, the one you met at lunch, into a party. It was like a Greek tragedy. I almost got fired because he kept running around pulling at different Bunny tails." He laughed. "I guess that's my uncle." A block from Katherine's apartment he cleared his throat. "Well, I hope you'll mull over my offer. Living in Athens is a dream for many people."

Katherine's eyes glistened. The hair on her arms tingled. "Wow. That's for sure. In a few years, I planned to return to Athens. It's funny when I was in Athens, I imagined a place right at the foot of the Acropolis."

"Well, most of my friends and I live in Attica, a northern suburb of Athens. If you decide to work with us, you can check out that neighborhood. In fact—"

"Katherine!" A breathless, shouting Neal rushed up the block toward them.

Katherine gasped. "Neal!"

He glared at Angelos. "This must be a friend?"

Katherine cleared hear throat and bit her lip. "Yes," she stuttered, raising her hand to Neal. "This is my friend Neal. Neal is also a friend of Charlotte's." Katherine turned to Neal and smiled. "He knows Charlotte too."

Neal removed his hands from his back and offered Angelos a limp handshake. "Hello. Sorry to barge in on you."

Angelos smiled and squeezed Neal's hand. "Nice to meet you. You're fine. I was just walking Katherine home. She's almost back, and you look like a strong protector. I'll leave you two now. My day starts early tomorrow." He turned to Katherine. "Thanks for a fun evening."

"I had a great time. And I'll be thinking about your suggestion."

The couple waved off Angelos and watched him walk down the street.

She turned to Neal, who looked like an angry bull ready to charge. "Well, if you walk me home, are you up for a glass of wine?"

Neal turned to Katherine and grabbed her hands. "I had to see you tonight. I'm leaving for my parents' cabin on Whidbey Island tomorrow and then to D.C. on Monday. They need me for a rush project. I start my job at the Justice Department two weeks earlier than expected." He released a deep breath. "I thought you'd like to see me before I go." He paused and turned in Angelos' direction. "But you didn't tell me about this guy. "

Katherine pulled her hands away from his grasp and flung them on her hips. "Hey, when did we become an item? You don't tell me everything, I bet!"

Neal rubbed his head. "You're right. I apologize."

Katherine put her arm in his. "Okay. Come. Let's have a bon voyage glass of wine."

Neal smiled and touched her hand. "Do you mean a 'hit-the-road-Jack drink' since you're busy with other things?"

Katherine attempted to slip her key into the door. She sighed when the door opened. "Come on in. Bear with me" She had envisioned Neal's first visit to her apartment since she had redecorated it in her style. It's wasn't a fantastic event since she rushed to hide the mess in her living room.

Neal walked in and headed toward the living room with the wall of windows open to a clear view of the glowing night-light of the moon shining on Lake Michigan, the lights of Lake Shore Drive, and the sparkling stars. "Wow. Cool place."

Katherine rubbed the back of her neck. "Would you like a glass of wine?"

Neal turned from the window and hugged Katherine. "Sure." He pulled her back and looked into her eyes. "This will be our last wine until we're in D.C."

Katherine wrinkled her brow and jerked back. "D.C.?"

"Yeah, just one week ago, in Ravinia, you hinted that you'd come to D.C. Right?"

"Right. We can talk about that, but let's have a glass of wine first."

Neal's forehead wrinkled, and his face flashed red like a raging forest fire. He surveyed the cluttered room to find a place to sit. He flung an old winter pea coat on the floor and plopped on the sofa. "Okay. Let's have a glass of wine."

Katherine lingered at the kitchen cabinets to give herself time to find a way to respond to Neal's question. Mesmerized with her thoughts, she clutched the stem of a wine glass. Last week, moving to Washington D.C. was tangling in her mind, but it was a fantasy, and now she had Athens to consider. Without a job, she needed a shelter but she didn't want Neal to be a haven in the storm. They had the beginnings of a relationship. *I can't lean on Neal. I have to be my person who can give and not take from him. Neal might be my future, but not my only hope for now.* Then, she tightened her fingers around the wine glass. It shattered. She shrieked. Neal rushed to mop up the blood dripping from her hand.

Neal wrapped paper towels around her hand and stared into her mist-filled eyes. "Are you okay? What's happening with you?"

She turned her face from his gaze and finished wiping the blood from her hand. "Excuse me. I'll be right back. I think I have gauze in the bathroom."

Closing the bathroom door, she leaned against it and sighed. Neal was the best, and she didn't want to ruin their relationship, but she couldn't just move in with him like that. *I'll just tell him we can call and write. I can't decide until I get an apartment and a job. If he's serious, he will slow down and wait.*

She returned to the living room with a big smile. Neal greeted her with a scowl accompanied by narrowed eyes like daggers. Neal's left hand crunched Angelos' tour business brochure. He waved it under her nose. "Is this from the guy you were with tonight? Is this why you didn't want to talk about D.C.?"

Katherine closed her eyes and rubbed her forehead. "No. He's a business acquaintance. He asked me if I'd like to work with the family tour business in Athens. I didn't seriously think about his offer. I only found out about it when he sprung it on me after we'd gone to see the Greek art exhibit. Heck, how could I decide on something I learned about two hours ago? Of course, I'm not planning to move Athens!"

"And you're not going to D.C. either, are you?" Neal shouted.

Katherine reached out for Neal's hand. He pulled it back and turned to walk out the door. "I thought you were different, that we had something. But I turned my back, and you're out on the town with a jerk from the Playboy Club. We had an exciting summer, but it's come to an end. Thanks."

The door slammed. Katherine stood in silence, her apartment encircling her with a darkness that made her chest fight for air.

42

LIKE AN ICE STATUE, Katherine remained in the center of the living room where she and Neal had embraced. Now her stomach jiggled with pain, and her heart thumped like a war dance drum. He'd come to see her. He'd wanted to tell her something. But then, it all changed with Angelos' tour agency brochure. Motionless, Katherine's mind flooded with images of her and Neal at the zoo, at the Gaslight Club, at Ravinia. Each gave her a beautiful warm glow like a warm winter fire. Together they'd woven a harbor of comfort and communion.

She rubbed her brow to find a calm place. The night had begun with balloons, champagne bubbles, and the promise of new endeavors and aspirations. A flow of tears streamed down her checks as Katherine walked around her empty living room. Its emptiness mirrored the void inside her. *I was full of love, excitement, and dreams and now they're gone? I didn't even admit my feelings for him to myself. Now I realize how much he was going to mean to me and did mean to me. I didn't want to harm our relationship.*

Katherine narrowed her eyes to block the last teardrops, but it was like squeezing water from a sponge. She spotted the crumpled brochure that Neal had flung. Katherine collapsed on the floor and slipped her legs into a yoga position. She ironed the wrinkles out of the Acropolis displayed in the center of the brochure. The next page was full of bullet points of tours: Greek Towns and Villages; Greek Islands; Best Castles and Forts; Best Beaches of Greece; Best Greek Archeological sites; Best Museums. Her shaking finger moved over each tour, awakening visions of Greece. She sighed. *I could have a job in Greece with these tours. What an incredible destiny. Is it mine?* Her finger flipped to the next page and crumbled yellow notepaper flew out and landed on the floor. Katherine's brow wrinkled as she grabbed the mysterious paper. She held the paper to her nose. "Neal?"

She held the crumbled note against her chest. She sniffled as she read Neal's handwritten note.

Dear Katherine,

I may not get a chance to see you tonight. If you're not home, I'll leave this with your doorman. I got a call to start my job at the Justice Department two weeks earlier than planned. My workday starts next Monday. I'm packed and ready to move out tomorrow morning. Tonight is the only time I have left to see you before I move to D.C. Are you still coming there?

I'm going to my parent's cabin on Whidbey Island for a couple of days to get some of my things. (You must go with me sometime, maybe when you get a Seattle layover.) While I'm there, I won't have phone connections. Then I'll fly from the island to D.C. I'll get in touch with you as soon as I can. I have an apartment in Georgetown (it may be yours too). I don't have a phone hooked up.

I'll miss you.
Neal

Katherine clutched the note to her chest. She jumped up and rushed to her bedroom. The neon light on the clock flashed the time: 12:30 a.m. It was too late to call him. She tumbled into bed and rolled around restless all night.

The next morning, Katherine awoke with her muscles strung tight, and her heart pounded like Beach Boys surf beat drums. Katherine rushed to get to Neal's apartment; she flung on her Jefferson Airplane T-shirt and jeans and climbed into her sneakers.

While she waited for a taxi, her rapid heartbeat continued. Her mantra galloped through her mind: *Neal has to be there, he has to be there, he has to be there.* A taxi interrupted her plea.

She hopped in the yellow cab. "Please rush to 546 Addison. My life depends on it!"

Right then, that's how she felt. Early that summer, her life had been moving on smooth waters. She was a stewardess with a life of travel fun and expectations. She'd had a growing relationship with a man who may be Mr. Right. How could this happen, when she was on a journey to help the Chippewa tribe, not to find romance?

The taxi driver stopped at Neal's Lincoln Park basement apartment and shouted, "Miss, this is your stop!" He shouted louder, "Miss this your stop!"

Katherine blinked and gasped. "Oh. I'm sorry." She paid him and descended the circular inlaid stairs to Neal's apartment. Closed blinds blacked out the windows. No noise or signs of people inside. *What if he is here? What if he has a woman with him?*

Before she could think of another question, a man called to her from the top of the stairs. "Hello, Miss. Are you looking for Neal Meyer?"

"Yes, I'm a friend."

"I'm the landlord." He started down the winding stairs in a rush. "Are you Katherine?"

"Yes."

"Neal stopped by last night to settle up with me since he was leaving early this morning. He took off at five." He reached into his jacket pocket and pulled out a notepaper. He handed it to Katherine. "He asked me to give this to you if you came here. He's an excellent young man. He was my best tenant."

Katherine ran up the steps and tripped on the last stone. Her elbows stopped her fall. Clutching the note in her fist, she pushed herself up and propelled herself into the street. Breathless, she plopped on a long low-rise cement wall. Her hands shook as she fought to open the folded paper. She wiped her eyes and read the note.

Dear Katherine,

I'm leaving this with Walt, my landlord, since I may not have a chance to see you before I leave. I want you to know how much I'll miss you and hope it won't be long until we are together in D.C.

Neal

The note fluttered in the breeze as Katherine clung to it. Closing her eyes, she saw Neal walking out the door and out of her life. The Thunderbird necklace struggled to calm the turbulence in her heart.

Why did I accept Angelos' invitation? It wasn't a romantic date. It turned out to be a job interview. And Neal hasn't pledged himself to me. I owe him nothing. I think I fell in love with him, but I don't know how he feels about me. What's the matter with me? I'm acting just like Emma Jean. I have my life waiting for me. I'm don't want a retro, submissive role.

Katherine jammed the note into her pocket, touched her Thunderbird, and heard it say, "Can you hear your life's summons? Get moving. You have lots of work to do."

Katherine turned on East Fullerton Avenue to take a long way home with a walk from Fullerton Beach to Oak Street Beach. Her gait increased along Lake Michigan, and she moved between a skip and dance.

43

"YOU ARE SCHEDULED TO meet in my office," the supervisor's letter read, "in full uniform without that necklace at 13:00 on July 27. Upon an acceptable appearance check, you will return to a full flight schedule starting on August 1."

The Warhol calendar on her desk said: "They always say time changes things, but you change them yourself." Katherine circled the current date, July 24, on her calendar. She had three days before her launch or skunk day.

Katherine leaned back and released her clasped hands to the ceiling. The phone rang. Like a ballerina completing her fifth position, Katherine answered the phone. "Hello."

"Hi, Katherine, How's everything?" Angelos' Greek accent jarred Katherine. *I forgot all about him. What does he want?*

Katherine sighed. "Super. And how's everything with you?"

"Well, my cousin leaves today for Washington D.C., and we'll take her to the airport. I wondered if you might be headed to the airport tomorrow. If so, do you have time for coffee to discuss my job offer?"

Any mention of Washington D.C. made Katherine's heart thump. Her body zoomed with adrenaline dashing to the crown of her head and the bottom of her feet. "Why is your cousin going to Washington D.C.?"

"She wants to visit the Smithsonian Museum. She hopes to learn more about American culture, and she told me to let you know that she's meeting with your anthropology professor. They are both on their way to Washington D.C. for a summer project at the Smithsonian." He coughed. "Both of us enjoyed visiting with you at the exhibition the other night."

The Castle at the Smithsonian Museum floated into her mind. *How could I forget the pull that the city gave me? I promised myself that I would go back. That's where I got my inspiration for anthropology.* "Give her my kind wishes. Yeah, that's Professor Margret Kingsley. She's kept my feet to the fire to complete a paper that I've owed her since I left Beloit."

Angelos cleared his throat. "Katherine, do you have any questions about the offer for you to work with our tour agency in Athens?"

The moment of truth was approaching for Katherine. Her heart fluttered as she took in a deep breath to stare at the date of her meeting: July 27. Her body and mind collided with energy and direction. An inspiration cloud floated over Katherine's head. The Smithsonian, my big mountain, and I'd never thought of it. But here it was waiting for her to climb on and up. *Okay, courage. Give me a shove.* "Well, I'm honored that you even thought of me. You, as a Greek, know the importance of following a personal destiny."

"Yes, we Greeks believe that a person must have the enthusiasm to help one's passions shine out. Do you know your future?"

"Eureka! Yes, thank you, you helped me get the spark. I'm going to check with Professor Kingsley to see if she can find me a student job at the Smithsonian!"

Angelos roared. "Certainly. I'll mention your interest to my cousin as well. That's what we thought."

"We?" Katherine asked.

"Yes, my cousin said that you have a huge interest in pursuing your anthropology degree. She wants to help women achieve bigger roles in the world. She noticed something in you. Not what I saw in you." A big sigh and then silence. "By the way, that Neal guy, is he your boyfriend?"

Katherine's body heat zoomed like stifling heat blazing off Key West's South Beach. *No,* she thought, *we're not even friends anymore.* "He's my old roommate's friend. Why?"

"Well, I didn't want to get you in trouble with him. I thought he was ready to slug me. I apologize if I caused you any problems."

"You're fine. Don't worry. I must be keeping you right now." She paused. "I wish that I could work with you, but my place is in the Smithsonian. Thanks again for understanding."

"I wish you could work with me too, but you have to do what you love."

"Exactly. Thank you. And I hope your tourism agency is your passion."

"Sure. I hope so. When you visit Athens, I'll give you a complimentary tour package."

Katherine wanted to give him a hug. "Thanks. I'll remember your offer."

"Definitely. Thanks. Say, can you meet me for a drink before I leave?"

"Darn it; I have a full schedule for the next couple weeks." Katherine smiled and mused. *Like becoming a warrior woman.*

"Then I guess I'll see you in Athens."

44

KATHERINE FLOATED THROUGH O'Hare International Airport. The thoughts of new ventures hummed in her mind along with the usual sounds of the airport: pages shouting passengers' names, jet engines roaring, and the constant chatter of passengers

"Hey, Katherine! Wait up!" Carol called from behind her.

Katherine jolted to a stop. *Be a good girl. I'll never see her again.* She hadn't connected with Carol. "Hi, Carol, how are you?"

"Wonderful!" She flashed a pearl ring under Katherine's nose. "This is from my agent and future husband. He's a drummer. We're moving to L.A. later this year. He's got a gig to finish up here at Universal Recording Studios." She took a breath. "Sorry, I'm rushing to check-in, but say, what's this rumor I heard about you?"

"That I'm resigning today? Is that what you heard?"

Carol's mouth flew open. "Oh, no! I wanted to ask if you needed a roommate for six months. Anita, you know, your almost flat mate, was my friend. I talked to her last week, and she wondered if you ever got a roommate. Well, my man can't leave Chicago until he finishes the recording session with Ramsey Lewis and Tony Bennett." She paused and let the name-dropping float around Katherine. "I want to move downtown to be closer to him. Right now, I'm living with three other stews in Schaumburg."

Wow, Katherine thought, *she is a genuine person. I rushed to judgment. I'm getting a nudge with my favorite quote again. As Anaïs Nin says, 'We don't see things as they are, we see them as we are.'* "What time is your check-in? Talk for another five minutes?"

"I have fifteen minutes before check-in." She pointed to a couple of bar stools at the snack bar inside the gift shop. "Let's get a quick Coke."

Resting on the stool and sipping on her Coke, Katherine leaned forward. "Can you keep a secret?"

Carol nodded.

Katherine's inner tuning hummed. *When I flew with her last month, I was so different. Time exploring myself gave me a treasure. I got to discover me and not what others thought I should be. I saw what I think of myself. What a lesson to learn. Now I can move forward and feel good.*

"I can't wait to turn in my resignation. I'm so thrilled since I'm starting a job at the Smithsonian in Washington D.C." She put her finger to her lips. "I'll be moving out of my apartment and need someone who needs a six-month lease. My parents promised to pay my half of the rent if I could find someone to move in and pay the other half. The rent is $250.00 a month for a one-bedroom apartment for you alone. The apartment is a block from Lincoln Park and the beach."

Carol squealed. "I love it, and I'll take it!" She hugged Katherine and flew off her stool. "Yikes. I'm late for check-in. Please put a note in the mailbox with the details. I'll call you tomorrow when I get home from my San Mateo layover." She hugged Katherine again.

"Have a safe trip. Talk to you tomorrow." Katherine watched her walk away. She rubbed the back of her neck and her brow wrinkled. *No more San Mateo layovers for me. Plus, I'll have no more one-bedroom apartment next to Lincoln Park and Lake Michigan.* She sighed and glided off the stool. Katherine gave the waitress a big smile and slipped five dollars on the counter. *I'm ready.*

At the crew lounge door, Katherine paused and rubbed her Thunderbird. As she opened the door, she inhaled the strong scent of Old Spice. A pilot reached from behind her to hold the door. Katherine smiled at the young pilot from her Las Vegas junket.

"Hi, Katherine! You look like you're ready for something exciting today."

Katherine walked through the open door and smiled. "Thanks." She wanted to shout out; *This is my liberation today.* "Oh, I have a few new things happening." She turned and smiled. "Have a great trip."

He waved and smiled.

Katherine peeked at the crew desk and smiled at stewardesses checking out their flight reports. Her mind zipped back to her first check-in two and half years ago. She'd been leaving her books, classes, and small-town life to travel the world and live in a city, Chicago. When she'd told her dad her plan to go back and study, she'd been trying to decide if she should be a cultural anthropologist or a social anthropologist. She hadn't believed in herself. It was a fantasy. But her journeys as a stewardess had led her through the stages of social anthropology in its way. As a stewardess, she'd seen people from different places and ways. She'd gotten a snapshot of what they think, how they organize their lives. Now she wanted to help people learn the wonders of the Chippewa. But now, she had to move on to her happy stewardess ending.

With a fixed smile, she strutted toward her supervisor's office. She passed the dreaded scale as an ashen-faced stewardess stepped onto it. *Now I can get fat and sassy.*

She stood outside her supervisor's office, grabbed at one more chunk of courage, and entered. Her supervisor looked up from her papers and screamed, "Katherine! What are you wearing? Where's your uniform?"

"My uniform is at home. I won't be wearing it anymore." She paused, breathed in strength, and continued. "I'm here to resign."

"Resign?" The supervisor looked away and shuffled papers on her desk. "You have a good record with lots of passenger orchid letters. All you needed to do was not wear that necklace." She raised her voice. "Did you misunderstand me?"

Katherine leaned forward and pulled out her Thunderbird. "This necklace means more to me than being a stewardess. I understand. You gave me an ultimatum: the necklace or the job. I chose the necklace. How do I resign?"

The supervisor wrinkled her brow and waved her hand to the door. She pointed to a woman at the desk outside her office. "Oh, just go to Betty, and she'll give you the details."

Katherine reached to shake her hand. "Thank you."

The supervisor gave her a limp handshake and a half smile.

Walking away from the supervisor's office, Katherine covered her lips to suppress her squeal. With her new wings, she floated above the clouds and gave a wink to Hanging Cloud. The drumbeat rhythm of her heart raised and lowered her treasured Thunderbird charm. *What's next?*

45

FRED, THE DOORMAN, smiled and waved at Katherine, "Hi, Miss Katherine, I hear that you're leaving us soon. Where are you going?"

Katherine appreciated Fred as her palace guard; he'd always been kind and protective of her. "I'm moving to Washington D.C."

"Are you transferring there?"

Katherine wanted to tell him she'd be working at the Smithsonian, but her Beloit College professor had not responded to her letter yet. It was still just a dream. "No, I quit my stewardess job, and I will find a job that's entirely different."

"Different? Like how?" He paused and rushed to the lobby cabinet and pulled out a large oversized envelope. "Golly, I forgot this. The mailman left it with me."

Katherine's eyes widened when she saw the large manila envelope. Its Beloit College logo raised her expectation and her heartbeat. *An envelope this large can't be a "Sorry, no thank you" letter from Professor Kingsley. She must have accepted me to work on the project, probably with a pittance for pay.* She crossed her fingers. *Thank you, Dad, for offering to give me an allowance and believing in me.* "Oh, thanks, Fred, I better go."

Fred grinned and pointed to the Beloit College logo on the envelope. "Are you going to that college?"

"Well, I'll be working for them. I hope. I'll tell you later."

Katherine dashed to her mailbox, still clutching the manila envelope. It tumbled from her hand when she reached for her mailbox key. Like a bird reaching for its morsel of food, she bent to retrieve it. She hoped there was a letter from her mom and dad with Dad's promised check. *Now I need my parents help for a few months. What a joke. I'm trying to be independent, and here I am with my arms outstretched for a brace from Mom and Dad.*

Katherine sighed and reached inside her mailbox. One piece of mail drifted into her hand, a soft pink envelope with camellias engraved around the corner. It looked like a perfect Southern belle envelope. *Emma Jean's wedding invitation! I wish that I'd said yes when she asked me to be one of her bridesmaids.* Katherine's eye overflowed with teardrops. *My life is in flux. I wish I could attend the wedding. Emma Jean, I'll miss you. When I get settled, I'll take a trip to Charleston sometime.* Katherine exhaled and swished her hands across her face. While she waited for her elevator, she opened Emma Jean's wedding invitation.

Emma Jean's note, enclosed with the request, enticed her to smile.

Dear Katherine,

I wish you could be in my wedding. Could you come for one night, or come the night before for the rehearsal dinner at the Charleston Harbor Club and attend our wedding the next day at the South Carolina Society Hall? Mama and Papa have an extra room for you. Please come.

Love, Emma Jean

The elevator began its slow ascent, and Katherine looked at her watch and tapped her fingers on the elevator door. With each floor, she made a list. Call Emma Jean. Call Mom and Dad. Find a place to live in Washington D.C. Call Angelos and thank him. Call Charlotte. At the fifteenth floor, the elevator door opened, and Katherine ran out like a race-horse out of the gate.

Katherine jammed her keys into her apartment door lock. Inside, she dropped her purse and keys in the entryway hall and dashed into the living room. Her palms sweat, and her heart pounded as she tore open the big manila envelope. A stack of paper two inches thick flew onto her lap. On top was the letter from her professor. She clutched the letter and skimmed to the lines that said, yes, she was part of the program. The more she read, the more green-lights of acceptance dashed off the page. Katherine's finger ran over the names of the people on the team, which included her professor, another Beloit College faculty member, a doctoral candidate, and her.

Katherine squealed, "I did it!"

Katherine wanted to burst her pride buttons since her professor told her that the idea of interns was new and not many people know how to use them. According to her instructor, her internship chances had been almost nil. Katherine raised her fisted arm in the air. *I'm a trailblazer.*

Her hand hit Betty Friedan's book *The Feminine Mystique*; it crashed to the floor and opened to an underlined quote: "The only way for a woman, as for a man, to find herself, to know herself as a person, is by creative work of her own."

Katherine clapped her hands. *I have to call Mom and Dad.*

Katherine's index finger reached to dial her parents when the phone rang.

"Hi, Katherine. Thanks for the note with your apartment details. Do you still want to sublease it?" Carol asked.

Katherine fought the urge to shout, *Come on over and move in tonight*. Lucky stars sparkled around her. "Why, yes, are you still interested?"

"I sure am. I'd like to move in as soon as possible."

Katherine looked at the start date in the letter: August 15. She looked around her bedroom stuffed with boxes addressed to Mr. and Mrs. Roebling, Chippewa Falls, Wisconsin. Many of these possessions had journeyed with her when she left home and now returned full circle. She smiled and touched her Thunderbird. *I already have all my real belongings with me.* "Well, how about the end of next week?"

Carol cheered, "Yes, I can come over tomorrow to pay you and sign the sublease. And look around the apartment. I can't wait to get downtown. My boyfriend works in the recording studio a few blocks from your apartment."

"Sure, the morning is better. I'm so glad that this works out for you."

"Oh, golly wally, I nearly forgot. I ran into one of my friends who transferred to Washington D.C. a month ago. She's looking for a roommate. Are you interested in finding a roommate?" She paused and giggled. "She lives in a neighborhood called Foggy Bottom. Can you beat that?"

Katherine needed a place to live, and Foggy Bottom was either her ship coming in or a port in a storm. "Sure. I could talk with her. So please have her call me."

"Okay. See you tomorrow."

Katherine's stomach danced to the rhythm of her heart beating. "Sure thing."

She clutched the handset of the pink princess phone and laughed. Katherine's chest tightened. She gasped. She was leaving her familiar sites—Lincoln Park and the zoo, Oak Street Beach, her Gold Coast neighborhood, and the cozy feeling of Greek Town—to live in a place called Foggy Bottom. Would she enjoy the new community?

She shrugged her shoulders and release a breath. And a new roommate! She'd never had a stranger as a roommate. She hoped the new roommate agreed with William Butler Yeats: "There are no strangers here; only friends you haven't yet met."

46

KATHERINE'S FIRST-CLASS FLIGHT to Washington's National Airport, her last crew pass, was the final remnant of her high-flying stewardess life. After this trip, she'd need to pay full price for her airplane tickets. Thoughts of her new life as an intern in one of the world's best museums replaced any regrets with visions of personal inspiration. *I am a trailblazer. And I'm no longer a jet model moving on a conveyor of uniformity.*

Katherine flipped through the pages of the visitor's guide to Washington D.C. She fanned herself and giggled at the descriptions of the White House, Capitol Hill, and the Smithsonian. All the new places to see and things to do caused her back to twitch with new visions sprouting from her heart to her mind.

A stewardess turned to Katherine and asked, "Excuse me, what's your lunch choice, chicken or beef?"

Katherine dropped her book and rubbed her eyes and looked up at the stewardess and smiled. "Hey, didn't we work together on a Las Vegas junket last month?"

The stewardess' face glowed with a broad smile. "Oh, yes. I thought I recognized you. Say what happened to you and those jerks with the offensive Indian shot glass?"

"Oh, nothing. Wasn't that a riot?"

The stewardess smiled. "I sympathized with you." She glanced at her book. "Hey, are you going on vacation?"

Katherine held up her book. "Oh, no, I'm moving to D.C."

"You're lucky to get a transfer to D.C. I have lots of friends who are based in D.C. Do you need help searching for a roommate?"

Katherine smiled. "I resigned for a new job in D.C. Thanks, but I have a roommate. She's a friend of a Chicago-based stew."

The stewardess put her palms over her face and furrowed her brow. "I know most of the Chicago stews with D.C. friends. If it's Carol and she referred a D.C. friend to you, you may want my friend's name. Just as a backup."

Katherine's stomach turned, and her mind filled with warning. "Oh, well, thanks, I'll keep them in reserve."

The stewardess nodded and smiled. "Sure, I'll give them to you before we land. You may have flown with them. They're former Chicago-based stews." She glanced over her shoulder. "Hey, I have to finish up in the galley."

Katherine smiled. *Wow, I won't have to do that again.* Katherine reached for her Thunderbird and placed it on the outside of her blouse. Freedom. Freedom must continue to grow, or it flows away. Yes, when she began as a stewardess, she'd had freedom. But freedom isn't stagnant. It's like a body that loses mature cells to grow new cells. Katherine wrapped her arms around her shoulders, leaned back in her chair, and dreamed.

The Washington D.C. humidity swarmed around Katherine. Her clothes stuck to her as she paced around her suitcases in the baggage pickup line. Katherine reread the letter from her new roommate to confirm the time and place for her pickup at the airport. Every ten minutes, she tried to call the new roommate's phone number with no luck. Thirty minutes and then forty-five minutes passed, but no blue Chevy Camaro with a red-haired woman driver appeared. Katherine put her hands on her hips and clenched her fists. She stroked the back of her neck to pad down the bristles. The crowd of passengers zoomed past her. Still no sign of her new roommate. Her veins pumped blood like a hot coffee percolator.

"Hey, Katherine." The stewardess from her flight motioned from the crew car.

Katherine nodded. "Hi."

The stewardess turned to the other crew members, whispered to them, and walked over to Katherine. "Are your still waiting for your new roommate?"

Katherine's face felt hot. *I'm not a little kid on my first day of school.* "Yeah. She's an hour late, and I tried calling her, but no luck."

The stewardess wrinkled her brow. "I bet she got called out on the flight and didn't know how to reach you. Let's check at the crew desk. I'll tell the team to go on to the hotel."

Katherine wanted to hide. *She thinks I'm a stupid idiot who got myself in a mess. I could hear that thought in her voice. Now, I'm a lost orphan, but it isn't the real me. I am a free, independent, in-charge-of-my-life person. I do need help right now, though.* "Thank you. I'll wait here."

"Okay, you can watch for her while I check with the D.C. crew desk." She paused and gave Katherine a look like a lost puppy that she wanted to help find a good home. "Okay?"

Katherine's stomach didn't send a message, but her

thumping heart delivered warning signs. "Sure. I appreciate your help, but what about your crew at the hotel? Please let me give you money for your taxi when you come back."

"It's nothing. We stews are an exclusive club. I'll be a clipped wing someday, and you may give me a hand. See you soon."

Katherine laughed. "I'll be here." The stewardess disappeared through the terminal doors. It was a symbolic image for Katherine; her closing one door while her other hand reached for the new door. Her mind drifted over her flight into Washington National Airport and the view of Washington from the air: National Mall and the Potomac River. All those times she'd flown into O'Hare International Airport with thousands and thousands of sparkling lights glowing from Chicago suburbs: Arlington Heights, Des Plaines, and Schaumburg. What a different a world she was entering. *Remember, relax and enjoy the ride.* The Smithsonian was a beginning of something on a bigger scale with more tests and trials. If she'd learned anything from her stewardess career, it was to expect the unexpected. Flight delays, canceled flights, and unexpected charter flights. *And now I have a new roommate who's missing in action.*

Katherine waved at the taxi drivers who called out to her. "Taxi?"

She released a breath and took in the air of Washington D.C. She wrinkled her nose and nodded. *Yep. Enjoy the fresh air. Soon, my daily work life will be full of stuffy air from old papers and old books, like my dad's old law books in the attic.*

A fat, lecherous man in a dark blue suit cleared his throat and smiled at Katherine. "Excuse me, miss; you look lost. Are you a new girl in town?" He paused and surveyed every part of Katherine from her mod shoes to her perfect face, which was framed by wavy blonde hair. He winked and pointed to the taxi. "I can give you a ride to a hotel downtown. I'm going to the Willard. It's a grand hotel."

Geez, I'm not even in uniform and lechers lurk from dark corners. Katherine put her hands on her hips and glared at the ruddy man with cigar stains on his fingers. "No, thanks. I work on Capitol Hill and know my way around the city." She turned her back and saw her new stewardess friend trotting toward her.

The stewardess with her proper training shouted, "Oh, Miss Roebling, your limo driver called, and he ran into traffic problems." She motioned for her to come with her. "He wants you to wait in the terminal, and he'll have you paged when he arrives out front."

Katherine seized her suitcases and glided into the terminal.

The stewardess motioned for her to join her. "Katherine, sit here." She motioned to a chair next to her.

The stewardess's face reminded her of her mother's face when she'd told Katherine that her favorite rabbit died. Katherine gulped. "Thanks. What's the news?"

The stewardess sat up and sighed. "Your new roommate got fired. She is a married woman. Two supervisors met her flight early this morning." She paused and looked at Katherine. Katherine nodded and motioned for her to continue. "Her husband met her flight and took her away somewhere."

Well, it could be worse. This stewardess could be a pilot telling me to prepare for an emergency landing. I can handle this. I'm jinxed. First Anita and now this woman. Hm, this must be a message for me. "Hm. I guess I can call Carol and see if she knows anything about this and where I can get in touch with her friend. I'd like my first month's rent back." Katherine wrinkled her brow. "If she was married, why did she want a roommate?"

"As a cover. Supervisors check the names of suspicious stewardesses' apartment listings. With two women listed, it looks right. Carol didn't tell me anything else. She gave me lots of details on how nice she is and that she's from Wyoming. You're lucky that this happened. Not because of the roommate. The location is terrible. Foggy Bottom is a bummer for commuting. You need a car. Do you have a place to stay? Maybe you could stay in my room at the hotel."

Katherine appreciated her kindness but staying in a crew hotel room with a stewardess was a move back to the door she'd closed. "You're super, but you've done more than enough for me. I'll get a hotel downtown and make a new plan tomorrow." She reached into her handbag and handed the stewardess a twenty-dollar bill. "Is this enough for the taxi to your hotel?" Katherine paused and laughed. "I can't give you my telephone number or address, but I'd like yours. When I get settled, I'll send my information to you. If you get Washington, D.C. layovers, we can have dinner or drinks. Okay?"

"Twenty is too much. I'm glad I could help. Say, check with the stews I gave you. They may need a roommate. I guarantee that they're single and lovely women."

"Thanks, I'm sure they're perfect. I'll start fresh tomorrow." Emma Jean appeared in her vision, and Katherine smiled. "You know, like Scarlett O'Hara."

47

KATHERINE WALKED OUT OF the Mayflower Hotel elevator and strode across the lobby's marble floors. At 6:30 a.m. political crowds merged in and out of the hallway. Katherine fought the urge to step in front of one of the handsome young men and trip him. Each one appeared more important than other. *What laws are they creating? What's going on at "the Hill?"*

"Katherine," a familiar voice shouted.

"Dad!" she roared. It was thrilling, meeting her dad in the Mayflower Hotel in Washington D.C. She grabbed his arm and led him to the breakfast buffet. "I could devour everything—the omelets, the pastries, and tons of pineapple bits."

The waiter poured coffee for Katherine and her father. "Welcome to our sunrise breakfast. We offer delectable food to get you ready for a busy day."

"Wonderful," Katherine said. For the last week, her breakfast had been a muffin and coffee. Now visions of crispy bacon, fluffy omelets, French toast, and pancakes danced across her mind.

Her mother and father's generosity in loaning her money to stay at the Mayflower for two months with extra for meals and personal needs overwhelmed her. She planned to pay them back when she had the money.

"Your special French toast, please, and a side of ham, orange juice, and lots of coffee."

After her father ordered, he sipped his coffee and wiped his glasses with his napkin. "Now I can see all the Washington movers and shakers."

Katherine's rash emerged undetected on her arms. She scanned her father for any clues of disapproval for his "loan" or her misstep with her new roommate. There was no evidence of the usual signs of anger: tapping fingers, a clearing of the throat, avoiding looking at her. Instead, her father leaned back in his dining chair and stretched like a Cheshire cat with an equally huge smile to match. *Okay,* she thought, *he must like this plan. But was he really here for business in D.C. or is he here to check on me?*

"You are a tremendously resourceful young woman," her father said with a smile. "Your job at the Smithsonian is the buzz of Chippewa Falls."

"What's all the fuss? I'm not the first intern at the Smithsonian. It's not a real job. At least not yet."

Her father laughed. "When you became a stewardess, that *was* a big deal. In Chippewa Falls, it was a glamorous job, and you were the only girl in town who'd ever been accepted as a stewardess. Didn't you notice the women with their eyes green with envy glaring at you on Main Street? But now the image of stewardess is sexy. And you're not that 'kinda' girl."

"Dad, how do you know that?"

"I read the newspapers with the ads. I hear men talking about stewardesses all the time."

Katherine frowned. "Dad! Men everywhere act like wolves waiting for lambs to walk by, sometimes literally. Women need equal rights and respect. My stewardess friends are the best women. Blame it on men's imagination and women's appearances. The airlines are just capitalizing on 'sex sells.'"

"You're right. Your mother and I bubble over with admiration when we see how you've grown up. You were Katherine, the stewardess, and now you're ready to become Katherine, the Pathfinder." He folded his napkin and dropped it on the table. "Okay, I'll be late for my committee meeting."

"Yikes. What time is it?"

"7:30. The meeting starts at 8:00. The American Bar Association building is one block away on Connecticut Street. So, I have a little time."

She clapped her hands and laughed. "I'm looking forward to a super first day. My first meeting with human resources is at 9:30. And my walk is the best, superior to walking along Lake Shore Drive. I walk past the White House and down the Mall. The high point is the Washington Monument. My morning starts with inspiration."

Her father gulped his last drop of coffee, paid the check, and grabbed his briefcase. "Goldie, you're a lucky girl. Let's meet for dinner tonight? Okay?"

"Meet you in the lobby?"

He reached for his wallet and handed her two five-dollar bills. "No, here's money for a taxi. My committee members are going for cocktails after our meeting. Take a cab to Martin's in Georgetown. You can give me a full report on your first day at the Smithsonian." He smiled and gave her a thumbs-up. "Can't wait for reconnecting tonight."

Katherine waved. "Okay."

Katherine gazed at her father's statesman-like gait as he sauntered away from her. *Wow, I may become my father's equal. And I'm in the city where people make changes that ripple around the world!*

Katherine brushed crumbs off her dusty pink skirt, straightened her black-and-pink-checkered box jacket, and raised her athletic body from the dining room chair. She touched the cherished turquoise charm and whispered, "I'm ready." Gliding out of the restaurant like an eagle soaring, she smiled at the waiters and the restaurant guests paying their bills. She gave them her best and thought, *I don't have to smile at you, but I can't help it. I'm part of something special.* She hummed as she recalled tribe wisdom from her youth: "A great vision is needed, and the man who has it must follow it as the eagle seeks the deepest blue of the sky." Katherine planned to take poetic license and replace the word man with the word woman.

"What a day," Katherine exhaled as she rushed into her hotel room. She tossed her pink suit on her bed to change for dinner with her father.

At Martin's Tavern, her father waved from a booth in the wood-paneled dining room.

"Wow. I must get a picture for your mother." Her father motioned for Katherine to sit on the bench across from him. "How was your day?"

"Oh, Dad, I had the most thrilling day. I can't wait to give you a full report. I have so much to add to my journal. I'll send it to you and Mom." She surveyed the wood paneling and the lines of booths around the restaurant. "I read about this place. It has a long history that goes back to the Depression. When we have time, I'd like to check all the president's favorite booths."

Her father tipped his thumb to a plaque on the wall. "Yeah. We're sitting in the booth where Jack Kennedy proposed to Jacqueline." He wiped a tear from his cheek.

Katherine thought of her father and his knight-like willingness to fight for underdogs. Now she understood part of the reason for his actions: Jack Kennedy. "He had the same effect on me," she sighed. "Dad, can you excuse for a minute? I have to hit the ladies' room."

"Sure."

Going past the crowded bar to the ladies' room, Katherine heard a familiar laugh; her head cocked over her shoulder. Before she could jerk her head back, the funny guy pulled his head back. Neal's eyes widened. "Katherine!"

"Neal?" Katherine smiled and leaned into Neal's embrace. Katherine released a deep breath of air. *Is this really happening?* Katherine touched her Thunderbird. *Back in Neal's arms, this is where I'm meant to be.*

48

KATHERINE'S JAW DROPPED, her eyes glistened. Her shoulders lifted high as tears streamed down her face. "I can't believe this!" *Is it destiny, fate, or Hanging Cloud?* Her heart hummed with the flutter of the turquoise Thunderbird necklace. Katherine rested her head next to his chest with his heart beating in time with the rhythm of her heart, mind, and soul; just like a symphony. Katherine moved away to look in his eyes. "Neal. How did this happen?"

"My magic powers."

Katherine's eyes danced. Her voice bubbled. "And you did it. I was wishing for this to happened."

A man at the bar with a boisterous laugh tugged at Neal's sleeve. "Hey, Neal, aren't you going to introduce us?" He turned and pointed to a group of four men, all dressed in the standard dress blue striped suit, white shirt, and assorted club ties. Katherine glanced at his dark red Cambridge University tie embroidered with golden lions.

Neal's face turned as red as his scarlet tie. He clutched Katherine's side and turned her toward the four other men. "Gentlemen, may I introduce my friend Katherine Roebling."

All four men leaned forward with outstretched hands. Like an assembly line, Katherine clasped each fellow's warm hands. She forced a heartfelt grin for each of them. *All I want to do right now is hold Neal's hand.*

A blond man standing next to Neal proffered a big smile. "Katherine, it's a pleasure to meet you." He stopped and tapped Neal's chest. "This gent almost hired a private detective to find you." He laughed. "And now here you are."

Neal's brow furrowed and released a sigh. Katherine placed her hand in Neal's clenched fist. *Another side of Neal. I'll remember this.* "Oh, Neal and I are old friends, and we always play games with each other."

Neal sighed and feigned a laugh. "Yeah."

Katherine remembered her father. She turned to his friends and smiled. "Do you mind if I take Neal to meet a friend of mine?"

Neal laughed. "Hank's not my mother. No need to ask his permission!" Neal smiled and took Katherine's hand. A couple of feet away from the blue squad, Neal whispered in her ear. "Your friend? Are you here on a date?"

"No. My father is calling out the bloodhounds; I left him to go the restroom."

"Your father?"

"Yep. That's my dad, the guy with white knuckles holding his beer mug." They walked to his table. "Hi, Dad, I'd like you to meet my friend, Neal Meyer."

Her father jumped up and flung his hand into Neal's open palm. "Hi, Neal. Would you like to join us?"

"Nice to meet you, Mr. Roebling." He looked at Katherine. "I don't want to intrude."

Katherine's heart pounded out a signal, and her voice quaked. "We'd like the company. Please join us." *I bet Dad wants to kick me under the table. I'll ask for forgiveness later.*

He's probably wondering if I let this guy pick me up. "Dad, here's an amazing coincidence. I know Neal from Chicago, and he moved here to take a job with the Justice Department." Katherine's mental frequency sensed her father's approval of Neal moved up the charts.

"Oh, I used to have friends at the Justice Department."

"I think Katherine mentioned that you're a lawyer."

"Yes, I have twenty-five practice years notched on my belt. How about you?"

"I just graduated from Northwestern University in the spring, passed the bar, and now I'm an attorney." Neal paused and smiled at Katherine. "It'll be three weeks tomorrow."

Katherine glanced at Neal and then turned to her father. Arrows pinged in her stomach and charged to her scalp to dart around her head. Her hand twisted the Thunderbird. The night Neal walked out of her apartment had run through her waking days and dreaming nights. *How did it all happen? Our misunderstanding? Now, maybe we can get back on track.*

Neal turned to Katherine and touched her hand. "How long have you been in D.C.? What's happening in your life?"

Katherine noticed the sweat rolling down her dad's brow. *I have to solve this. I want to have dinner with Dad, and I want to talk to Neal. What to do?*

"Gosh. That'll take a while. How about meeting for a drink tomorrow? I'm staying at the Mayflower Hotel."

"The Mayflower Hotel? Sounds good. How about I meet you in the lobby at six. I'm glad I found you. I called Charlotte over ten times to see if she knew how to find you. I thought she'd have your phone number."

Katherine smiled. "I'll give her a call soon. It's amazing to see you; we'll catch up tomorrow."

"I'm heading to Germany in a few days. I know you've been there. Maybe you'll give me useful tourist tips tomorrow night." He offered his hand to Katherine's father. "Mr. Roe-bling, it was a pleasure meeting you. Have a good visit with your daughter."

Katherine's dad put his handkerchief back in his jacket pocket after wiping his brow. He smiled and offered Neal his hand. "A pleasure meeting you."

Neal turned to Katherine, smiled, and squeezed her hand "See you tomorrow."

49

THE MUSTY SMELL OF OLD manuscripts, pictures, and artifacts in the Smithsonian Castle's archive room smothered her wanderlust. Now she had a real calling. *I can't believe it, but I may be on the road to becoming a leader in archeology.* Pounding heart, shaking knees, collapsing walls without windows chimed in tune with wonder. She couldn't believe how lucky she'd gotten to have her internship changed to a paying position right off the bat. *I will be a warrior for discovery and truth about ancient people and cultures whose stories are waiting for me to tell.*

Boxes and boxes lined the stadium-long mahogany tables. Katherine reviewed the list of exhibits for the 1968 Festival of American Folk Art and bounded along the long row of files, reading the marking labels: Native American Program: Lummi Indians, City-Country, bluegrass, jazz, and Cajun; Crafts: sheep shearing, soap, candy, and sorghum making. Katherine chuckled.

"Hey, Katherine, how's it going?" a familiar voiced shouted from the entry.

Dr. Margaret Kingsley, her Beloit College anthropology professor, walked over and sat in a chair across from Katherine. She pointed to the massive conference room table covered with boxes. "I hope you're not upset about the internship falling apart. Will this fit with your plans? A medieval décor work environment isn't glamorous. At least you have a job for a year and maybe longer. It's exceptional for this grade level job if it's right for you. I hope you won't get bored."

Katherine's tongue pushed at her teeth like a protective guard ready to charge through the bolted door. *How can I ever show this woman the amazing gift that she's given me and the opportunity that the American Folk Festival offered me?* In the future, she could help promote and educate the world on the art and gifts that Chippewa tribes bring to the world. Katherine raised her hands to her face to suppress her tears of joy, so she could replace them with a grin that slipped from cheek to cheek. "Oh, Professor Kingsley, I don't know how to thank you. You've opened more doors for me than I could ever imagine. I only hope that I can walk through each one and come out a better person. I hope I can make you proud of me as my thank-you to you."

Katherine's eyes widened when the professor stood up, lifted her chin, and released a booming laugh. "Hey, you're one of my star students, even if you take long sabbaticals for high-flying glamor. I had my fingers crossed that you would return and give me a chance to have one shining star in my teaching career." Her professor sat down and leaned back in the chair. She folded her arms over her chest. "I was even jealous of you when came to tell me you were leaving school to become a stewardess. Wow. Wasn't it exciting?"

Katherine didn't want to disillusion herself. "Yeah. It was cool. But I couldn't do it forever." She swept her hands across the room. "With this beginning assignment, I might have a long-term career."

Professor Kingsley raised herself from the comfortable chair and strolled to Katherine. She put her hand on her shoulder. "Keep in touch. We're leaving for Athens tomorrow. But I have high expectations for you." She started to walk away but turned and gave her a big smile and offered her a thumbs-up.

"Thanks, Dr. Kingsley. Have a great trip. I'll keep you updated on my progress."

Katherine turned to the never-ending row of boxes and sighed. "Athens."

She strolled over to land in the chair that had just been occupied by her professor. Two weeks ago, she couldn't even have imagined this place. She even got tempted to work in Athens with Angelos. Katherine's eyes glistened. *Hanging Cloud, you guided me to this like a straight-arrow aimed at a bull's eye. Everyone carries a destiny. I cherish the people and friends that have journeyed with me: Mom and Dad, Dr. Kingsley, Emma Jean, Charlotte, Adam, Angelos, Fred, and all the people along the way as part of my thread of destiny. My magic thread entwined in colors. Brown, the color of roots, a steady shelter for my life with family. Green is the color of new beginnings, for my college life at Beloit College. Orange is the color of expansion, spontaneity for life as a stewardess in Chicago. Indigo blue, the color of professionalism, credibility for this new life at the Smithsonian.* Katherine raised her hands over her head to straighten her back. *My hope for the next roll out of colors: Deep purple, the color of the visionary, for my new plans to help the Chippewa tribe; and okay, a dream, but light pink, the color of romance and affection, for a long, lasting relationship with Neal.*

Katherine leaned forward, brushed her hands across her face, and crossed her legs. Swish. With the crossover leg, she bumped the draft booklet for next season 1968 Festival of American Folk Art. It tumbled to the floor. The Thunderbird necklace flopped away from her chest.

A gust of wind flipped the pages to page ten. *What is Folklore?*

Katherine closed her eyes, sighed, and knelt next to the paper. With trembling hand, she picked up the manuscript and read it:

> *Folklore is the culture of the people. It is the submerged underground culture lying in the shadow of a whole civilization about which historians write. Schools and churches, legislatures and courts, books and concerts represent the institutions of culture. But surrounding them are other cultural systems based on tradition, systems that directly govern the ideas, beliefs, and behavior of most of the world's peoples.*

Katherine smiled and raised her eyes to the trompe l'oeil celling. "I have a mountain to climb."

50

KATHERINE TURNED THE TINY umbrella in her daiquiri glass and listened to Neal's proposition. She sighed with a sense of freedom. Glancing around the Mayflower lobby bar, she envisioned what it would be like if she stayed at the Mayflower for another month, and another month. *Hotels are nice, but they're not home*, she thought.

Neal picked up his beer glass and took a swig. He wiped the foam from his lips. "So, what do you say? My place is big enough for both of us: four bedrooms, three bathrooms, and lots of closet space in one of them for your clothes. Capitol Hill is the best location for you to get work at the Smithsonian. And we can even walk to work together. The Department of Justice is on the way, and the Castle is on the same route."

The buzz of voices and the clinking of glasses floated around the room like the sound of jet engines ready for takeoff.

"Neal," she blurted, "I saw a red cardinal on the Mall this morning when I walked to the Smithsonian."

Neal's eye pinched together. "A red cardinal? Is this your way of saying no thanks?"

Katherine swallowed and licked her lips. "I meant the opposite. Native Americans believe that birds or spirits are medicine animals. They are messengers from the Great Spirit." She paused and looked around the lobby again. "The cardinal symbolizes relationships, courtships, and," she paused again. "Monogamy."

Neal's mouth dropped opened, and he laughed. "Why didn't I expect your response? You are not the ordinary woman." He paused and scratched his head. "You know, I saw a cardinal a few days ago too. Is this considered an omen?"

Katherine put her hands on her lap and smiled. *Did he see a cardinal or is he playing along with me?*

"Yes."

Walking around Neal's Capitol Hill townhouse, Katherine thought, *Is this a dream? Life moves magically. One month ago, Chicago was my home. My one bedroom apartment that I shared with Charlotte fit just right.* Katherine's skin tingled like waves rippling on a quiet lake. She glanced up at the intricate fanlight windows surrounding the rotunda. When she first saw them, she'd told Neal that his semi-circular windows looked like Southern belle fans. His warm-hearted squeeze had overwhelmed her when he'd whispered in her ear, "I can't wait to lift you and carry you into my arms and life forever. I want you beside me and, in my heart, forever."

I never thought I'd like having a man take me under his wing and carry me into eternity.

Katherine danced and whirled around the rotunda room with empty shelves encircling the room; awaiting books and art objects. She'd never had this much space for her belongings. Katherine's heart zoomed like a motor ready to start at the Indianapolis 500.

Katherine dashed to the phone. She gasped. "Hello."

"Hello, dear. Are you okay? You sound out of breath."

Katherine's parents had surprised her with their acceptance of her moving in with Neal. Her mother always concurred with her father on sensitive matters. Neal had impressed her father when they'd met at Martin's. Katherine admired her father's fine people skills, gained in his years as an attorney. He'd even given Katherine pointers on how to spot a phony, a jerk, and of course, a real person. Katherine had relied on her Native American instincts and her father's shrewd skills to navigate the skies as a stewardess. "Oh, Mom, I can't wait until you and Dad can visit and see my new place with Neal."

"Can you give me a preview?

"Neal is the humblest person. He underplayed the place he bought."

"Are they good-sized rooms?"

"Oh, dear, Mother. Yes. I'm living in a whole row house on East Capitol Street." Katherine caught her breath and continued. "Can you imagine that there are rooms that are waiting for us to use? I climbed the winding stairs to the third floor to see the additional three bedrooms, the attic, and a maid's room. It's five times bigger than my one-bedroom apartment in Chicago."

Katherine's mother chuckled. "I guess you'll have room enough for your dear parents."

"Yep. And Neal plans to stay in Washington D.C."

"And do you plan to stay?"

"Wow, Mom, yes. All the signs guided me here. I've moved from a jet goddess to Hanging Cloud, or as the Ojibwe say, *Aazhawigiizhigokwe*, Goes Across the Sky Woman. As a stewardess, I flew across the sky. Now I'm flying to something more lasting." Katherine sighed and paused.

"I've never heard you mention Ojibwe."

"Maybe it's because no one could pronounce Ojibwe and changed our tribe name to Chippewa." Katherine took a breath. "Guess what else? I feel like I've lost a layer so a new me could live. I'm becoming a warrior like Hanging Cloud."

Katherine's mother chuckled. "Maybe the women's movement is helping you feel like you can charge ahead."

"Yep, it might be the outer world that's making the path easier, but my secret dream gives me the strength. Like the Ojibwe say, 'You cannot destroy one who has a dream of mine.'"

Katherine sensed her mother nodding in pleasure with her. "Does your dream have wings?"

"Yes, to start. I'm transferring from Beloit to American University to complete my bachelor's degree, and maybe I'll continue and get a Ph.D. That will give me solid support in my life plans for the Chippewa. As you know, it will take shape as I grow."

Katherine heard her mother clap. "My daughter. I can't wait to share in your journey."

"I hope to make it remarkable."

"Wonderful. How about living in D.C.?"

"Right here. I found a garden where I can plant seeds for a rich future harvest right here at the Smithsonian. Neal and I step outside, and we're right in the center of history: the past, the present, and the future of our country. And Neal and I dig into the history. It's thrilling to live next door to the Capitol. Right now, the city is fiery with anti-war protests and race riots. Our nation's capital is the center for people from everywhere, who either come to rumble and riot or to come build on their dreams."

"You father crosses his heart that you'll stay safe."

"Neal is street smart and knows how to avoid danger. And I have my protectors who guide me. You already knew that. When are you and Dad planning on visiting D.C.?"

"Probably not until the fall. Is that good for you?" Katherine's mother coughed, and her voice cracked. "One thing, your father and I wonder what's happening with you and Neal?"

Katherine smiled. "I was going to tell you and Dad about our plans. Yes, Neal and I love each other and plan to marry. When our plans our set, you and Dad will get all the details for our wedding. Right now, we are enjoying each other and letting each other grow and become separate individuals, like in Kahlil Gibran's marriage poem,

> 'Give your hearts, but not into each other's keeping.
> For only the hand of Life can contain your hearts.
> And stand together yet not too near together:
> For the pillars of the temple stand apart,
> and the oak tree and the cypress grow not in each
> other's shadow.'"

Katherine paused and looked at her watch. "Hey, Mom, I have to get dinner ready for Neal. He's been working late on his first big case at the Justice Department. I can't wait for you and Dad to visit."

"We can't wait to visit either. We're so proud of you. Dad glows whenever someone asks him what you're doing. So he'll jump at the chance to come for a visit. Love you."

"Love you and Dad too. Bye."

Katherine sauntered into the kitchen, put her hands on her hips, and sighed. *What a change.* From ready-to-serve food on airplane galleys to her kitchen full of ingredients ready to prepare. Her hands opened the cabinets, her eyes searched for a cookbook, and her mind wanted an answer. *Mom never gave me any cooking lessons.*

Rushing to find the right cookbook, Katherine's hand rushed over a pile of papers and envelopes on the kitchen counter that she hadn't read. An unopened envelope plummeted to the kitchen floor. It was from her mom and dad. It had come the day she'd moved in, and she'd forgotten about it. *I wonder why Mom didn't mention it to me today. Probably, nothing important, right now. I have to find a recipe for dinner.*

Katherine started to toss the envelope back on the pile of papers but then thought twice. It was a manila envelope, the kind her dad used for his legal work. Maybe it was urgent, perhaps about her outstanding loans to them.

Katherine opened the envelope and out tumbled three photos of young Ojibwe girls dressed in their native clothes. Then, a legal document entitled the Termination Act flopped in full view.

Katherine dropped to the floor and sat cross-legged. Her hand's shook as she picked up the official legal document. Clipped to the document was a handwritten note from Katherine's father.

Dear Goldie,

I know you haven't finished your degree and made your way into the vast career world. Now is time to start understanding the challenges you'll face. To prepare you for your mission, as a good father, I thought you should become aware of the troubles that plague the Chippewa and all Native Americans. Briefly, this Indian Termination Policy attempts to assimilate American Indians into the mainstream. You may ask, is this a problem? Yes, it will end tribal rights. Worst of all, the Indian tribes will lose their community.

And the photos of the charming young Chippewa girls dressed in the tribal clothes are from your mother. She helped plan a Native American art festival.

Katherine rubbed her fingers over the photo. *Wow, this picture glistens with the beauty and honesty of the Native American's respect for nature.* Katherine grinned. *Now I appreciate the fun I had with Mom when we walked into the woods, zoos, and farms to find porcupine quills, bird feathers, and bark fraying off broken branches so Mom's Chippewa art students could sew their native clothing. Doing this taught me what my Chippewa ancestors believed—to respect all of nature and all of the animals that gave their lives for humans.*

Katherine raised herself from the floor. Katherine's muscles tightened as she clutched her father's note and the photo against her chest. *I'll never let you down. I'm at the bottom of the mountain, but I will climb it and make certain that you will not lose your culture and community.*

51

MY DEAR NEAL. Katherine sighed as she settled into her mahogany armchair with its curved leather back, perfect to nestle around her spine. *This antique chair is the best gift from you. Now I have to fulfill my destiny and dreams.* Katherine's hands rubbed the companion gift from Neal, a nineteenth-century mahogany rolltop desk.

When she and Neal went shopping at the corner antique shop in Georgetown, he had told her the desk and chair were symbols for her years ahead. He added that a future archeologist needed an antique desk to channel her peers. *And Soaring Eagle too, my shaman. He guided and protected me this far. He won't leave me now. I've only begun my mission.*

Barbara Streisand's Christmas music drifted around Katherine's study on the top floor of Neal's townhouse. The midnight blue sky's full golden moon faded behind the fluffy crystals of white floating past the bay window. Katherine's mind and spirit wandered into the mood of the festive holiday music and the comforting warmth of the steam heat's gurgle. Her head waved and bowed to meet her chest. Soothing sleep joined the festive Christmas music as it faded under the melodic flute music of a Chippewa dream song. It swept Katherine into a magical realm, chanting the Ojibwe Dream Catcher lyrics into her inner ear.

Sleep well sweet child
Don't worry your head
Your Dream Catcher is humming
Above your bed
Listen so softly
I know you can hear
The tone of beyond
Close to your ear
Love is alive
And living in you
Beyond all your troubles
Where good dreams are true.

A loud clamor rang from the antique brass telephone that jolted her from her dream world. Katherine's mouth opened, and her head jerked. Katherine coughed with a muffled voice. "Hello."

"Hi, sweets. Sorry, I'm so late. Did you fall asleep?" Neal asked.

Katherine raised her hands to stretch and laughed. "No, I'm pondering the questions of the universe."

"I wish I were there to help you find the answers, but I have another hour to finish this brief. We have to file it with the court of appeals by eight tomorrow morning. Go ahead and have dinner. I'll grab something here. When I get home, let's pop champagne. This afternoon, the Arboretum confirmed our April wedding date."

Katherine's eyes glistened while her heart twirled. She raised her shoulders and released a soft squeal. *We're getting married*. When her parents had visited in October, they had visited the National Arboretum. Her mother had smiled at the two of them and, with a twinkle in her eye, exclaimed that the young couple could have a special private wedding at this particular place. Again her mother's prescient nature moved into Katherine's life. After wandering around the rural retreat in the center of Washington's concrete jungle and exploring the scattered foliage, the boxwood shrubs, and the herb garden, Katherine and Neal had agreed with her mother. Once again, the mystical hand of destiny slipped into Katherine's life.

"Wow. I'll put the bubbly on ice. And I know you're excited that we'll take our vows between the Arboretum's massive Corinthian columns."

Neal laughed. "After we say, 'I do,' can we dive into the reflecting pool for a swim?"

Katherine shrugged. "Let's talk later. Get to work on that brief so you can hurry home and hug me."

"Yeah. Love you."

Katherine gave herself a kick. She secretly wanted time. Time to regroup. Time to realign. Time alone to plan.

<hr>

With a quivering hand, Katherine opened her new red leather-bound journal with the gold-engraved title, Good Deed Book. It wasn't just any book; it would be a road map and record to keep her on track with her destiny. The picture from her parents of the three young Chippewa girls found their place on the first page of her new Good Deed Book. *These ladies are my constant reminder and lodestar.*

A glossy golden quill pen slipped into the inkwell. With a magic motion, Katherine wrote the title page, *My Life for the Ojibwe, the First Nations People, Turtle Island.*

Next, she pasted a map of the Chippewa tribes with the notation: "Create a four-year scholarship for one talented young woman from each reservation."

On the next page of the journal, she unrolled yellow paper about Ojibwe medicine, an example of the circle of life where all things are connected. The four-column list showed each nature element: White: North, Air; Red: South, Earth; Yellow: East, Fire; and Blue: West, Water.

Katherine took her pen and inked the title: *My Circle of Life Journey.*

Number one: Air . My first stage completed.

Katherine pasted her stewardess photo.

Number two: Earth. My next stage and work in progress to be an archeologist.

Under number two, she pasted the Ojibwe thoughts on the earth. The earth would be her inspiration for this cycle.

"To the Earth. Our Mother Earth is the source of all life, whether it be the plants, the two-legged, four-legged, winged ones, or human beings. Mother Earth is the greatest teacher, if we listen, observe, and respect her. When we live in harmony with Mother Earth, she will recycle the things we consume and make them available to our children and their children. As an Indian I must teach my children how to care for the Earth, so it is there for the future generations. So, from now on:

I realize the Earth is our mother. I will treat her with honor and respect.

I will honor the interconnectedness of all things and all forms of life. I will realize the Earth does not belong to us, but we belong to the Earth.

The natural law is the ultimate authority upon the lands and water. I will learn the knowledge and wisdom of the natural laws. I will pass this knowledge on to my children.

Mother Earth is a living entity that maintains life. I will speak out in a good way whenever I see someone abusing the Earth. Just as I would protect my mother, so will I protect the Earth. I will ensure that the land, water, and air will be intact for my children and my children's children—unborn."

Katherine's life story continues.

THERE'S MORE TO COME.

You've finished this chapter in Katherine Roebling's life, but Katherine's life adventures continue. The last pages of *Sky Queen* are inviting you to continue with Katherine Roebling's story with another nature element (sky, earth, water, fire). Life on earth is next for Katherine.

For more details on Katherine's next journey please visit my website: www.judykundert.com.

Acknowledgments

"NO MAN IS AN ISLAND. No man stands alone." John Donne's quote is valid for writers. Writing is done in solitude, but it comes alive with the help and support of other writers. Reading is the solitary partner in the writer's craft journey. A writer needs another partner to grow, and that's why I want to call out the wonderful writers and groups that are part of my writing journey.

My journey began and continues with the Rocky Mountain Fiction Writers. From the critique groups to their annual Colorado Gold Conference, I have gained friendship, writing techniques, and writing inspiration.

Other places on my writing journey include:

The Lighthouse Writers, Denver, Colorado, who offer courses packed with inspiration and talented instructors.

And other workshops:

Phil Sexton's Writer Digest Scituate Writer's Retreat, Scituate, MA, led by Paula Munier, agent at Talcott Literary Services, and Hallie Ephron, award winning writer, was a fantastic experience in writing and sharing the craft with others.

Mara Purl's, National Best Seller of Women's Fiction, workshop that gives insightful help in writing self-discovery.

My husband, Pat Kundert whose eagle editor eyes provided a valuable service to help polish my writing.

And thank you to all the others who have shared their talents with me.

About the Author

JUDY KUNDERT, a recipient of the Marquis Who's Who Excellence in Authorship award, loves storytelling, from folk and fairy tales to classics for elementary school children. She authors award-winning middle-grade novels designed to inspire and intrigue children. After she left her career as a United Airlines stewardess, she earned a Bachelor of Arts degree from Loyola University, Chicago and a Master of Arts from DePaul University, Chicago. Most recently, she completed a master's Certificate in Public Relations and Marketing from the University of Denver. For fun, she likes reading (usually three or four books at a time), watching movies from the oldies to the current films, traveling, biking, and hiking in the vast Colorado outdoors with her husband. Learn more at www.judykundert.com.

Author photo © TK

SELECTED TITLES FROM SHE WRITES PRESS

She Writes Press is an independent publishing company founded to serve women writers everywhere. Visit us at www.shewritespress.com.

Beautiful Garbage by Jill DiDonato. $16.95, 978-1-938314-01-8. Talented but troubled young artist Jodi Plum leaves suburbia for the excitement of the city—and is soon swept up in the sexual politics and downtown art scene of 1980s New York.

Cleans Up Nicely by Linda Dahl. $16.95, 978-1-938314-38-4. The story of one gifted young woman's path from self-destruction to self-knowledge, set in mid-1970s Manhattan.

The Geometry of Love by Jessica Levine. $16.95, 978-1-938314-62-9. Torn between her need for stability and her desire for independence, an aspiring poet grapples with questions of artistic inspiration, erotic love, and infidelity.

Play for Me by Céline Keating. $16.95, 978-1-63152-972-6. Middle-aged Lily impulsively joins a touring folk-rock band, leaving her job and marriage behind in an attempt to find a second chance at life, passion, and art.

Just the Facts by Ellen Sherman. $16.95, 978-1-63152-993-1. The seventies come alive in this poignant and humorous story of a fearful rookie reporter at a small-town newspaper who uncovers a big-time scandal.

The Lucidity Project by Abbey Campbell Cook. $16.95, 978-1-63152-032-7. After suffering from depression all her life, twenty-five-year-old Max Dorigan joins a mysterious research project on a Caribbean island, where she's introduced to the magical and healing world of lucid dreaming.